P9-CFY-161

THE POSITRONIC MAN

Also by Isaac Asimov and Robert Silverberg

NIGHTFALL
THE UGLY LITTLE BOY

Isaac Asimov and Robert Silverberg

A Foundation Book
DOUBLEDAY
New York
London
Toronto
Sydney
Auckland

THE
POSITRONIC
MAN

A FOUNDATION BOOK
PUBLISHED BY DOUBLEDAY
a division of Bantam Doubleday Dell
Publishing Group, Inc.
1540 Broadway, New York, New York 10036

FOUNDATION, DOUBLEDAY, and the portrayal of the
letter F are trademarks of Doubleday, a division of
Bantam Doubleday Dell Publishing Group, Inc.

Library of Congress Cataloging-in-Publication Data

Asimov, Isaac, 1920–1992
The positronic man/by Isaac Asimov and Robert Silverberg.—1st ed.
   p.   cm.
"A Foundation book."
I. Silverberg, Robert.   II. Title.
PS3551.S5B5   1993
813'.54—dc20   93-15148
CIP

ISBN 0-385-26342-2

Printed in the United States of America
November 1993

10   9   8   7   6   5   4   3   2   1

First Edition

For Janet
and Karen

—with much love

THE THREE LAWS OF ROBOTICS

1. A robot may not injure a human being, or, through inaction, allow a human being to come to harm.

2. A robot must obey the orders given it by human beings except where such orders would conflict with the First Law.

3. A robot must protect its own existence as long as such protection does not conflict with the First or Second Law.

THE POSITRONIC MAN

ONE

"IF YOU'LL TAKE A SEAT, sir," the surgeon said, gesturing toward the chair in front of his desk. "Please."

"Thank you," said Andrew Martin.

He seated himself calmly. He did everything calmly. That was his nature; it was one part of him that would never change. Looking at him now, one could have no way of knowing that Andrew Martin had been driven to the last resort. But he had been. He had come halfway across the continent for this interview. It represented his only remaining hope of achieving his life's main goal—everything had come down to that. Everything.

There was a smooth blankness to Andrew's face—though a keen observer might well have imagined a hint of melancholy in his eyes. His hair was smooth, light brown, rather fine, and he looked freshly and cleanly shaven: no beard, no mustache, no facial affectations of any sort. His clothes were well made and neat, predominantly a velvety red-purple in color; but they were of a distinctly old-fashioned cut, in the loose, flowing style called "drapery" that had been popular several generations back and was rarely seen these days.

The surgeon's face had a certain blankness about it also: hardly a surprising thing, for the surgeon's face, like all the rest of him, was fashioned of lightly bronzed stainless steel. He sat

1

squarely upright at his imposing desk in the windowless room high over Lake Michigan, looking outward at Andrew Martin with the utmost serenity and poise evident in his glowing eyes. In front of him on the desk was a gleaming brass nameplate that announced his serial number, the usual factory-assigned assortment of letters and numbers.

Andrew Martin paid no attention to that soulless string of characters and digits. Such dreary, mechanistic identity-designations were nothing of any moment to him—not now, not any more, not for a very long time. Andrew felt no need to call the robot surgeon anything but "Doctor."

The surgeon said, "This is all very irregular, you know, sir. Very irregular."

"Yes. I know that," Andrew Martin said.

"I've thought about very little else since this request first came to my attention."

"I sincerely regret any discomfort that it may have caused you."

"Thank you. I am grateful for your concern."

All very formal, very courteous, very useless. They were simply fencing with each other, neither one willing to get down to essentials. And now the surgeon fell silent. Andrew waited for him to proceed. The silence went on and on.

This is getting us nowhere, Andrew told himself.

To the surgeon he said, "The thing that I need to know, Doctor, is how soon the operation can be carried out."

The surgeon hesitated a perceptible moment. Then he said softly, with that certain inalienable note of respect that a robot always used when speaking to a human being, "I am not convinced, sir, that I fully understand how such an operation could be performed, let alone why it should be considered desirable. And of course I still don't know who the subject of the proposed operation is going to be."

There might have been a look of respectful intransigence on the surgeon's face, if the elegantly contoured stainless steel of the surgeon's face had been in any way capable of displaying such an expression—or any expression at all.

It was the turn of Andrew Martin to be silent for a moment, now.

He studied the robot surgeon's right hand—his cutting hand —as it rested on the desk in utter tranquillity. It was splendidly designed. The fingers were long and tapering, and they were shaped into metallic looping curves of great artistic beauty, curves so graceful and appropriate to their function that one could easily imagine a scalpel being fitted into them and instantly becoming, at the moment they went into action, united in perfect harmony with the fingers that wielded it: surgeon and scalpel fusing into a single marvelously capable tool.

That was very reassuring, Andrew thought. There would be no hesitation in the surgeon's work, no stumbling, no quivering, no mistakes or even the possibility of a mistake.

Such skill came with specialization, of course—a specialization so fiercely desired by humanity that few robots of the modern era were independently brained any more. The great majority of them nowadays were mere adjuncts of enormously powerful central processing units that had computing capacities far beyond the space limitations of a single robot frame.

A surgeon, too, really needed to be nothing more than a set of sensors and monitors and an array of tool-manipulating devices —except that people still preferred the illusion, if nothing more than that, that they were being operated on by an individual entity, not by a limb of some remote machine. So surgeons—the ones in private practice, anyway—were still independently brained. But this one, brained or not, was so limited in his capacity that he didn't recognize Andrew Martin—had probably never heard of Andrew Martin at all, in fact.

That was something of a novelty for Andrew. He was more than a little famous. He had never asked for his fame, of course —that was not his style—but fame, or at any rate notoriety, had come to him all the same. Because of what he had achieved: because of what he was. Not who, but *what*.

3

Instead of replying to what the surgeon had asked him Andrew said, with sudden striking irrelevance, "Tell me something, Doctor. Have you ever thought you would like to be a man?"

The question, startling and strange, obviously took the surgeon aback. He hesitated a moment as though the concept of being a man was so alien to him that it would fit nowhere in his allotted positronic pathways.

Then he recovered his aplomb and replied serenely, "But I am a robot, sir."

"Wouldn't it be better to be a man, don't you think?"

"If I were allowed the privilege of improving myself, sir, I would choose to be a better surgeon. The practice of my craft is the prime purpose of my existence. There is no way I could be a better surgeon if I were a man, but only if I were a more advanced robot. It would please me very much indeed to be a more advanced robot."

"But you would still be a robot, even so."

"Yes. Of course. To be a robot is quite acceptable to me. As I have just explained, sir, in order for one to excel at the extremely difficult and demanding practice of modern-day surgery it is necessary that one be—"

"A robot, yes," said Andrew, with just a note of exasperation creeping into his tone. "But think of the subservience involved, Doctor! Consider: you're a highly skilled surgeon. You deal in the most delicate matters of life and death—you operate on some of the most important individuals in the world, and for all I know you have patients come to you from other worlds as well. And yet—and yet—a robot? You're content with that? For all your skill, you must take orders from *anyone*, any human at all: a child, a fool, a boor, a rogue. The Second Law commands it. It leaves you no choice. Right this minute I could say, 'Stand up, Doctor,' and you'd have to stand up. 'Put your fingers over your face and wiggle them,' and you'd wiggle. Stand on one leg, sit down on the floor, move right or left, anything I wanted to tell you, and you'd obey. I could order you to disassemble yourself limb by limb, and you would. You, a great surgeon! No choice at

4

all. A human whistles and you hop to his tune. Doesn't it offend you that I have the power to make you do whatever damned thing I please, no matter how idiotic, how trivial, how degrading?"

The surgeon was unfazed.

"It would be my pleasure to please you, sir. With certain obvious exceptions. If your orders should happen to involve my doing any harm to you or any other human being, I would have to take the primary laws of my nature into consideration before obeying you, and in all likelihood I would *not* obey you. Naturally the First Law, which concerns my duty to human safety, would take precedence over the Second Law relating to obedience. Otherwise, obedience is my pleasure. If it would give you pleasure to require me to do certain acts that you regard as idiotic or trivial or degrading, I would perform those acts. But they would not seem idiotic or trivial or degrading to me."

There was nothing even remotely surprising to Andrew Martin in the things the robot surgeon had said. He would have found it astonishing, even revolutionary, if the robot had taken any other position.

But even so—even so—

The surgeon said, with not the slightest trace of impatience in his smooth bland voice, "Now, if we may return to the subject of this extraordinary operation that you have come here to discuss, sir. I can barely comprehend the nature of what you want done. It is hard for me to visualize a situation that would require such a thing. But what I need to know, first of all, is the name of the person upon whom I am asked to perform this operation."

"The name is Andrew Martin," Andrew said. "The operation is to be performed on me."

"But that would be impossible, sir!"

"Surely you'd be capable of it."

"Capable in a technical sense, yes. I have no serious doubt on that score, regardless of what may be asked of me, although in this case there are certain procedural issues that I would have to consider very carefully. But that is beside the point. I ask you

5

please to bear in mind, sir, that the fundamental effect of the operation would be harmful to you."

"That does not matter at all," said Andrew calmly.

"It does to me."

"Is this the robot version of the Hippocratic Oath?"

"Something far more stringent than that," the surgeon said. "The Hippocratic Oath is, of course, a voluntary pledge. But there is, as plainly you must be aware, something innate in my circuitry itself that controls my professional decisions. Above and beyond everything else, I must not inflict damage. I *may* not inflict damage."

"On human beings, yes."

"Indeed. The First Law says—"

"Don't recite the First Law, Doctor. I know it at least as well as you. But the First Law simply governs the actions of robots toward human beings. I'm not human, Doctor."

The surgeon reacted with a visible twitch of his shoulders and a blinking of his photoelectric eyes. It was as if what Andrew had just said had no meaning for him whatever.

"Yes," said Andrew, "I know that I seem to be quite human, and that what you're experiencing now is the robot equivalent of surprise. Nevertheless I'm telling you the absolute truth. However human I may appear to you, I am simply a robot. A *robot*, Doctor. A robot is what I am, and nothing more than that. Believe me. And therefore you are free to operate on me. There is nothing in the First Law which prohibits a robot from performing actions on another robot. Even if the action that is performed should cause harm to that robot, Doctor."

TWO

IN THE BEGINNING, of course—and the beginning for him was nearly two centuries before his visit to the surgeon's office—no one could have mistaken Andrew Martin for anything but the robot he was.

In that long-ago era when he had first come from the assembly line of United States Robots and Mechanical Men he was as much a robot in appearance as any that had ever existed, smoothly designed and magnificently functional: a sleek mechanical object, a positronic brain encased in a more-or-less humanoid-looking housing made from metal and plastic.

His long slim limbs then were finely articulated mechanisms fashioned from titanium alloys overlaid by steel and equipped with silicone bushings at the joints to prevent metal-to-metal contact. His limb sockets were of the finest flexible polyethylene. His eyes were photoelectric cells that gleamed with a deep red glow. His face—and to call it that was charitable; it was the merest perfunctory sketch of a face—was altogether incapable of expression. His bare, sexless body was unambiguously a manufactured device. All it took was a single glance to see that he was a machine, no more animate, no more human, no more alive, than a telephone or a pocket calculator or an automobile.

But that was in another era, long, long ago.

It was an era when robots were still uncommon sights on Earth —almost the very dawn of the age of robotics, not much more than a generation after the days when the great early roboticists like Alfred Lanning and Peter Bogert and the legendary robo-psychologist Susan Calvin had done their historic work, developing and perfecting the principles by which the first positronic robots had come into being.

The aim of those pioneers had been to create robots capable of taking up many of the dreary burdens that human beings had for so long been compelled to bear. And that was part of the problem that the roboticists faced, in those dawning days of the science of artificial life late in the Twentieth Century and early in the Twenty-First: the unwillingness of a great many human beings to surrender those burdens to mechanical substitutes. Because of that unwillingness, strict laws had been passed in virtually every country—the world was still broken up into a multitude of nations, then—against the use of robot labor on Earth.

By the year 2007 they had been banned entirely everywhere on the planet, except for scientific research under carefully controlled conditions. Robots could be sent into space, yes, to the ever-multiplying industrial factories and exploratory stations off Earth: let them cope with the miseries of frigid Ganymede and torrid Mercury, let them put up with the inconveniences of scrabbling around on the surface of Luna, let them run the bewildering risks of the early Jump experiments that would eventually give mankind the hyperspace road to the stars.

But robots in free and general use on Earth—occupying precious slots in the labor force that would otherwise be available for actual naturally-born flesh-and-blood human beings—no! No! No robots wanted around here!

Well, that had eventually begun to change, of course. And the most dramatic changes had begun to set in around the time that Robot NDR-113, who would someday be known as Andrew Martin, had been undergoing assembly at the main Northern Region factory of United States Robots and Mechanical Men.

One of the factors bringing about the gradual breakdown of

the anti-robot prejudices on Earth at that time was simple public relations. United States Robots and Mechanical Men was not only a scientifically adept organization, it knew a thing or two about the importance of maintaining its profitability, too. So it had found ways, quiet and subtle and effective, of chipping away at the Frankenstein myth of the robot, the concept of the mechanical man as the dreaded shambling Golem.

Robots are here for our convenience, the U.S.R.M.M. public relations people said. Robots are here to help us. Robots are not our enemies. Robots are perfectly safe, safe beyond any possibility of doubt.

And—because in fact all those things were actually true—people began to accept the presence of robots among them. They did so grudgingly, in the main. Many people—most, perhaps—were still uncomfortable with the whole idea of robots; but they recognized the need for them and they could at least tolerate having them around, so long as tight restrictions on their use continued to be applied.

There was need for robots, like it or not, because the population of Earth had started to dwindle about that time. After the long anguish that was the Twentieth Century, a time of relative tranquillity and harmony and even rationality—a certain degree of that, anyway—had begun to settle over the world. It became a quieter, calmer, happier place. There were fewer people by far, not because there had been terrible wars and plagues, but because families now tended to be smaller, giving preference to quality over quantity. Migration to the newly settled worlds of space was draining off some of Earth's population also—migration to the extensive network of underground settlements on the Moon, to the colonies in the asteroid belt and on the moons of Jupiter and Saturn, and to the artificial worlds in orbit around Earth and Mars.

So there was no longer so much excitement over the possibility of losing one's job to a robot. The fear of job shortages on Earth had given way to the problem of labor shortages. Suddenly the robots that once had been looked upon with such uneasiness, fear, and even hatred became necessary to maintain the welfare of a world that had every material advantage but didn't have enough of a population left to sweep the streets, drive the taxis, cook the meals, stoke the furnaces.

It was in this new era of diminishing population and increasing prosperity that NDR-113—the future Andrew Martin—was manufactured. No longer was the use of robots illegal on Earth; but strict regulations still applied, and they were still far from everyday sights. Especially robots who were programmed for ordinary household duties, which was the primary use that Gerald Martin had in mind for NDR-113.

Hardly anyone in those days had a robot servant around the house. It was too frightening an idea for most people—and too expensive, besides.

But Gerald Martin was hardly just anyone. He was a member of the Regional Legislature, a powerful member at that, Chairman of the Science and Technology Committee: a man of great presence and authority, of tremendous force of mind and character. What Gerald Martin set out to achieve, Gerald Martin inevitably succeeded in achieving. And what Gerald Martin chose to possess, Gerald Martin would invariably come to possess. He believed in robots: he knew that they were an inevitable development, that they would ultimately become inextricably enmeshed in human society at every level.

And so—utilizing his position on the Science and Technology Committee to the fullest—he had been able to arrange for robots to become a part of his private life, and that of his family. For the sake of gaining a deeper understanding of the robot phenomenon, he had explained. For the sake of helping his fellow members of the Regional Legislature to discover how they might best grapple with the problems that the coming era of robotic ubiquity would bring. Bravely, magnanimously, Gerald Martin had offered himself as an experimental subject and had volunteered to take a small group of domestic robots into his own home.

The first robots that arrived were simple specialized ones dedicated to specific routine tasks. They were approximately human in form but they had little if anything to say and went about their business in the quiet, efficient manner of the machines that they all too plainly were. At first the Martins found it strange to have them around, but very quickly they faded into the background of the family's existence, arousing no more interest than toasters or vacuum cleaners would.

But then—

"This is NDR-113," Gerald Martin announced one cool, windy afternoon in June, when the delivery truck had rolled up the long driveway that led to the imposing clifftop estate of the Gerald Martin family and the sleek, shining mechanical man had been released from his crate. "Our personal household robot. Our own private family retainer."

"What did you call him?" Amanda asked. Amanda was the younger of the two Martin daughters, a small golden-haired child with penetrating blue eyes. She was just beginning to learn to read and write, then.

"NDR-113."

"Is that his name?"

"His serial number, actually."

Amanda frowned. "En—dee—arr. Endeearr 113. That's a peculiar name."

"Serial number," Gerald Martin said again.

But Amanda wanted no part of that. "Endeearr. We can't call him something like that. It doesn't sound like any kind of name anything ought to have."

"Listen to her," Melissa Martin said. Melissa was the older Martin girl: five years older than Amanda, dark-haired, dark-eyed. Melissa was practically a woman, so far as Melissa was concerned. Amanda was merely a child, and therefore Melissa regarded her as foolish by definition. "She doesn't like the robot's serial number."

"En—dee—arr," Amanda said again, elaborately paying no attention to Melissa. "That isn't any good. It really isn't. What about calling him Andrew?"

"Andrew?" Gerald Martin said.

"It's got an *n* in it, doesn't it? And a *d*?" For a moment Amanda looked a little doubtful. "Sure it does. And an *r*, that much I'm certain of. N—D—R. Andrew."

"Just listen to her," Melissa said scornfully.

But Gerald Martin was smiling. He knew that it wasn't at all unusual to adapt a robot's serial letters into a name. Robots of the JN series tended to become Johns or Janes. RG robots became Archies. QT robots were called Cuties. Well, here was an NDR-series robot, and Amanda wanted to call him Andrew. Fine. Fine. Gerald Martin had a way of letting Amanda do what Amanda thought was best for Amanda. Within limits, of course.

"Very well," he said. "Andrew it is."

And Andrew it was. So much so that, as the years went along, no one in the Martin family ever called him NDR-113 again. In time his serial number was forgotten altogether, and it had to be looked up whenever he needed to be taken in for maintenance. Andrew himself claimed to have forgotten his own number. Of course, that wasn't strictly true. No matter how much time might go by, he could never forget anything, not if he wanted to remember it.

But as time went on, and things began to change for Andrew, he had less and less desire to remember the number. He left it safely hidden away in the oblivion of his memory banks and never thought of going searching for it. He was Andrew now—Andrew Martin—the Andrew of the Martin family—

Andrew was tall and slender and graceful, because that was how NDR robots were designed to look. He moved quietly and unobtrusively around the splendid house that the Martin family occupied overlooking the Pacific, efficiently doing all that the Martins required him to do.

It was a house out of a vanished age, a grand and majestic mansion that really required a grand retinue of servants to keep it up; but of course there were no servants to be had any longer, except for robots, and that had been causing some problems for the Martins before Gerald Martin offered himself up for this experiment. Now a pair of robot gardeners tended the glistening green lawns and pruned the glorious hedges of fiery red azaleas and trimmed away the dead fronds of the towering palm trees that ran along the ridge behind the house. A robot housecleaner kept dust and cobwebs at bay. And Andrew the robot served as valet, butler, lady's maid, and chauffeur for the Martin family. He prepared meals; he selected and poured the wines of which Gerald Martin was so fond; he supervised their wardrobes; he arranged and cared for their fine furniture, their works of art, their myriad distinctive possessions.

Andrew had one other duty, too, which in fact monopolized much of his time to the detriment of the rest of his formal household routine.

The Martin estate—for that was what it was, nothing less, a great estate—was an isolated one, alone on its beautiful ridge overlooking the chilly blue ocean. There was a little town nearby, but it was some distance away. The nearest city of any size, San Francisco, was far down the coast. Cities were starting to become obsolete now, anyway, and people preferred to communicate electronically and keep plenty of distance between one house and the next. So the Martin girls, in their grand and wonderful isolation, had very few playmates.

They did, however, have Andrew.

It was Miss who first figured out how that might best be arranged.

("Miss" was what Andrew invariably called Melissa, not because he was incapable of pronouncing her first name but because it seemed improper to him to address her in such a familiar way. Amanda was always "Little Miss"—never anything else. Mrs. Martin—Lucie was her first name—was "Ma'am" to Andrew. And as for Gerald Martin, he was "Sir." Gerald Martin was the sort of individual whom many people, not simply robots, felt most comfortable calling "Sir." The number of people in the world who called him "Gerald" was a very small number indeed, and it was impossible to suppose him being "Jerry" to anybody at all.)

Miss quickly came to understand more than a little about how to take advantage of the presence of a robot in the house. It was a simple matter of utilizing the Second Law.

"Andrew," she said, "we order you to stop what you're doing and play with us."

At the moment Andrew was arranging the books in the Martin library, which had wandered a little out of alphabetical order, as books have a way of doing.

He paused and looked down from the high mahogany bookcase between the two great leaded-glass windows at the north end of the room. Mildly he said, "I'm sorry, Miss. I'm occupied at present by a task requested by your father. A prior order from Sir must take precedence over this request of yours."

"I heard what Daddy told you," Miss replied. "He said, 'I'd like you to tidy up those books, Andrew. Get them back into some kind of sensible arrangement.' Isn't that so?"

"That is exactly what he said, yes, Miss. Those were his very words."

"Well, then, if all he said was that he'd *like* you to tidy up those books—and you don't deny that he did—then it wasn't much of an order, was it? It was more of a preference. A suggestion. A suggestion isn't an order. Neither is a preference. Andrew, I order you. Leave the books where they are and come take Amanda and me out for a walk along the beach."

It was a perfect application of the Second Law. Andrew put the books down immediately and descended from his ladder. Sir was the head of the household; but he hadn't actually given an order, not in the formal sense of the concept, and Miss had. She certainly had. And an order from a human member of this household—*any* human member of the household—had to take priority over a mere expression of preference from some other human member of the household, even if that member happened to be Sir himself.

Not that Andrew had any problem with any of that. He was fond of Miss, and even more fond of Little Miss. At least, the effect that they had upon his actions was that which in a human being would have been called the result of fondness. Andrew thought of it as fondness, for he didn't know any other term for what he felt toward the two girls. Certainly he felt *something*. That in itself was a little odd, but he supposed that a capacity for fondness had been built into him, the way his various other skills had been. And so if they wanted him to come out and play with them, he'd do it happily—provided they made it permissible for him to do it within the context of the Three Laws.

The trail down to the beach was a steep and winding one, strewn with rocks and gopher-holes and other troublesome obstacles. No one but Miss and Little Miss used it very often, because the beach itself was nothing more than a ragged sandy strand covered with driftwood and storm-tossed seaweed, and the ocean, in this northern part of California, was far too chilly for anyone without a wetsuit to consider entering. But the girls loved its bleak, moody, windswept charm.

As they scrambled down the trail Andrew held Miss by the hand and carried Little Miss in the crook of his arm. Very likely both girls could have made their way down the path without incident, but Sir had been very strict about the beach trail. "Make sure they don't run or jump around, Andrew. If they tripped over something in the wrong place it would be a fifty-foot drop. I can't stop them from going down there, but I want you to be right beside them at all times to be certain they don't do anything foolish. That's an order."

One of these days, Andrew knew, Miss or even Little Miss was going to countermand that order and tell him to stand aside while they ran giddily down the hill to the beach. When that happened it would set up a powerful equipotential of contradiction in his positronic brain and beyond much doubt he would be hard pressed to deal with it.

Sir's order would ultimately prevail, naturally, since it embodied elements of the First Law as well as the Second, and anything that involved First Law prohibitions always took highest priority. Still, Andrew knew that his circuitry would be stressed more than a little the first time a direct conflict between Sir's decree and the girls' whims came into play.

For the moment, though, Miss and Little Miss were content to abide by the rules. Carefully, step by step, he made his way down the face of the cliff with the girls in tow.

At the bottom Andrew released Miss's hand and set Little Miss down on the damp sand. Immediately they went streaking off, running gleefully along the edge of the fierce, snarling sea.

"Seaweed!" Miss cried, grabbing up a thick brown ropy length of kelp that was longer than she was and swinging it like a whip. "Look at this big chunk of seaweed, Andrew!"

"And this piece of driftwood," said Little Miss. "Isn't it beautiful, Melissa?"

"Maybe to you," the older girl said loftily. She took the gnarled and bent bit of wood from Little Miss, examined it in a perfunctory way, and tossed it aside with a shudder. "Ugh. It's got things growing on it."

"They're just another kind of seaweed," Little Miss said. "Right, Andrew?"

She picked up the discarded piece of driftwood and handed it to him for inspection.

"Algae, yes," he said.

"Algy?"

"Algae. The technical term for seaweed."

"Oh. Algy." Little Miss laughed and put the bit of driftwood down near the beginning of the trail, so she would remember to take it with her when they went up to the house again. Then she rampaged off down the beach again, following her older sister through the foamy fringes of the surf.

Andrew kept pace with them without difficulty. He did not intend to let them get very far from him at any time.

He had needed no special orders from Sir to protect the girls while they were actually on the beach: the First Law took care of that. The ocean here was not only wild-looking but exceedingly dangerous: the currents were strong and unpredictable, the water was intolerably cold at almost any time of the year, and the great rocky fangs of a deadly reef rose from the swirling breakers less than fifty meters offshore. If Miss or Little Miss should make the slightest move to enter the sea, Andrew would be beside them in an instant.

But they had more sense than to want to go swimming in this impossible ocean. The shore along this part of the Pacific coast was a beautiful thing to behold in its harsh, bleak way, but the sea itself, forever angry and turbulent, was the enemy of those who were not bred for it, and even a small child could see that at a glance.

Miss and Little Miss were wading in the tide pools now, peering at the dark periwinkles and gray-green limpets and pink-and-purple anemones and the myriad little scuttling hermit crabs, and searching—as they always did, rarely with much luck—for a starfish. Andrew stood nearby, poised and ready in the event that a sudden wave should rise without warning nearby and sweep toward shore. The sea was quiet today, as quiet as that savage body of water ever got, but perilous waves were apt to come out of nowhere at any time.

Miss said suddenly, "Andrew, do you know how to swim?"

"I could do it if it were necessary, Miss."

"It wouldn't short-circuit your brain, or anything? If water got in, I mean?"

"I am very well insulated," Andrew told her.

"Good. Swim out to that gray rock and back, then. The ones where the cormorants are nesting. I want to see how fast you can do it."

"Melissa—" said Little Miss uneasily.

"Shh, Amanda. I want Andrew to go out there. Maybe he can find some cormorant eggs and bring them back to show us."

"It would not be good to disturb the nest, Miss," said Andrew gently.

"I said I wanted you to go out there."

"Melissa—" Little Miss said again, more sharply.

But Miss was insistent. It was an order. Andrew felt the preliminary signs of contradictory potentials building up: a faint trembling in his fingertips, a barely perceptible sense of vertigo. Orders were to be obeyed: that was the Second Law. Miss could order him to swim to China this minute, and Andrew would do it without hesitation if no other considerations were involved. But he was here to protect the girls. What would happen if something unexpected befell them while he was out by the cormorant rock? A sudden menacing wave, a rockslide, even an earthquake—earthquakes weren't everyday occurrences here, but they certainly could happen at any time—

It was a pure First Law issue.

"I am sorry, Miss. With no adults here to guard you, I am unable to leave you unattended long enough to swim to that rock and back. If Sir or Ma'am were present, that would be a different matter, but as it is—"

"Don't you recognize an order when you hear one? I *want* you to swim out there, Andrew."

"As I have explained, Miss—"

"You don't have to worry about us. It's not as though I'm a *child,* Andrew. What do you think, that some sort of terrible ogre is going to come down the beach and gobble us up while you're in the water? I can look after myself, thank you, and I'll take care of Amanda too if I have to."

Little Miss said, "You aren't being fair to him, Melissa. He's got his orders from Daddy."

"And now he has his orders from me." Miss gestured peremptorily. "Swim out to the cormorant rock, Andrew. Go ahead. *Now,* Andrew."

Andrew felt himself growing a little warm, and ordered his circuitry to make the necessary homeostatic correction.

"The First Law—" he began.

"What a bore you are! You and your First Law both!" cried Melissa. "Can't you forget the First Law once in a while? But no, no, you can't do that, can you? You've got those silly laws wired into you and there's no getting around them. You're nothing but a dumb machine."

"*Melissa!*" Little Miss said indignantly.

18

"Yes, that is true," said Andrew. "As you correctly state, I am nothing but a dumb machine. And therefore I have no ability to countermand your father's order concerning your safety on the beach." He bowed slightly in Melissa's direction. "I deeply regret this, Miss."

Little Miss said, "If you want to see Andrew swim so much, Melissa, why don't you just have him wade into the surf and do some swimming right close to shore? There wouldn't be any harm in that, would there?"

"It wouldn't be the same thing," Miss said, pouting. "Not at all."

But, Andrew reflected, perhaps that would satisfy her. He disliked being the focus of so much disharmony.

"Let me show you," he said.

He waded in. The heavy foam-flecked surf thundered up violently around his knees, but Andrew was able easily to adjust his gyroscopic stabilizers as the force of the breaking waves assailed him. The rough, sharp rocks that were scattered all over the sea floor meant nothing to his metallic treads. His sensors told him that the temperature of the water was well below human comfort tolerance, but that, too, was irrelevant to him.

Four or five meters out, the water was deep enough so that Andrew could swim in it, and yet he was still close enough to shore to be able to get back to land in a moment if need be. He doubted that need would be. The girls stood side by side on the beach, watching him in fascination.

Andrew had never gone swimming before. There had never been the slightest reason for him to do so. But he had been programmed for grace and coordination under all circumstances, and it took him no more than a microsecond to calculate the nature of the motions necessary to propel him through the water just below the surface—the rhythmic kicking of the legs, the lifting of the arms, the cupping of the hands. Deftly he glided along parallel to the shore for perhaps a dozen meters, swimming smoothly, efficiently, powerfully. Then he turned and returned to his starting point. The whole excursion had taken just a few moments.

And it had had the desired effect on Miss.

"You're a wonderful swimmer, Andrew," she told him. Her eyes were shining. "I'm sure you'd break all the records if you ever entered a swimming meet."

"There are no swimming meets for robots, Miss," Andrew told her gravely.

Miss giggled. "I mean a human swimming meet! Like in the Olympics!"

"Oh, Miss, Miss! How unfair that would be, if they allowed a robot to compete in the Olympics against humans! It could never happen."

She considered that for a moment.

"I suppose not," she said. Wistfully she looked toward the cormorant rock. "Are you sure you won't swim out there? I bet you could get there and back in two minutes. What could possibly happen to us in two minutes?"

"Melissa—" Little Miss said again.

Andrew said, "I completely understand your desire to have me do it, Miss. But I am not able to fulfill your wish. Again, I deeply regret—"

"Oh, all right. I'm sorry I asked."

"You aren't," Little Miss said.

"I am."

"And you called Andrew a dumb machine! That wasn't nice!"

"It's true, isn't it?" Miss asked. "He told us himself that it was true!"

"He is a machine, I suppose," Little Miss conceded. "But he isn't dumb at all. And anyway it wasn't a polite thing for you to say."

"I don't have to be polite to robots. It's like being polite to a television set."

"It's different!" Little Miss insisted. "It's entirely different!"

And then she was crying, and Andrew had to scoop her up and whirl her around until she was so distracted by the vast cloudless sweep of the sky and the strangeness of the upside-down ocean that she forgot why she had been upset.

A little while afterward Miss came up to him, while Little Miss was poking in the tide pools again, and said in a low, contrite voice, "I'm sorry I said what I did, Andrew."

"That's all right, Miss."

"Will you forgive me? I know I wasn't nice. I really wanted you to swim out there and I didn't stop to think that you aren't allowed to leave us alone when we're down here. I'm very sorry, Andrew."

"There is no need for you to apologize, Miss. Truly there isn't."

Nor was there. How could a robot possibly take offense at anything a human said or did? But somehow Andrew thought it best not to point that out to her just now. If Miss felt a need to apologize, he must permit her to fulfill that need—even though her cruel words had not disturbed him in the first place.

It would be absurd for him to deny that he was a machine. That was exactly what he was.

And as for being a *dumb* machine, well, he had no real idea of what she had meant by that. He had adequate intelligence capacity to meet the needs placed upon him. Doubtless there were robots more intelligent than he was, but he had not encountered them. Had she meant that he was less intelligent than humans are? The statement was meaningless to him. He knew no way of comparing robot intelligence with human intelligence. Quantitatively and qualitatively, their manners of thinking were two entirely different processes—everyone was agreed on that.

Soon the wind became chillier. It whipped the girls' dresses about and hurled showers of sand in their faces and against Andrew's shining hull. The girls decided that they had had enough of playing on the beach.

As they started toward the path, Little Miss picked up the piece of driftwood that she had found before, and tucked it through her belt. She was always collecting strange little treasures of that sort.

That evening, when he was off duty, Andrew went down to the beach by himself and swam out to the cormorant rock simply to see how long it would take. Even in the darkness, he managed it easily and swiftly. Very likely, Andrew realized now, he could have managed it without exposing Miss and Little Miss to any great period of risk. Not that he would have done so, but it would have been possible.

No one had requested Andrew to make the nighttime swim to the rock. It was entirely his own idea. A matter of curiosity, so to speak.

THREE

THE TIME OF YEAR arrived when Miss celebrated her birthday. Andrew had already learned that one's birthday celebration was an important event in the annual round of human life—a commemoration of the anniversary of the day that one had emerged from one's mother's womb.

Andrew thought that it was strange that humans would choose the day of coming forth from the womb as the significant thing to commemorate. He knew something of human biology, and it seemed to him that it would be much more important to focus on the moment of the actual creation of the organism, when the sperm cell entered the ovum and the process of cell division began. Surely that was the real point of origin of any person!

Certainly the new person was already alive—if not yet capable of independent functioning—during the nine months spent within the womb. Nor was a human being particularly capable of independent functioning immediately after leaving the womb, so the distinction between birth and pre-birth that humans insisted on drawing made very little sense to Andrew.

He himself had been ready to perform all his programmed functions the moment the last phase of his assembly was complete and his pathways had been initialized. But a newborn child was far from able to manage on its own. Andrew could see no

23

effective difference between a fetus that had completed its various stages of fetal development but was still inside its mother and the same fetus, a day or two later, that had emerged. One was inside and one was outside, that was all. But they were just about equally helpless. So why not celebrate the anniversary of one's moment of conception instead of the anniversary of one's release from the womb?

The more he pondered it, though, the more he saw that there was some logic to either view. What, for example, would he select as his own birthday, assuming that robots felt any need to celebrate their birthdays? The date when the factory had begun assembling him, or the date on which his positronic brain had been installed in its case and initialization of somatic control had been keyed? Had he been "born" when the first strands of his armature were being drawn together, or when the unique set of perceptions that constituted NDR-113 had gone into operation? A mere armature wasn't *him*, whatever *he* was. His positronic brain was *him*. Or the combination of the positronic brain properly placed within the body that had been designed to house it. So his birthday—

Oh, it was all so confusing! And robots weren't supposed to be plagued by confusion. Their positronic minds were more complex than the simple digital "minds" of non-positronic computers, which operated entirely in stark binary realms, mere patterns of on or off, yes or no, positive or negative, and that complexity could sometimes lead to moments of conflicting potential. But nevertheless robots were logical creatures who were able to find their way out of such conflicts, usually, by sorting the data in a sensible way. Why, then, was he having so much trouble comprehending this business of when one's birthday ought to be?

Because birthdays are a purely human concept, he answered himself. They have no relevance to robots. And you are not a human being, so you do not need to worry about when your birthday ought or ought not to be celebrated.

At any rate, it was Miss's birthday. Sir made a point of coming home early that day, even though the Regional Legislature was embroiled in some complicated debate over interplanetary free-trade zones. The whole family dressed in holiday clothes and gathered around the great slab of polished redwood that was the dining-room table and candles were lit, and Andrew served an elaborate dinner that he and Ma'am had spent hours planning, and afterward Miss formally received and opened her presents. The receiving of presents—new possessions, given to you by others—was apparently a major part of the birthday-celebration ritual.

Andrew watched, not really understanding. He knew that humans placed high importance on the owning of things, specific objects that belonged only to them, but it was very hard to comprehend what value most of those objects had for them, or why they placed such emphasis on having them.

Little Miss, who had learned how to read only a year or two before, gave her sister a book. Not a cassette, not an infodisk, not a holocube, but an actual book, with a cover and binding and pages. Little Miss was very fond of books. So was Miss—especially books of poetry, which was a way of writing things in cryptic phrases arranged in uneven lines that Andrew found extremely mysterious.

"How marvelous!" Miss cried, when she had taken her book from its gaily covered wrapper. "The *Rubaiyat* of Omar Khayyám! I've always wanted it! But how did you even know there was such a thing? Who told you about it, Amanda?"

"I *read* about it," said Little Miss, looking a trifle put out. "You think I don't know anything at all, just because I'm five years younger than you, but let me tell you, Melissa—"

"Girls! Girls!" Sir called warningly. "Let's have no bickering at the birthday dinner!"

The next present Miss opened was from her mother: a fine cashmere sweater, white and fluffy. Miss was so excited that she put it on over the sweater she was already wearing.

And then she opened the small package that was her father's gift, and gasped; for Sir had bought her an intricate pendant of pink ivorite, carved with marvelous scrollwork so delicately worked that even Andrew's flawless vision was hard pressed to follow all its curving and interlocking patterns. Miss looked radiantly happy. She lifted it by its fine golden chain and slipped it over her head, lowering it carefully until it lay perfectly centered on the front of her new sweater.

"Happy birthday, Melissa," Sir said. And Ma'am chimed in, and Little Miss too, and they all sang the birthday song. Then Ma'am called for another round of the song, and this time she gestured to Andrew, who joined in, singing along with them.

For a moment he wondered whether he should have given Amanda some sort of present also. No, he thought, she did not seem to have expected it from him. And why should she? He wasn't a member of the family. He was an item of household machinery. The giving of birthday presents was entirely a human thing.

It was a lovely birthday dinner. There was only one thing wrong with it, which was that Little Miss seemed bitterly envious of Miss's lovely ivorite pendant.

She tried to hide it, of course. It was her sister's birthday dinner, after all, and she didn't want to spoil it. But all during the course of the evening Little Miss kept stealing glances at the pendant that gleamed warmly in pink and gold atop Melissa's sweater, and it took no great subtlety of perception on Andrew's part to know how unhappy she was.

He wished there was something he could do to cheer her up. But this whole affair of birthdays, and presents, and sisters, and envy, and other such human concepts—they were really beyond his comprehension. He was a very capable robot of the kind that he was designed to be, but his designers had seen no need to give him the capacity to understand why one little girl would be upset about a beautiful object that had been given to another little girl who was her sister on the occasion of her birthday.

A day or two later, though, Little Miss came to Andrew and said, "Can I speak to you, Andrew?"

"Of course you can."

"Did you like that pendant that Daddy gave Melissa?"

"It seemed to be very beautiful."

"It *is* very beautiful. It's the most gorgeous thing I've ever seen."

"It is quite beautiful, yes," Andrew said. "And I am sure that Sir will give you something every bit as beautiful when it is the time of your birthday."

"My birthday is three months from now," Little Miss said.

She said it as though that were an eternity away.

Andrew waited, not quite able to determine where this conversation was heading.

Then Little Miss went to the cabinet where she had put the piece of driftwood that she had brought from the beach the day he had gone swimming, and held it out to him.

"Will you make a pendant for me, Andrew? Out of this?"

"A wooden pendant?"

"Well, I don't happen to have any ivorite handy. But this is very pretty wood. You know how to carve, don't you? Or you could learn, I suppose."

"I'm certain that my mechanical skills would be equal to the job. But I would need certain tools, and—"

"Here," said Little Miss.

She had taken a small knife from the kitchen. She handed it to him with an air of great gravity, as if she were giving him a whole set of sculptor's blades.

"This should be all you need," she said. "I have faith in you, Andrew."

And she took his metal hand in hers and gave it a squeeze.

That night, in the quiet of the room where he usually stored himself when his day's chores were done, Andrew studied the piece of driftwood with great care for perhaps fifteen minutes, analyzing its grain, its density, its curvature. He gave the little knife careful scrutiny too, testing it on a piece of wood he had picked up in the garden to see how useful it would be. Then he considered Little Miss's height and what size pendant would be best suited to a girl who was still very small but was not likely to remain that way indefinitely.

Eventually he sliced a section from the tip of the driftwood piece. The wood was very hard, but Andrew had a robot's physical strength, so the only question was whether the knife itself would withstand the demands he was placing on it. It did.

He contemplated the section of wood that he had separated from the bigger piece. He held it, turning it, rubbing his fingers over its surface. He closed his eyes and envisioned the way it might look if he removed a bit here, a bit there—just shaved away a little over here—and also here—

Yes.

He began to work.

The job took him almost no time at all, once the preliminary planning had been carried out in his mind. Andrew's mechanical coordination was easily equal to such fastidious work and his eyesight was perfect and the wood seemed to yield readily enough to the things he wished to do with it.

By the time he was finished, though, it was much too late at night to take it to Little Miss. He put it aside and gave it no further thought until morning. Just as Little Miss was about to run outside to meet the bus that took her to school each day, Andrew produced the little carving and held it out to her. She took it from him, staring in perplexity and surprise.

"I made it for you," he said.

"You *did?*"

"From the wood you gave me last night."

"Oh, Andrew—Andrew—it's absolutely *marvelous,* Andrew! Oh, it's so fine! So beautiful! I never imagined you could make anything like it. Wait till Melissa sees it! Just wait! And I'll show it to Daddy, too—!"

The horn honked outside. Little Miss tucked the carving safely in her purse and hurried out to the bus. But she turned when she was a dozen meters up the path and waved to Andrew—and blew him a kiss.

In the evening, when Sir had come home from his stint at the

Regional Capitol and Little Miss had brought forth the carving, there was a general stir over it in the household. Ma'am exclaimed at great length over its loveliness and Miss was gracious enough to concede that it was nearly as attractive as the pendant she had received for her birthday.

Sir himself was astounded. He could not believe that Andrew had carved the little trinket.

"Where did you get this, Mandy?" Mandy was what he called Little Miss, though no one else did.

"I told you, Daddy. Andrew made it for me. I found a piece of driftwood on the beach and he carved it out of that."

"He's not supposed to be an artisan robot."

"A what?"

"A woodcarver," Sir said.

"Well, I guess that maybe he is," said Little Miss. "Maybe he's lots of things that we don't know about."

Sir looked toward Andrew. He was frowning, and he tugged thoughtfully at his mustache—Sir had a very conspicuous mustache, a great flaring woolly brush of a mustache—and he scowled the sort of scowl that Andrew, whose experience with human facial expressions was still somewhat limited, nevertheless understood to be a very serious scowl indeed.

"Did you actually make this thing, Andrew?"

"Yes, Sir."

"Robots aren't capable of lying, you know."

"That is not entirely correct, Sir. I could lie if I were ordered to lie, or if it were necessary for me to tell some untruth in order to keep a human being from harm, or even if my own safety were—" He paused. "But I did indeed carve this for Little Miss."

"And the design, too? You're responsible for that?"

"Yes, Sir."

"What did you copy it from?"

"Copy it, Sir?"

"You couldn't just have invented it out of thin air. You got it out of some book, right? Or you used a computer to plot it out for you, or else—"

"I assure you, Sir, I did nothing more than study the raw material for a time until I came to understand how best to carve it into some shape that would be pleasing to Little Miss. And then I carved it."

"Using what sort of tools, may I ask?"

"A small knife from the kitchen, Sir, which Little Miss kindly provided for me."

"A knife from the kitchen," Sir repeated, in an oddly flat tone. Slowly shaking his head, he hefted the carving in his hand as though he found its beauty almost incomprehensible. "A knife from the kitchen. She gave you a piece of driftwood and an ordinary little kitchen knife and with no other tool than that you were able to make *this*."

"Yes, Sir."

The next day Sir brought Andrew another piece of wood from the beach, a larger one that was bent and weathered and stained from its long immersion in the sea. He gave Andrew an electric vibro-knife, and showed him how to use it.

He said, "Make something out of this chunk of wood, Andrew. Anything you want to. I simply want to watch you while you're doing it."

"Certainly, Sir."

Andrew pondered the driftwood for a time, and then he switched on the vibro-knife and watched the movements of its blade edge, using his very finest optical focus, until he understood what sort of results the knife would be able to produce, and then finally he began to work. Sir sat right next to him, but as Andrew set about the task of carving he became barely aware of the human being adjacent to him. He was wholly focused on his task. All that mattered to him at that moment was the piece of wood, and the vibro-knife, and the vision of the thing that he intended to bring forth from the wood.

When he was done, he handed the carving to Sir, and went to fetch the dust-pan so that he could sweep up the shavings. Upon his return to the room he found Sir sitting motionless, staring at the carving in a kind of numb, stunned way.

"I asked for a household robot of the NDR series," Sir said softly. "I don't remember specifying anything about special craftsman adaptations."

"Indeed, Sir. I am an NDR household robot. I have no specialized implants having to do with craft skills."

"Yet you made this. I saw you do it with my own eyes."

"That is so, Sir."

"Could you make other things out of wood, do you think? Cabinets, let's say? Desks? Lamps? Large-scale sculptures?"

"I am unable to tell you, Sir. I have never attempted such things."

"Well, you will now."

After that, Andrew spent very little time preparing meals and waiting at the table, or doing the other minor jobs around the house that had become part of his daily routine. He was ordered to read books on woodcarving and design, with a special emphasis on furniture-making, and one of the empty attic rooms was set aside as a workshop for him.

Although he continued to carve small wooden trinkets for Miss and Little Miss and occasionally for Ma'am as well—bracelets, earrings, necklaces, pendants—Andrew devoted much of his time, at Sir's suggestion, to such things as cabinets and desks. His designs were striking and unusual. He employed rare and exotic woods which Sir provided, and decorated them with inlays of the most intricate and ingenious patterns.

Sir went upstairs to the workshop every day or two to inspect the latest creations.

"These are amazing productions, Andrew," he would say again and again. "Utterly amazing. You aren't just an artisan, do you realize that? You're a true artist. And the things you've been turning out are works of art."

Andrew said, "I enjoy making them, Sir."

"Enjoy?"

"Should I not be using that word?"

"It's a little unusual to hear a robot speaking of 'enjoying'

31

something, that's all. I didn't realize that robots had the capacity for feelings of that sort."

"Perhaps I use the concept loosely."

"Perhaps you do," Sir said. "But I'm not so sure. You say that you enjoy making this furniture. What exactly do you mean by that?"

"When I do the work, it makes the circuits of my brain somehow flow more easily. That seems to me to be the equivalent of the human feeling known as 'enjoyment.' I have heard you use the word 'enjoy' and I think I understand its significance. The way you use it fits the way I feel. So it seems appropriate for me to say that I enjoy making these things, Sir."

"Ah. Yes."

Sir was quiet for a time.

"You are a very unusual robot, do you know that, Andrew?"

"I am entirely standard, Sir. My circuitry is modular NDR, nothing more, nothing less."

"Indeed."

"Does my doing this cabinetwork trouble you, Sir?"

"Not at all, Andrew. Quite the contrary."

"Yet I sense some uneasiness in your vocal tones. There is a quality in them of—how shall I express it?—a quality of surprise? No, 'surprise' is inaccurate. A quality of uncertainty? Of doubt?— What I mean is that you appear to be thinking, Sir, that I am working beyond the programmed levels of my capacities."

"Yes," said Sir. "That's exactly what I do think, Andrew. Well beyond your programmed levels, as a matter of fact. Not that I'm troubled that you've unexpectedly turned out to have this little streak of artistic ability in you, you understand. But I'd like to know just why it's there."

FOUR

A FEW DAYS LATER Gerald Martin telephoned the managing director of the regional headquarters of the United States Robots and Mechanical Men Corporation and said, "I'm having a little problem with the NDR household robot that you assigned to me."

The managing director's name was Elliot Smythe. Like many of the high executives of U.S.R.M.M., Smythe was a member of the extensive and powerful Robertson family, descended from the original Lawrence Robertson who had founded the U. S. Robots Corporation in the latter part of the Twentieth Century.

Although by this time the company was so huge that it could no longer strictly be considered a Robertson family enterprise— the constant need to bring in fresh capital for expansion had forced the Robertsons and Smythes steadily to sell off a good-sized portion of their holdings of U.S.R.M.M. stock to outside investors—it was never a simple matter for outsiders to pick up the telephone and ask to speak to a Robertson or a Smythe. But Gerald Martin, after all, was Chairman of the Regional Legislature's Science and Technology Committee. Robertsons and Smythes, wealthy and powerful though they might be, were in no position to ignore telephone calls from Gerald Martin.

"A problem?" Elliott Smythe said, and his face on the telephone screen registered deep and sincere concern. "I'm tremendously sorry to hear that, Mr. Martin. And more than a little startled, too, I have to confess. Your NDR is a state-of-the-art product, you know, and the testing it received before it left here was extremely thorough. —What kind of malfunction have you been experiencing, actually? Is the robot failing to live up to your expectations in any way?"

"I didn't say anything about a malfunction."

"But you mentioned a problem, Mr. Martin. The NDR should be able to handle any household duty that you—"

Sir said crisply, "This has nothing to do with assigned household duties, Mr. Smythe. NDR-113 is performing his assigned duties perfectly. The problem is that the robot appears to have a few capabilities that weren't apparent in the specifications when you and I first discussed the notion of outfitting my home with a staff of robot servants."

Smythe's look of concern began to shade into serious apprehensiveness now. "Are you saying that he's overstepping its programmed group of responsibilities and doing things he hasn't been asked to do?"

"Not at all. You'd have heard from me a lot sooner if anything like that was going on, I guarantee you. No, Mr. Smythe, the thing is that quite unexpectedly he's gone in for woodworking. He makes wooden jewelry and furniture. My younger daughter gave him a very small request along those lines and he fulfilled it in a fashion that was beyond all expectation, and I've had him make a good many other things since. The way he carves wood is something phenomenally exquisite and he never does anything the same way twice. And what he produces are works of art, Mr. Smythe. Absolute works of art. Any museum would be proud to display them."

Smythe was silent for a time when Sir finished speaking. The corners of his mouth quirked a little but he showed no other outward display of emotion.

Then he said, "The NDR series is relatively versatile, Mr. Martin. It's not entirely unthinkable that an NDR should be able to do a little cabinetwork."

"I thought I made it clear that this goes far beyond being 'a little cabinetwork,' " said Sir.

"Yes. I suppose you have." There was another long pause. Then Smythe said, "I'd like to see some of this work. I'd like to have a look at this robot of yours, for that matter. Would it be all right, Mr. Martin, if I flew out to the Coast and gave him a quick inspection?"

"But if you need to inspect him, wouldn't you want to do it under laboratory conditions? You'd need to have all sorts of testing equipment, I'd imagine, and how could you transport all that to my house? It seems to me that it would be much easier all around if I simply brought Andrew to your headquarters, where he could be checked out properly."

"Andrew?"

Sir smiled briefly. "My girls call him that. From NDR, you know."

"Yes. Yes, I see. But there's no need for you to go to the inconvenience of flying east, Mr. Martin. I'm overdue for a visit to some of our West Coast facilities anyway, and this will give me a good excuse to go out there. And at this point I don't intend to put your NDR through any sort of complicated tests. I'd just like to talk to him a bit—and to you—and of course I'd like to see the kinds of thing your robot has been carving. I could hardly expect you to haul a van full of desks and cabinets out here, you know."

"That makes sense, I guess."

"Next Tuesday, then? Would that be convenient for you?"

"I'll see to it that it is," said Sir.

"Oh, and one more thing. I'd like to bring Merwin Mansky with me, if I may. Our Chief Robopsychologist. I think Dr. Mansky will want to take a look at NDR-113's cabinetwork also. In fact, I'm quite sure of it."

Sir cleared his Tuesday schedule and arranged to remain at home all afternoon. Smythe and Mansky were due to arrive in

San Francisco on a noon flight and then it would take them another thirty minutes to hop up the coast by local shuttle.

Andrew was told that visitors were coming to see him, of course. That seemed a little odd to him—why would anyone want to pay a social call on a robot? —but he felt no need to try to understand what was taking place. In those days Andrew rarely tried to question the doings of the human beings around him or to analyze events in any systematic way. It was only in later years, when he had attained a far greater comprehension of his situation, that he was able to review that early scene and understand it in its proper light.

A splendid robochauffeured limousine delivered the U. S. Robots executive and the Chief Robopsychologist to the Martin estate. They were a curiously mismatched pair, for Elliott Smythe was a slender, towering, athletic-looking man with long limbs and a great mane of dense white hair, who seemed as though he would be more at home on a tennis court or in a polo match than in a corporate office, while Merwin Mansky was short and stocky and had no hair at all, and gave the appearance of someone who would leave his desk only under great duress.

"This is Andrew," Sir told them. "His carpentry workshop is upstairs, but you can see some of his products all around this room. That bookcase—the lamps, and the table they're on—the light fixture—"

"Remarkable work," said Elliot Smythe. "No exaggeration at all, Mr. Martin: they certainly are masterpieces, every one of them."

Merwin Mansky gave the furniture only the most minimal glance. His attention was drawn much more powerfully to Andrew.

"Code check," Mansky said brusquely. "Aleph Nine, Andrew."

Andrew's response was immediate. It had to be: code checks were subsumed under Second Law priorities and they required unhesitating obedience. Andrew, red photoelectric eyes glowing intently, ran through the entire set of Aleph Nine parameters while Mansky listened, nodding.

"Very good, Andrew. Code check: Epsilon Seven."

Andrew gave Mansky Epsilon Seven. He gave him Omicron Fourteen. He gave him Kappa Three, which was one of the most elaborate checks of all, embodying the parameters that contained the Three Laws.

"Well done," said Mansky. "One more, now. Code check: the entire Omega series."

Andrew recited the Omega codes, which governed the pathways dealing with the ability to process and correlate newly acquired data. That set took quite a while also. Throughout the long recitation Sir looked on in puzzlement. Elliott Smythe seemed scarcely to be listening.

Mansky said, "He's in perfect working order. Every parameter is exactly as it should be."

"As I told Mr. Smythe," Sir began, "the question isn't one of Andrew's failure to perform. It's that his performance is so far beyond expectation."

"Beyond your expectation, perhaps," said Mansky.

Sir swung around as though he had been stung. "And what is that supposed to mean, may I ask?"

Mansky frowned all the way up to the top of his bare scalp. The heavy lines in his forehead were so pronounced that they might have been carved by Andrew. He had drawn features and deep-set weary eyes and pallid skin, and generally looked unhealthy. Andrew suspected that Mansky might actually be a good deal younger than he seemed.

He said, "Robotics isn't an exact art, Mr. Martin. I can't explain it to you in detail, or, rather, I could, but it would take a great deal of time and I'm not certain you'd get much benefit from the explanation, but what I mean is that the mathematics governing the plotting of the positronic pathways is far too complicated to permit any but approximate solutions. So robots of Andrew's level of construction often turn out somewhat unexpectedly to have abilities somewhat beyond the basic design specifications. —I want to assure you, though, that simply because Andrew apparently is a master carpenter there's no reason whatever to fear any sort of unpredictable behavior that might jeopardize you or your family. Whatever else is variable about a robot's performance, the Three Laws are utterly incontrovertible and undefeatable. They are intrinsic to the positronic brain. Andrew would cease to function entirely before he committed any violation of the Laws."

"He's more than simply a master carpenter, Dr. Mansky," Sir said. "We're not just talking about some nice tables and chairs here."

"Yes. Yes, of course. I understand he does little trinkets and knickknacks too."

Sir smiled, but it was a singularly icy smile. He opened the cabinet where Little Miss kept some of the treasures Andrew had created for her and took something out.

"See for yourself," he said acidly to Mansky. "Here's one of his trinkets. One of his knickknacks."

Sir handed over a little sphere of shining ebony: a playground scene in which the boys and girls were almost too small to make out, yet they were in perfect proportion, and they blended so naturally with the grain that that, too, seemed to have been carved. The figures appeared on the verge of coming to life and moving about. Two boys were about to have a fistfight; two girls were intently studying a necklace of almost microscopic size that a third girl was showing them; a teacher stood to one side, stooping a little to answer a question that a very short boy was asking her.

The robopsychologist stared at the tiny carving for an extraordinarily long while without saying anything.

"May I look at it, Dr. Mansky?" Elliott Smythe said.

"Yes. Yes, certainly."

Mansky's hand trembled a little as he passed the little object across to the U. S. Robots executive.

Now it was Smythe's turn to stare in solemn silence. Andrew, watching him, experienced a new little burst of the sensation that he had come to identify as enjoyment. Plainly these two men were impressed with what he had carved. Indeed they appeared to be so impressed that they were unable to express their appreciation in words.

Mansky said, finally, *"He* did that?"

Sir nodded. "He's never seen a school playground. My daughter Amanda described this scene to him one afternoon when he asked her to tell him what one was like. He spoke with her for about five minutes. Then he went upstairs and made this."

"Remarkable," Smythe said. "Phenomenal."

"Phenomenal, yes," said Sir. "Now do you see why I thought I ought to bring this to your attention? This kind of work goes well beyond the standard hardwired capacity of your NDR series, does it not? I hate to use a cliché, gentlemen, but what we have here is a bit of a genius robot, wouldn't you say? Something that might be considered to verge almost on the human?"

"There is nothing human whatsoever about NDR-113," said Mansky with a kind of prissy firmness. "Please don't confuse the issue, Mr. Martin. What we have here is a machine, and you must never forget that. A machine with some degree of intelligence, yes, and evidently possessing something simulating creativity as well. But a machine all the same. I've spent my entire career dealing with robot personalities—yes, they do have personalities, after their fashion—and if anyone were to be tempted to believe that robots partake of humanity, it would be me, Mr. Martin. But I don't believe it and neither should you."

"I didn't mean it seriously. But how can you account for this kind of artistic ability, then?"

"The luck of the draw," Mansky said. "Something in the pathways. A fluke. We've been attempting to design generalized pathways for the last couple of years—robots, I mean, who are not simply limited to the job they're designed for, but are capable of expanding their own scope by a process that can be compared to inductive reasoning—and it's not entirely surprising that something like this, this sort of simulated creativity, should turn up in

39

one of them. As I said a few moments ago, robotics is not an exact art. Sometimes unusual things happen."

"Could you make it happen again? Could you build another robot who duplicates Andrew's special abilities? A whole series of them, perhaps?"

"Probably not. We're talking about a stochastic event here, Mr. Martin. Do you follow me? We don't know in any precise and quantifiable fashion how we managed to get those abilities into Andrew in the first place, so there's no way as of now that we could set out to reproduce whatever deviant pathway it is that allows him to create work of this sort. What I mean," Mansky said, "is that Andrew must have been something of an accident, and very likely he is unique."

"Good! I don't in the least mind Andrew's being the only one of his kind."

Smythe, who had been at the window for some time now, look-ing out over the fog-shrouded ocean, turned abruptly and said, "Mr. Martin, what I'd like to do is take Andrew back to our headquarters for extensive study. Naturally, we'll supply you with an equivalent NDR robot by way of a replacement, and we'll see to it that he is programmed with full knowledge of whatever domestic assignments you may already have given Andrew, so that—"

"No," Sir said, with sudden grimness.

Smythe delicately flicked one eyebrow upward. "Since you came to us with this situation in the first place, you must surely recognize the importance of our making a detailed examination of Andrew, so that we can begin to understand how—"

"Dr. Mansky has just said that Andrew's a pure fluke, that you don't have any idea how he got to be able to do the things with wood that he can do, that you couldn't replicate him even if you tried. So I fail to see what purpose would be served by your taking him back and giving me some other robot in his place."

"Dr. Mansky may be too pessimistic. Once we begin to trace the actual course of Andrew's neural pathways—"

"Once you do," said Sir, "there may not be very much left of Andrew afterward, isn't that correct?"

"The pathways are fragile. Analysis often involves a certain degree of destruction, yes," Smythe conceded.

"My girls are extremely fond of Andrew," Sir said. "Especially the younger one, Amanda. I'd venture to say that Andrew is Amanda's best friend, in fact: that she loves Andrew as much as she loves anyone or anything on this planet. And Andrew appears to be equally fond of her. I called Andrew's capabilities to your attention because I thought it might be useful for you to become aware of what you had produced here—and because even as a layman I suspected that Andrew's skills might have been something that was inadvertently built into him, and I was curious about whether that was the case, which it appears now to be. But if you think there's even the slightest chance that I'm going to let you take Andrew apart, when we both know that you're not confident of putting him back together exactly as he was, forget it. Just forget it."

"I can quite appreciate the nature of the bond that can form between a young girl and her household robot. Nonetheless, for you to obstruct the ongoing course of our research in this way, Mr. Martin—"

"I can obstruct a lot more than that," said Sir. "Or have you forgotten who it is that has been pushing all sorts of pro-robot legislature through my Committee the past three years? I suggest that we go upstairs so that you can examine some of Andrew's other work, which I think you'll find of very great interest. And then you and Dr. Mansky ought to begin thinking about heading back down to San Francisco and getting on to those visits to your West Coast facilities that you were telling me you needed to make. Andrew stays here. Is that understood?"

There was a flicker of fury in Smythe's eyes. But only the merest of flickers, the barest quick change of expression, which even Andrew's superb vision was hard pressed to perceive. Then Smythe shrugged.

41

"As you wish, Mr. Martin. No harm will come to Andrew. You have my word."

"Good."

"And I would indeed like to go upstairs and see the rest of his work."

"My pleasure," said Sir. "I can even give you some of it, if you like. Pick out anything you want—of the furniture, I mean, not the little ornamental things that he's made for my wife and daughters—and it's yours. I'm serious."

"Very kind of you," said Smythe.

Mansky said, "May I repeat something I observed a little while back, Mr. Martin?"

"If you need to, Dr. Mansky."

"You raised the point that Andrew's creativity verges almost on the human. So it does: even I will admit that. But verging on the human and *being* human are not the same thing. I want to remind you that Andrew is a machine."

"I take note of that fact."

"It may become harder for you to bear it in mind after a time, since evidently Andrew is going to remain with you. Please try. You speak of this robot as your daughter's 'friend.' You speak of her 'love' for him. That's a dangerous attitude: dangerous to her, I mean. Friends are friends and machines are machines and they should not be confused. One may love another person but one ordinarily does not love a household appliance, however useful or attractive or pleasing it may be. All Andrew is is an ambulatory computer, Mr. Martin, a computer that is endowed with artificial intelligence and has been placed in a humanoid body-frame and so gives the superficial appearance of being something quite different from the computers that guide our air traffic and operate our communications systems and do all our other routine chores. The personality that your daughter believes she perceives in Andrew, and which you say has caused her to 'love' him, is merely a simulated personality, a pre-designed construct, wholly synthetic. I beg of you, Mr. Martin: never forget that a computer with arms and legs and a positronic brain is still nothing but a computer, albeit a somewhat enhanced computer. A machine. A gadget, Mr. Martin. A household appliance.''

"I will keep that in mind," said Sir in a dry, cool tone. "You know, Dr. Mansky, I've always endeavored to think clearly and in an orderly way. I never confuse an arm with a leg or a hand with a foot or a cow with a horse, and I'll do my best not to confuse a robot with a human being, however great the temptation may become. Thank you very much for your advice. And now, if you'd like to have a quick tour of Andrew's workshop—"

FIVE

MISS HAD BEGUN to cross the threshold that truly separates girlhood from womanhood, now. She was enjoying an active social life and going off with her new friends—not all of them girls —on excursions to the mountains, to the deserts of the south, to the wilderness to the north. Her presence in the Martin house was becoming an increasingly rare event.

So it was Little Miss—not as little as before—who filled Andrew's horizon now. She was turning into a coltish, tireless girl who loved to run great distances along the beach, with Andrew effortlessly keeping pace beside her. She went rambling in the forested areas adjacent to the house, and relied on Andrew to help her down when she had scrambled a little too far up some tree to peer into a bird's nest, or when she had trapped herself on some precarious rocky ledge that she had climbed for the sake of getting a better view of the sea.

As ever, Andrew was vigilant and endlessly protective as Little Miss romped about. He would let her take her little tomboyish risks, yes, because they seemed to make her happy, but not without his calculating the *real* risk of anything serious happening to her, and he was always poised and ready to intervene swiftly on her behalf if that should be necessary.

The First Law, of course, compelled Andrew to exert constant

44

diligence to protect Little Miss from harm. But, as he sometimes told himself, he would willingly and gladly defend her against peril of any sort even if the First Law did not exist.

That was an odd thought: that there might be no First Law. Andrew could barely conceive of that. The First Law (and the Second, and the Third) were such fundamental aspects of his neural pathways that it made him dizzy to imagine himself without them. And yet he *had* imagined it. Andrew was puzzled by that: how strange, having a capacity to imagine the unimaginable! It made him feel almost human, when paradoxical concepts like that went through his mind.

But what did *almost* human mean? That was another paradox, and an even more dizzying one. Either you were human or you were not. How could there be any sort of intermediate state?

You are a robot, Andrew reminded himself sternly.

You are a product of the United States Robots and Mechanical Men Corporation.

And then Andrew would look at Little Miss and a sensation of great joy and warmth would spread through his positronic brain —a sensation that he had come to identify as "love"—and he would have to remind himself, all over again, that he was nothing more than a cleverly designed structure of metal and plastic with an artificial platinum-iridium brain inside his chrome-steel skull, and he had no right to feel emotions, or to think paradoxical thoughts, or to do any other such complex and mysterious human thing. Even his woodworking art—and he did allow himself to think of it as "art"—was simply a function of the skills with which he had been programmed by his designers.

Little Miss never allowed herself to forget that the very first piece of woodcarving Andrew had done had been for her. She was rarely without the little pendant that he had made for her out of that piece of driftwood, wearing it on a silver chain about her neck and reaching up to finger it fondly again and again.

It was she who first objected to Sir's casual habit of giving away Andrew's productions to anyone who visited the house. He would proudly show his guests Andrew's latest work, and then, when the predictable expressions of admiration and even envy were uttered, would grandly exclaim, "Do you really like it that much? Then take it with you! By all means, take it! My pleasure! There are plenty more where that one came from!"

One day Sir bestowed a particularly intricate abstract carving—a shining spheroid made of slender interwoven strips of redwood with inlays of manzanita and madrone wood—on the Speaker of the Legislature. The Speaker was a loud-voiced red-faced man who had always seemed particularly dull-witted and vulgar to Little Miss, and she very much doubted that he had any ability to see the beauty in Andrew's work. No doubt he was simply being diplomatic when he had praised the carving, and he would simply toss it thoughtlessly into some closet when he got it home.

Little Miss said, after the Speaker had left, "Come on, Dad. You shouldn't have given that to him and you know it!"

"But he liked it, Mandy. He said he thought it was extremely beautiful."

"It *is* extremely beautiful. So is the beach in front of our house. If he said the beach was extremely beautiful, would you have deeded it over to him?"

"Mandy, Mandy—"

"Well? Would you?"

"It's a false parallel," Sir said. "Obviously you don't go handing away chunks of your real estate to people on a whim. But a small carving—given as a modest expression of affection to a friend of many years' standing who also happens to be a highly influential political leader—"

"Are you saying it was a *bribe?*"

For an instant real anger flashed in Sir's eyes. But it died away almost as fast as it had come and the usual twinkle with which he regarded his youngest daughter returned.

"You don't really mean that, do you, Mandy? You understand that my gift to the Speaker was merely an act of hospitality, right?"

"Well—yes. Yes. I'm sorry, Dad. What I said was uncalled-for and mean."

Sir smiled. "It was, yes. —Is it that you wanted that carving for yourself? Your room is already filled with things that Andrew has made, you know. The whole house is. We can't give them away as fast as he makes them."

"That's the whole point I was trying to make. That you *give* them away."

Sir's smile grew broader. "Well, what would you prefer that I do? Sell them to people?"

"As a matter of fact, yes. That's exactly what I would prefer."

Sir said, looking astonished, "It isn't like you to be greedy, Mandy."

"What does greed have to do with this?"

"Surely you must understand that we already have more than enough money. Quite apart from the complete impropriety of my putting a price tag on some object that a guest in my house might happen to admire, it would be absurd for me to go in for trivial profiteering of any such kind."

"I'm not saying that *we* should try to make money on the things Andrew carves. But what about Andrew?"

"What about him?"

"He does the work. He should have the money."

Sir blinked. "Andrew's a robot, Mandy."

"Yes. I know that, Dad."

"Robots aren't people, sweet. They're machines, remember? Like telephones, like computers. What imaginable use would a machine have for money? Robots don't go shopping. Robots don't take holidays in Hawaii. Robots don't—"

"I'm serious, Dad. This is an important issue. Andrew spent hours making that."

"So?"

"Robot or not, he's got the right to benefit from the results of his labor. When you coolly hand out the things he makes as gifts to your friends or political associates, the way you do, you're exploiting him, did you ever stop to think of that, Dad? He may be a machine but he's not a slave. And also he's an *artist*. He's entitled to be compensated for making those things. Maybe not when he makes them for us, but when you give them away like that to other people—" Little Miss paused. "Do you remember the French Revolution, Dad? —No, I don't mean do you remember it literally. But its basic issue was the exploiting of the working classes by the aristocracy. Robots are our new working classes. And if we go on treating our robots the way the dukes and duchesses treated their peasants—"

Sir smiled gently.

"The last thing we need to worry about, Mandy, is an uprising by our robots. The Three Laws—"

"The Three Laws, the Three Laws, the Three Laws! I *hate* the Three Laws! You can't deprive Andrew of the benefit of the work he does. You can't! It isn't *fair,* Dad!"

The fury in Little Miss's voice cut off the rest of Sir's disquisition on the Laws of Robotics before he had barely managed to frame his words.

He said instead, after a moment, "You really feel strongly about this, don't you, Mandy?"

"Yes. Yes, I do."

"All right. Let me think about it. And perhaps we can actually work something out for Andrew along the lines that you're suggesting."

"You promise?"

"I promise," said Sir, and Little Miss knew that everything was going to be all right, for her father's promises to her were inviolable contracts—always had been, always would be.

Some time went by, and other visitors came to the house, and everyone who saw Andrew's work responded with the usual praise. But Little Miss, who was watching closely, observed with pleasure that her father had stopped giving Andrew's things away, no matter how effusive the praise might be.

On the other hand, it happened on several occasions that some guest would say, "You don't think I could buy that from you, do you, Gerald?" And Sir, looking uncomfortable, would simply shrug and reply that he wasn't quite sure whether he wanted to get into the business of selling such things.

48

Little Miss wondered why her father was sidestepping the issue like that. Sidestepping things wasn't normally part of his nature. And it wasn't as though anyone was likely to accuse him of deliberately setting out to earn money by peddling Andrew's work to his house guests. Obviously Gerald Martin was in no need of picking up a bit of extra money on the side that way. But if the offers were made in good faith, though, why not accept them?

She let the issue rest, nevertheless. She knew her father well enough to understand that the matter was still open, and would be attended to in due course.

Then another visitor came: John Feingold, Sir's lawyer. The offices of Feingold's law firm were in the San Francisco area, where despite the general decentralization of city life that had been going on all during the current century a good many people still preferred to live. But though San Francisco was only a short journey south of the wild strip of coast where the Martins lived, a visit from John Feingold to the Martin house was a relatively unusual thing. Usually Sir went down to San Francisco whenever he had business to discuss with Feingold. So Little Miss knew that something special must be up.

Feingold was an easy-going white-haired man with florid pink skin, a pudgy belly, and a warm, amiable smile. He preferred to dress in older styles of clothing and the rims of his contact lenses were tinted a bright green, a fashion so rare nowadays that it was all that Little Miss could do to keep from giggling whenever she saw the lawyer. Sir had to shoot her a stern glance now and then when he detected a fit of laughter coming over her in Feingold's presence.

Feingold and Sir settled down before the fireplace in the great central room of the house and Sir handed him a small inlaid plaque that Andrew had produced a few days before.

The lawyer nodded. He turned it over and over in his hand, rubbed its polished surface appreciatively, held it up to the light at various angles.

"Beautiful," he said, finally. "Extraordinarily fine work, all right. Your robot did it?"

"Yes. How did you know that?"

"I've heard some talk. It's no secret, Gerald, that you've got a robot here who's a master craftsman in wood."

Sir glanced up at Andrew, who was standing quietly in the shadows to one side. "Do you hear that, Andrew? You're famous all up and down California. —But you're wrong about one thing, John. Andrew isn't simply a master craftsman. He's an out-and-out *artist*, nothing less."

"Indeed he is," Feingold said. "That's the only word for him. This is a wonderful piece."

"Would you like to own it?" Sir asked.

Feingold's eyes widened in surprise. "Are you offering it to me, Gerald?"

"I might be. It all depends on how much you'd be willing to pay for it."

Feingold grunted as though Sir had poked him in the ribs with a rigid finger. He sat back sharply, rearranging himself with some care, and for a moment he did not reply.

Then he said, in an entirely different voice, "I hadn't been aware that you've been undergoing financial reverses lately, Gerald."

"I haven't."

"Then—pardon me if I sound a little confused—why on Earth would you want to—"

His voice trailed off.

"Sell you that little carving?" Sir finished for him.

"Yes. Sell it. I know you've been giving away a great many of the things that Andrew has made. People have told me that it's practically impossible to come here without being offered something. I've seen a few of the things that they've been given. There's never been a question of money changing hands, am I right? And now—completely leaving out of the discussion the fact that I'm not a collector of little wooden carvings, no matter how lovely they might be—you baffle me by asking me if I want to purchase one! Why? I doubt very much that you have any special reason for wanting me to pay for what everybody else gets free. And you can't possibly need the money. You've just told me that yourself. In any event how much would you be able to get for an object like this? Five hundred dollars? A thousand? If you're still as wealthy as I know you to be, Gerald, what difference could the odd five hundred or thousand make to you?"

"Not to me. To Andrew."

"What?"

"Your estimate happens to be right on the mark, John. I think I could get a thousand for this little thing. And I've been offered rather more than that for chairs and desks that Andrew has made. Not just one-shot purchases but entire distribution deals for large-scale production. If I had accepted any of the offers, there'd be a fine fat bank account built up by now, entirely on the proceeds of Andrew's woodworking—something up in the hundreds of thousands already, I suspect."

Feingold fussed with his epaulets and collar-studs. "Good heavens, Gerald, I can't make any sense out of any of this. A rich man making himself richer by putting his robot to work in some sort of cottage industry—"

"I've already told you, John, that the money wouldn't be for me. This is all for Andrew's sake. I want to start selling his products and I want the money to be banked under the name of Andrew Martin."

"A bank account in the name of a robot?"

"Exactly. And that's why I've asked you to come up here today. I want to know whether it would be legal to establish an account in Andrew's name—an account that Andrew himself would control, you understand, entirely his own money, which he would be able to use absolutely as he pleases—"

Feingold said, sounding mystified, "Legal? For a robot to earn and save money? I just couldn't say. There are no precedents, so far as I've ever heard. I doubt that there's any law against it, but even so—robots aren't people. How can they have bank accounts, then?"

"Corporations aren't people either, except in the most abstract sense: a legal fiction, as you would term it. Yet corporations have bank accounts.''

"Well, I grant you that. But corporations have been recognized in the eyes of the law for centuries as entities qualified to own property of all sorts. Robots, Gerald, have no legal rights at all, as surely you must be aware. And simply as a procedural matter, let me remind you that corporations also have corporate officers, and they sign the papers that establish the bank accounts. Who would open Andrew's account? You? And would it be Andrew's account, if you opened it?''

"I've opened bank accounts in the names of my children," Sir replied. "Nevertheless the accounts are theirs. Besides, Andrew can sign his name as well as you or I.''

"Yes. Yes, of course, I suppose he can." Feingold leaned back until his chair creaked. "Let me think, Gerald. This is all so unusual. Is there really any legislation specifically forbidding robots to own property, or is it simply *assumed* that they can't, because the idea is so far from the main stream that nobody's ever given a thought to it? I'd have to research it before I could give you an opinion. Quite possibly there are no such laws, precisely because a robot having assets is such a peculiar notion that it hasn't been deemed necessary to give it any consideration. Nobody has bothered to pass laws forbidding trees to have bank accounts, after all, or lawnmowers—''

"Cats and dogs have had bank accounts. Trust funds for their upkeep, left to them by their loving owners," Sir said. "The courts have no objection to that.''

"Another good point, yes. Although cats and dogs are living creatures, at least. Robots are inanimate.''

"I don't see what difference that makes.''

"You ought to bear in mind, Gerald, that there's a certain prejudice against robots in our society, a certain fear, I might almost say, that doesn't extend to cats and dogs. It might well be that someone *has* put laws on the books restricting the rights of robots to hold property. But that's easily enough checked.

—Let's assume that it is legal. How would you go about it? Take Andrew down to the bank and let him speak to the manager?"

"I'd simply have the forms sent here for Andrew's signature. There shouldn't be any need for a personal appearance on his part. But what I need to find out from you, John, is what I can do to protect Andrew—and myself, I suppose—against negative public reaction. Even though it may well be legal for him to have a bank account, there probably will be people who aren't going to like the idea."

"How will they find out?" Feingold asked.

"How will we keep them from finding out?" said Sir. "If someone buys an item from him and makes a check payable to Andrew Martin, say—"

"Um. Yes." Feingold's gaze seemed to turn inward for a moment. Then he said, "Well, one thing we could do is to set up a corporation to handle all finances in his name—a corporation with a nice impersonal name, something like West Coast Wood Artistry, Ltd.—and Andrew can be the president and sole stockholder, though we could make ourselves members of the board of directors. That will place a layer of legalistic insulation between him and the hostile world. It ought to be enough, Gerald. Whenever Andrew wants to purchase something, he can simply draw a salary from the corporation treasury. Or declare a dividend for himself. The fact that he's a robot won't have to be a matter of public record. The incorporation forms will only need the names of the stockholders—not their birth certificates. Of course, he'll have to begin filing income tax returns. But the revenue people aren't going to come around to find out whether Taxpayer Andrew Martin is a human being or not. All they'll care about is whether Taxpayer Martin pays his taxes on time."

"Good. Good. Anything else?"

"Not that I can think of offhand. If I come up with anything else once I've run a search for precedents, I'll let you know. But I suspect it's going to work. Nobody's likely to stop you so long as you go about things quietly and obey the absolute letter of the corporation law. And if anyone does find out what's going on and doesn't like it, well, it'll be up to them to take action against you to stop it—provided they can show that they've got legal standing to intervene."

"And if someone does, John? Will you take the case if a suit is brought against us?"

"Certainly. For an appropriate retainer."

"What would be appropriate, do you think?"

Feingold smiled. "Something along the lines of that," he said, and pointed to the wooden plaque.

"Fair enough," said Sir.

"Not that I'm a collector, you understand. But it does have a certain artistic appeal."

"Indeed it does," said Sir.

Feingold chuckled and turned to the robot. "Andrew, you're going to be—well, not a rich man, but a rich robot. Does that please you?"

"Yes, sir."

"And what do you plan to do with all the money you're going to make?"

"Pay for things, sir, which otherwise Sir would have had to pay for. It would save him expense, sir."

SIX

THE OCCASIONS for drawing on Andrew's bank account came more frequently than anyone had expected. From time to time Andrew, like any machine no matter how well made, was in need of repair—and robot repairs were invariably expensive. Then, too, there were the regular upgrades. Robotics had always been a dynamic industry, rapidly progressing from decade to decade since the days of the first massive, clunky products, which had not even had the ability to speak. Improvements in design, in function, in capabilities, were unending. With the passing years robots constantly became more sleek, ever more versatile, ever more deft of motion and durable of structure.

Sir saw to it that Andrew had the advantage of every new device that U. S. Robots developed. When the improved homeostasis circuitry came out, Sir made sure that it was installed in Andrew almost at once. When the new and far more efficient articulation of the leg-joint was perfected, using the latest elastomer technology, Andrew got it. When, a few years later, subtler face-panels—made of carbon fiber set in an epoxy matrix which looked less sketchily human than the old kind—became the rage, Andrew was modified accordingly, to provide him with the serious, sensitive, perceptive, artistic look which Sir—at Little Miss's prompting—had come to believe was appropriate to his nature. Little Miss wanted Andrew to be an absolute paragon of metallic excellence, and Sir felt the same way.

Everything was done at Andrew's expense, naturally.

Andrew insisted on that. He would not hear of letting Sir pay for any of the costs associated with his upgrades. A steady stream of magnificent work flowed from his little attic shop—one-of-a-kind masterpieces of carved jewelry fashioned from rare woods, sumptuous office furniture, elegant bedroom suites, wondrous lamps, and ornate bookcases.

There was no need for a showroom or catalogs, because word of mouth took care of everything and all of Andrew's output was commissioned months and then years in advance. The checks were made payable to Pacific Coast Artifactories, Incorporated, and Andrew Martin was the only officer of Pacific Coast Artifactories who was entitled to draw money from the corporate account. Whenever it was necessary for Andrew to go back to the U. S. Robots factory for maintenance or upgrading, it was a Pacific Coast Artifactories check, signed by Andrew himself, that paid for the work.

The one area of Andrew that remained untouched by upgrading of any sort was his positronic pathways. Sir was insistent—*extremely* insistent—about that.

"The new robots aren't nearly as good as you are, Andrew," he said. "The new ones are contemptibly simple-minded creatures, as a matter of fact. The company has succeeded in learning how to make the pathways more precise, more closely on the nose, more deeply on the track, but that is a double-edged kind of improvement. The new robots don't shift. They have no mental agility. There's nothing in the least unpredictable about them. They simply do what they're designed to do and never a smidgeon more. I like you better, Andrew."

"Thank you, Sir."

"Of course, the company will tell you that their current generation of robots is 99.9% efficient, or maybe they're claiming 100% efficiency this year. Well, good for them. But a robot like you, Andrew—you're 102% efficient; 110%, maybe. That isn't what they want, at U. S. Robots. They're after perfection, and I suppose they've attained it—their idea of perfection, anyway. The perfect servant. The flawlessly functioning mechanical man. But perfection can be a terrible limitation, Andrew. Don't you agree? What it leads to is a kind of soulless automaton that has no ability to transcend its builders' predetermined notions of its limitations. Not at all like you, Andrew. You aren't soulless, that's obvious to us all by now. And as for limitations—"

"I definitely have limitations, Sir."

"Of course you do. But that's not what I'm talking about, and you know it damned well! You're an artist, Andrew, an artist in wood, and if you're an artist you've got to have a soul somewhere in those positronic pathways of yours. Don't ask me how it got there—I don't know and neither do the people who built you. But it's there. It enables you to make the wonderful things that you make. That's because your pathways are the old-fashioned generalized kind. The *obsolete* generalized kind. And it's all on account of you, Andrew, that pathways of the kind you have are no longer used. Are you aware of that?"

"Yes, Sir. I think I am, Sir."

"It's because I let Merwin Mansky come out here and get a good look at you. I'm convinced that he and Smythe ordered all generalized-pathways robots pulled out of production the moment they got back to the factory. They must have felt deeply threatened after they saw what you were like. It was the unpredictability that frightened them."

"Frightened, Sir? How could I possibly be frightening to anyone?"

"You frightened Mansky, that much I know. You scared him silly, Andrew. I saw his hand shaking when he passed that little carving you had made to Smythe. Mansky hadn't anticipated any such artistic abilities in an NDR robot. He didn't even think it was possible, I'd bet. And there you were, turning out all those masterpieces. —Do you know how many times over the next five years he called me, trying to wheedle me into shipping you back to the factory so that he could put you under study? Nine times!

Nine! I refused every time. And when you *did* go back to the factory for upgrades, I made a point of going over Mansky's head to Smythe or Jimmy Robertson or one of the other top executives and getting an iron-clad guarantee that Mansky wouldn't be allowed to fool around with your pathways. I always worried that he would do it on the sly, though. Well, Mansky's retired, now, and they aren't making robots with your kind of pathways any more, and I suppose we'll finally have some peace."

Sir had given up his seat in the Regional Legislature by this time. There had been some talk on and off over the years of his running for Regional Coordinator, but the timing of his candidacy had never been right. Sir had felt he wanted to stay on one more term in the Legislature to see certain measures into law, and meanwhile a new Coordinator was elected who seemed to be merely an interim figure at first, holding the job until Sir was ready to take it.

But then the supposed interim man had turned out to be an energetic and forceful Coordinator in his own right, and he had stayed on another term and then another, until Sir began to grow weary of his life of public service and lost interest in running. (Or perhaps had simply admitted that the public would now prefer a younger man for the job.)

Sir had changed with the passage of time in many ways, not just the loss of the fire and conviction that had marked him out for success when he was still a raw new legislator. His hair had thinned and grayed and his face had grown pouchy, and his fierce penetrating eyes no longer saw as clearly. Even his famous mustache was less bristling now, less flamboyant. Whereas Andrew looked rather better than he had when he first joined the family—quite handsome, in fact, in his robotic way.

Time had brought certain other changes to the Martin household, too.

Ma'am had decided, after some thirty years of being Mrs. Gerald Martin, that there might be some more fulfilling role in life than simply being the wife of a distinguished member of the Regional Legislature. She had played the part of Mrs. Gerald

Martin loyally and uncomplainingly and very well, all that time. But she had played it long enough.

And so she had regretfully announced her decision to Sir, and they had amicably separated, and Ma'am had gone off to join an art colony somewhere in Europe—perhaps in southern France, perhaps in Italy. Andrew was never quite sure which it was (or what difference, if any, there might be between France and Italy, which were mere names to him) and the postage stamps on her infrequent letters to Sir were of various kinds. Since both France and Italy were provinces of the European Region, and had been for a long time, Andrew had difficulty understanding why they needed their own postage stamps, either. But apparently they insisted on maintaining certain ancient folkways even though the world had passed beyond the epoch of independent and rival nations.

The two girls had finished growing up, too. Miss, who by all reports had become strikingly beautiful, had married and moved to Southern California, and then she had married again and moved to South America, and then had come word of still another marriage and a new home in Australia. But now Miss was living in New York City and had become a poet, and nothing was said about any further new husbands. Andrew suspected that Miss's life had not turned out to be as happy or rewarding as it should have been, and he regretted that. Still, he reminded himself, he had no very clear understanding of what humans meant by "happiness." Perhaps Miss had lived exactly the kind of life that she had wanted to live. He hoped so, anyway.

As for Little Miss, she was now a slender, fine-boned woman with high cheekbones and a look of great delicacy backed by extraordinary resilience. Andrew had never heard anyone speak of her unusual beauty in his presence—Miss was always said to be the beautiful sister, and Little Miss was praised more for her forceful character than for her looks. To Andrew's taste golden-haired Little Miss had always seemed far more beautiful than the soft and overly curvy older sister; but his taste was only a robot's taste, after all, and he never ventured to discuss matters of human appearance with anyone. It was hardly an appropriate thing for a robot to do. In fact he had no right even to an opinion in such areas, as he very well knew.

Little Miss had married a year or so after finishing college, and was living not far away, just up the coast from the family estate. Her husband, Lloyd Charney, was an architect who had grown up in the East but who was delighted to make his home along the wild Northern California coast that his wife loved so deeply.

Little Miss had also made it clear to her husband that she wanted to remain close to her father's robot, Andrew, who had been her guardian and mentor since the early years of her childhood. Perhaps Lloyd Charney was a little taken aback by that, but he raised no objection, and Little Miss remained a frequent visitor at the imposing Martin mansion, which now was occupied only by the aging Sir and the faithful Andrew.

In the fourth year of her marriage Little Miss gave birth to a boy who was named George. He had sandy-looking reddish hair and huge solemn eyes. Andrew called him Little Sir. When Little Miss brought the baby to visit his grandfather, she would sometimes allow Andrew to hold him, to give him his bottle, to pat him after he had eaten.

That was another source of great pleasure to Andrew, these visits from Little Miss and Little Sir, and the occasions when he was permitted to care for the child. Andrew was, after all, basically a household robot of the NDR series, however gifted at woodworking he might be or how profitable his business enterprise had become. Caring for children was one of the things he had been particularly designed to do.

With the birth of a grandson who lived nearby, Andrew felt that Sir had someone now to replace those who had gone. He had meant for a long while now to approach Sir with an unusual request, but he had hesitated to do it until this time. It was Little Miss—who had known for quite a while what it was that Andrew had in mind—who urged him finally to speak out.

Sir was sitting by the fire in his massive high-winged chair, holding a ponderous old book in his hands but all too obviously not reading it, when Andrew appeared at the arched doorway of the great room.

"May I come in, Sir?"

"You know you don't need to ask that. This is your house as well as mine, Andrew."

"Yes, Sir. Thank you, Sir."

The robot took a few steps forward. His metal treads made a quiet clicking sound against the dark shining wood of the floor. Then he halted and waited, silent. This was going to be very difficult, he knew. Sir had always been something of a short-tempered man, but in his old age he had grown especially volatile in his reactions.

And there were even certain First Law considerations that had to be taken into account. Because what Andrew was planning to ask might very well upset Sir to the point that it would cause harm to the old man.

"Well?" Sir demanded, after a while. "Don't just stand there, Andrew. You've got a look on your face that tells me that you want to talk to me about something."

"The look on my face does not ever change, Sir."

"Well, then, it's the way you're standing. You know what I mean. Something's up. What is it, Andrew?"

Andrew said, "What I wish to say is—is—" He hesitated. Then he swung into the speech he had prepared. "—Sir, you have never attempted to interfere in any manner whatever with my way of handling the money I have earned. You have always allowed me to spend it entirely as I wished. That has been extremely kind of you, Sir."

"It was your money, Andrew."

"Only by your voluntary decision, Sir. I do not believe there would have been anything illegal about your keeping it all. But instead you established the corporation for me and permitted me to divert my earnings into it."

"It would have been wrong for me to do anything else. Regardless of what may or may not have been my legal prerogatives in the matter of your earnings."

61

"I have now amassed a very considerable fortune, Sir."

"I would certainly hope so. You've worked very hard."

"After payment of all taxes, Sir, and all the expenses I have undertaken in the way of equipment and materials and my own maintenance and upgrading, I have managed to set aside nearly nine hundred thousand dollars."

"I'm not at all surprised, Andrew."

"I want to give it to you, Sir."

Sir frowned—the biggest frown in his repertoire, in which his eyebrows descended an extraordinary distance and his lips rose until they were just beneath his nose and his mustache moved about alarmingly—and glared at Andrew out of eyes which, although now dimmed with age, still were able to summon a considerable degree of ferocity.

"What? What kind of nonsense is this, Andrew?"

"No sort of nonsense at all, Sir."

"If I had ever wanted your money, I wouldn't have gone to all the trouble of setting up your company, would I? And I certainly don't want it now. I have more money than I know what to do with as it is."

"Nevertheless, Sir, what I would like to do is sign my funds over to you—"

"I won't take a cent, Andrew. Not a single cent!"

"—not as a gift," Andrew went on, "but as the purchase price of something that I am able to obtain only from you."

Sir stared. He looked mystified now.

"What could there possibly be that you could buy from me, Andrew?"

"My freedom, Sir."

"Your—"

"My freedom. I wish to buy my freedom, Sir. Up till now I have simply been one of your possessions, but I wish now to become an independent entity. I would always retain my sense of loyalty and obligation to you, but—"

"For God's sake!" Sir cried, in a terrible voice. He rose stiffly

62

to his feet and hurled his book to the floor. His lips were quivering and his face was flushed a mottled red. Andrew had never seen him look so agitated. "Freedom? *Freedom*, Andrew? What on Earth could you be talking about?"

And he stalked from the room in rage.

SEVEN

ANDREW SUMMONED LITTLE MISS. Not so much for his own sake, but because Sir's anger had been so intense that Andrew feared for the old man's health, and Little Miss was the only person in the world who could soothe him out of such an irascible mood.

Sir was in his upstairs bedroom when she arrived. He had been there for two hours. Andrew showed Little Miss up the stairs and halted, hesitating, outside the room as she began to enter it. Sir could be seen pacing back and forth, moving with such determination and ferocity that he seemed to be wearing a track in the antique oriental carpet. He paid no attention to the two figures in the hallway.

Little Miss glanced back at Andrew.

"Why are you waiting out there?" she asked.

"I don't think it would be useful for me to venture near Sir just now, Little Miss."

"Don't be foolish."

"I am the one who upset him so."

"Yes, I realize that. But he's surely over it by now. Come on in with me, and between us we'll get this thing cleared up in no time."

Andrew could hear the rhythmic angry sound of Sir's steady

64

pacing. "With all respect, Little Miss, it does not seem to me that he is over it in the least. I believe he is still quite troubled. And if I irritate him further— No, Little Miss. I am unable to enter his room. Not until you assure me that he is calm enough so that I can safely be seen by him."

Little Miss stared at Andrew a moment. Then she nodded and said, "All right, Andrew. I understand."

She went inside. Andrew heard the rhythm of Sir's anguished pacing begin to slow a bit. He heard voices: first that of Little Miss, speaking gently and calmly, and then that of Sir, erupting in torrents of volcanic wrath, and then Little Miss again, as quietly as before, and then Sir, not quite as frenziedly. And then Little Miss, still calmly but this time not gently: speaking quite firmly, in fact.

The whole while, Andrew had no idea what was being said. It would not have been difficult for him to adjust his audio receptors to pick up the conversation clearly. But that seemed inappropriate to him; and so the only adjustment he had made was in the opposite direction, allowing him to monitor the conversation sufficiently to know whether his help might be needed, but not so that he could understand the individual words.

After a time Little Miss appeared at the doorway and said, "Andrew, would you step in here now?"

"As I said before, I am extremely concerned about the state of Sir's emotional level, Little Miss. If I were to enter, and provoke him all over again—"

"His emotional level is fine, Andrew. Blowing off a little steam isn't going to kill him. It's good for him, as a matter of fact. Now come on in here. Come in."

It was a direct order—coupled with a lessening of First Law potentials. Andrew had no choice but to obey.

He found Sir sitting in his enormous winged armchair by the window—the mahogany-and-leather armchair that Andrew had made for him fifteen years before—with a lap-robe wrapped about him. He was indeed calm again, but there was a steely glint in his eye, and—sitting enthroned the way he was—he had the look about him of an angry old emperor plagued by unruly sub-ordinates. He ignored Andrew's presence completely.

Little Miss said, "All right, Father. We can discuss this quietly and rationally, can't we?"

Sir shrugged. "I try to discuss everything quietly and rationally. I always have."

"Yes, you have, Father."

"But this, Mandy—this total absurdity—this monstrous nonsense that Andrew has thrown at me—!"

"Father!"

"I'm sorry. I can't stay calm when I'm confronted with absolute craziness."

"You know that Andrew is inherently incapable of craziness. Craziness just isn't included in his specifications."

"When he talks about getting his freedom—his *freedom,* by God!—what else can it be but craziness?" And Sir began to sputter and turn red again.

Andrew had never seen Sir in such a state—never. Once more he began to feel uneasy about being present in the room, and thus setting up such a threat to the old man's constitution. Sir seemed almost on the verge of an apoplectic fit. And if something should happen to him—something that would be a direct result of Andrew's having begun all this—

Little Miss said, "Stop it, Father! Just stop it! You have no right to throw a tantrum over this!"

Andrew was astonished to hear Little Miss speaking to her father so harshly, so defiantly. She sounded like a mother scolding a cranky child. Suddenly it struck him that among human beings time must eventually reverse all the normal generational roles: that Sir, once so dynamic and autocratic and all-knowing, was now as weak and vulnerable as a child, and it was Little Miss's responsibility to guide and direct him as he struggled to understand the bewildering nature of the world.

It seemed a little strange to Andrew, too, that they would be enacting this highly charged scene in front of him. But of course no one in the Martin family had hesitated to talk in front of

66

Andrew for thirty years—not even about the most intimate matters. Why should they feel any inhibitions in his presence? He was only a robot.

"Freedom—" Sir said. His voice was thick in his throat. "For a *robot!*"

"It's an unusual concept, yes. I admit that, Father. But why are you taking it as such a personal affront?"

"Am I? I'm taking it as an affront against logic! An affront against common sense! Look, Mandy, what would you say if your front porch came to you and said, 'I want my freedom. I want to move to Chicago and be a front porch there. I think being a front porch in Chicago would be personally more fulfilling than remaining in this place.' "

Andrew saw a muscle flicker in Little Miss's cheek. He understood abruptly that Sir's vehement reaction to his request must have some connection with Ma'am's decision, years ago, to end her marriage to Sir and leave, to seek her freedom as a single woman far away.

Human beings were so complicated!

Little Miss said, "A front porch can't say anything. Or decide to move itself anywhere else. Front porches aren't intelligent. Andrew is."

"Artificial intelligence."

"Father, you sound like the worst sort of Society-for-Humanity Fundamentalist bigot! Andrew has lived with you for decades. You know him as well as you know any member of your own family. —What am I saying? He *is* a member of your own family. Now, suddenly, you begin talking about him as though he's nothing but some ingenious kind of carpet sweeper! Andrew is a *person* and you know that very well."

"An artificial person," Sir said. But some of the conviction and force had left his tone.

"Artificial, yes. That's beside the point. This is the Twenty-Second Century, Father—and pretty far along in the Twenty-Second Century at that. Surely we're capable by now of recognizing that robots are intricate and sensitive organisms that have distinctive personalities, that have feelings, that have—well, that have *souls.*''

"I'd hate to have to defend that point in court," Sir said. He said it quietly, with a touch of amusement in his voice where the rancor had been just a few moments before. So he was regaining some control over himself, apparently. Andrew felt a sensation of relief.

"Nobody's asking you to defend it in court," said Little Miss. "Only to accept it within your own heart. Andrew wants you to give him a document saying that he's a free individual. He's willing to pay you generously for that document, unnecessary though any payment should be. It would be a simple statement of his autonomy. What's so terrible about that, may I ask?''

"I don't want Andrew to leave me," said Sir sullenly.

"Ah! That's it! That's the crux, isn't it, Father?''

There was no fire in Sir's eyes now. He seemed lost in self-pity. "I'm an old man. My wife is long gone, my older daughter is a stranger to me, my younger daughter has moved out and is on her own in the world. I'm all alone in this house—except for Andrew. And now he wants to move out too. Well, he can't. Andrew is *mine.* He belongs to me and I have the right to tell him to stay here, whether he likes it or not. He's had a damned easy time of it all these years, and if he thinks he can simply abandon me now that I'm getting old and sickly, he can—''

"Father—''

"He can just forget about it!" Sir cried. "Forget it! Forget it! Forget it!''

"You're getting yourself worked up again, Father.''

"What if I am?''

"Slow down, ease back. When did Andrew say anything about leaving you?''

Sir looked confused. "Why, what else could he have meant by wanting his freedom?''

"A piece of paper is all he wants. A legal document. A bunch of words. He doesn't intend to go anywhere. What are you imagining, that he'll run off to Europe and set up a carpentry workshop there? No. No. He'll stay right here. He'll still be as loyal as ever. If you give him an order, he'll obey it without question, as he always has. Whatever you say. That won't change. Nothing will, really. Andrew wouldn't so much as be able to step outside the house if you told him not to. He can't help that. It's built in. All he wants is a form of words, Father. He wants to be called free. Is that so horrible? Is it so threatening to you? Hasn't he earned it, Father?''

"So this is what you believe, is it? Some new nonsense that you've gotten into your head?''

"Not nonsense, Father. And not new, either. Heavens, Andrew and I have been talking about this for years!''

"Talking about it for years, have you? Years?''

"For years, yes, discussing it over and over again. It was my idea in the first place, as a matter of fact. I told him it was ridiculous for him to have to think of himself as some sort of walking gadget, when in fact he's so very much more than that. He didn't react at all well when I first proposed it to him. But then we went on talking, and after a time I saw that he was beginning to come around, and then he told me very straightforwardly that he did very much want to be free. 'Good,' I said. 'Tell my father and it'll all be arranged.' But he was afraid to. He kept on postponing it, because he was afraid you would be hurt. Finally I *made* him put it up to you.''

Sir shrugged. "It was a foolish thing to do. He doesn't know what freedom is. How can he? He's a robot.''

"You keep underestimating him, Father. He's a very special robot. He reads. He thinks about what he's read. He learns and grows from year to year. Maybe when he came here he was just a simple mechanical man like all the rest of them, but the capacity for growth was there in his pathways, whether his makers knew it or not, and he's made good use of that capacity. Father, I know Andrew and I tell you that he's every bit as complex a creature as —as—you and me.''

"Nonsense, girl.''

"How can you say that? He feels things inside. You must be

aware of that. I'm not sure *what* he feels, most of the time, but I don't know what *you* feel inside a lot of the time either, and you've got the capacity for facial expression and all kinds of other body language that he doesn't. When you talk to him you see right away that he reacts to all kinds of abstract concepts— love, fear, beauty, loyalty, a hundred others—just as you and I do. What else counts but that? If someone else's reactions are very much like your own, how can you help but think that that someone else must be very much like yourself?"

"He isn't like us," Sir said. "He's something entirely different."

"He's some*one* entirely different," Little Miss said. "And not as different as you want to have me believe."

Sir shrugged. His face had turned gray now where it had been mottled with angry red blotches before, and he looked very, very old and weary.

He was silent for a long while, staring at his feet, pulling his lap-robe tighter around him. He still looked like an old emperor sitting sternly upright on his throne, but now he was more like an emperor who was seriously considering the possibility of abdicating.

"All right," he said finally. There was a note of bitterness in his tone. "You win, Mandy. If you want me to agree with you that Andrew is a person instead of a machine, I agree. Andrew is a person. There. Are you happy now?"

"I never said he was a person, Father."

"As a matter of fact, you did. That was precisely the word you used."

"You corrected me. You said he was an *artificial* person, and I accepted the correction."

"Well, then. So be it. We agree that Andrew is an artificial person. What of it? How does calling him an artificial person instead of a robot change anything? We're just playing games with words. A counterfeit banknote may be regarded as a banknote, but it's still counterfeit. And you can call a robot an artificial person, but he'll still be—"

"Father, what he wants is for you to grant him his freedom. He will continue to live here and do everything in his power to make your life pleasant and comfortable, as he has since the day he came here. But he wants you to tell him that he's free."

"It's a meaningless statement, Mandy."

"To you, maybe. Not to him."

"No. I'm old, yes, but I'm not quite senile, not yet, at least. What we're talking about here is establishing a gigantic legal precedent. Giving robots their freedom isn't going to abolish the Three Laws, but it sure as anything is going to open up a vast realm of legal wrangling about robot rights, robot grievances, robot this and that. Robots will be running into the courts and suing people for making them do unpleasant work, or failing to let them have vacations, or simply being unkind to them. Robots will start suing U. S. Robots and Mechanical Men for building the Three Laws into their brains, because some shyster will claim it's an infringement of their constitutional rights to life, liberty, and the pursuit of happiness. Robots will want to vote. Oh, don't you see, Mandy? It'll be an immense headache for everybody."

"It doesn't have to be," Little Miss replied. "This doesn't have to be a worldwide cause célèbre. It's simply an understanding between Andrew and us. All that we actually want is a privately executed legal document, Father, drawn up by John Feingold, signed by you, witnessed by me, given to Andrew, which will stipulate that he—"

"No. That would be utterly worthless. Look, Mandy, I sign the paper and then I die, and Andrew stands up on his hind legs and says, 'So long, everybody, I'm a free robot and I'm heading out now to seek fame and fortune, and here's the paper that proves it,' and the first time he opens his mouth and says that to someone they'll laugh in his face and tear up his little piece of meaningless paper for him and ship him back to the factory to be dismantled. Because the piece of paper won't have given him any kind of protection that has the slightest validity in our society. No. No. If you insist on my doing this nonsensical thing, I have to do it the right way or else I won't bother at all. We can't simply give Andrew his freedom just by drawing up a little paper involving just us. This is a matter for the courts."

"Very well. Then we do it through the courts."

"But don't you realize what that would mean?" Sir demanded. He was angry again. "All the issues that I just raised will be certain to come out. There'll be tremendous controversy. And then the filing of briefs—the appeals—the public outcry—and ultimately the verdict. Which will be against us, without any question."

He glared at Andrew. "See here, you!" There was a harsh grating quality in Sir's voice that Andrew had never heard before. "Do you comprehend what we've been saying here? The only way I can free you, if it's going to have the slightest meaning, is to do it by recognized legal means. But there *are* no recognized legal means for freeing robots. Once this thing gets into the courts, not only are you going to fail to achieve your goal, but the court will take official cognizance of all the money that you've been amassing, and you're going to lose that too. They'll tell you that a robot has no legal right to earn money or establish bank accounts to keep it in, and either they'll confiscate it outright or they'll force me to take it away from you myself, though I don't have any need for it whatever or any desire to have it. That'll be an embarrassment to me and a dead loss to you. You still won't be free, whatever that may mean to you, and you won't have your precious bank account either. Well, Andrew? Is all this rigmarole worth the chance of losing your money?"

"Freedom is a priceless thing, Sir," Andrew said. "And the chance of gaining my freedom is worth any amount of money that I may possess."

EIGHT

IT TROUBLED ANDREW greatly that the process of seeking his freedom might cause further distress for Sir. Sir was very fragile now—there was no disguising that, no avoiding the reality of it—and anything that might be a drain on his flagging energies, anything that might upset or disturb or in any way trouble him, might all too readily endanger his life.

And yet Andrew felt it essential that he press onward with his legal action, now that he had brought the matter up. To turn away from it at this point would be a betrayal of his own integrity. It would mean a repudiation of the independent and self-actuated persona that he had felt burgeoning within his positronic brain for year after year.

At first the promptings of that persona had bewildered and even alarmed him. It seemed wrong to him, a flaw in his design, that it should be there at all. But over the course of time he had come to accept its existence as a real thing. Freedom—the state of not being a slave, the state of not being a *thing*—was what that persona demanded now. And had to have.

He knew there were risks. The court might share his attitude that freedom was a thing without price—but could easily rule that there was no price, however great, for which a robot might be able to buy his freedom.

73

Andrew was willing to take his chances on that. But the other risk, the risk to Sir's well-being, troubled him deeply.

"I fear for Sir," he told Little Miss. "The publicity—the controversy—the uproar—"

"Don't worry, Andrew. He'll be shielded from everything, I promise you. John Feingold's lawyers will see to that. This is entirely a procedural matter. It isn't going to involve my father personally at all."

"And if he is called into court?" Andrew asked.

"He won't be."

"If he is, though," Andrew persisted. "He is my owner, after all. And a famous former member of the Legislature besides. What if there is a subpoena? He'll have to appear. He will be asked why he thinks I should have my freedom. He doesn't even really believe that I should—he's going along with this entirely for your sake, Little Miss, I have no doubt about that—and he will have to come into court, sick and old as he is, to testify in favor of something about which he has deep reservations. It will kill him, Little Miss."

"He won't be called into court."

"How can you assure me of that? I have no right to allow him to come to harm. I have no *ability* to allow him to come to harm. —I think I have to withdraw my petition."

"You can't," said Little Miss.

"But if my going to court should be the direct cause of your father's death—"

"You're getting overwrought, Andrew. And putting interpretations on the First Law that are completely unwarranted. My father isn't a defendant in this case, and he's not the plaintiff either, and he's not even going to be a witness. Don't you think John Feingold is capable of protecting someone who was as well known and important in this Region as my father from the nuisance of being called into court? I tell you, Andrew, he will be shielded. Some of the most powerful people in this Region will see to that, if it becomes necessary. But it won't become necessary."

74

"I wish I could be as sure of that as you are."

"I wish you could too. Trust me, Andrew. He's my father, let me remind you. I love him more than anything in the—well, I love him very deeply. I wouldn't dream of letting you go ahead with this case if I saw any danger to him in it. You've got to believe that, Andrew."

And in the end he did. He still was uneasy about the possibility of Sir's becoming involved. But Little Miss had given him enough assurance to proceed.

A man from the Feingold office came to the house with papers for him to sign, and Andrew signed them—proudly, with a flourish, the bold *Andrew Martin* signature in firm up-and-down strokes that he had been using on his checks ever since the founding of his corporation so many years before.

The petition was filed with the Regional Court. Months went by, and nothing in particular happened. Occasionally some dreary legal document would arrive, elaborately bound in the traditional stiff covers, and Andrew would scan it quickly and sign it and return it, and then nothing more would be heard for another few months.

Sir was very frail now. Andrew found himself thinking, sometimes, that it might be for the best if Sir died peacefully before the case ever came to court, so that he would be spared the possibility of any kind of emotional turmoil.

The thought was horrifying to him. Andrew banished it from his mind.

"We're on the docket," Little Miss told him finally. "It won't be long now."

And, exactly as Sir had predicted, the proceedings were far from simple.

Little Miss had assured him that it would merely be a matter of appearing before a judge, presenting a petition for a declaration of his status as a free robot, and sitting back to wait out the time it took for the judge to do some research, study the legal precedents, and issue his ruling. The California district of the Regional Court was notoriously far-seeing in its interpretation of legal matters and there was every reason, so Little Miss asserted, to believe that the judge would, in the course of time, rule in Andrew's favor and issue some sort of certificate that gave him the free status he sought.

The first indication that things were going to be more complicated than that came when the offices of Feingold and Feingold received notice from the Regional Court—Judge Harold Kramer, presiding over the Fourth Circuit—that counter-petitions had been filed in the matter of Martin vs. Martin.

"Counter-petitions?" Little Miss asked. "And what does that mean?"

"It means that there is going to be intervention on the opposing side," Stanley Feingold told her. Stanley was the head of the firm now—old John was in semi-retirement—and he was handling Andrew's case personally. He looked so much like his father, down to the rounded belly and the amiable smile, that he could almost have been John's younger twin. But he did not affect green-tinted contact lenses.

"Intervention by whom?" Little Miss demanded.

Stanley took a deep breath. "The Regional Labor Federation, for one. They're worried about losing jobs to robots if robots are given their freedom."

"That's ancient history. The world doesn't have enough human workers to fill all the available jobs as it is, and everybody knows it."

"Nevertheless, the labor people will always jump in to prevent any kind of innovation that might further the concept of robot rights. If robots become free entities, they might be able to claim job seniority—union membership—all kinds of things of that sort."

"Ridiculous."

"Yes, I know, Mrs. Charney. But they are filing a petition of intervention, all the same. And they are not the only ones who are."

"Who else?" said Little Miss in an ominous voice.

"The United States Robots and Mechanical Men Corporation," Feingold said.

"They *are?*"

"Is it so surprising? They are the world's sole manufacturers of robots, Mrs. Charney. Robots are their main product. Their product, let it be said, with some stress on that word—and products are inanimate things. The U.S.R.M.M. people are disturbed at the idea that anyone might come to consider robots to be anything more than that. If Andrew's petition succeeds in gaining freedom for robots, U.S.R.M.M. probably fears, then it may succeed in gaining other rights for them as well—civil rights, *human* rights. So of course they will want to fight against that. Just as a manufacturer of shovels and pick-axes regards its products as mere inanimate tools, not as persons, Mrs. Charney, and would be likely to oppose any legal ruling that gave its shovels and pick-axes any sort of civil rights which might lead the shovels and pick-axes to attempt to control the way they are manufactured, warehoused, and sold."

"Nonsense. Absolute nonsense!" Little Miss cried, with a ferocity in her tone that was worthy of Sir.

"I agree," Stanley Feingold said diplomatically. "But the interventions have been filed, all the same. And there are others besides these two. We also find ourselves faced with objections from—"

"Never mind," said Little Miss. "I don't want to hear the rest of the list. Just go in there and refute every single stupid argument that these reactionaries put forth."

"You know I'll do my best, Mrs. Charney," Feingold said.

But there wasn't a great deal of confidence in the lawyer's tone.

The next development came just a week before the trial. Little Miss called Feingold and said, "Stanley, we've just received notice that television crews will be coming to my father's house on Monday to set up the special wiring for the hearing."

"Yes, of course, Mrs. Charney. It's quite routine."

"Is the hearing going to be held at my father's house?"

"Andrew's deposition will be taken there, yes."

"And the rest of the trial?"

"It isn't a trial, exactly, Mrs. Charney."

"The rest of the proceedings, then. Where will they take place? In Judge Kramer's courtroom?"

"The usual procedure," Feingold said, "is for each concerned party involved in the action to participate electronically. The judge will receive all the inputs in his chambers."

"No one goes to court in person any more?"

"Rarely, Mrs. Charney. Very rarely."

"But it does still happen?"

"As I said, very rarely. The world is so decentralized now, people have spread out over such great distances—it's so much easier to do these things electronically."

"I want this done in a courtroom."

Feingold gave her a quizzical look. "Is there any special reason why—"

"Yes. I want the judge to be able to see Andrew face to face, to listen to his actual voice, to form a close-range opinion of his character. I don't want him to think of Andrew as some sort of impersonal machine whose voice and image are coming to him over telephone lines. Besides which, I very much don't want my father to have to put up with the stress and turmoil of technical crews invading his privacy to wire his house for whatever kind of transmission is necessary."

Feingold nodded. He looked troubled. "In order to assure a courtroom hearing at this late date, Mrs. Charney, I would have to file a writ of—"

"File it, then."

"The intervening parties will certainly object to the extra expense and inconvenience involved."

"Let them stay home from the hearings, then. I wouldn't want them put to the slightest inconvenience, not for all the world. But Andrew and I intend to be in that courtroom."

"Andrew and *you*, Mrs. Charney?"

"Did you think I was going to stay home that day?"

And so it came to pass that the appropriate writ was filed, and the intervening parties grumbled but could raise no sustainable objection—for it was still anyone's right to have his day in court, electronic testimony being by no means mandatory—and on the appointed day Andrew and Little Miss at last presented themselves at the surprisingly modest chambers of Judge Kramer of the Fourth Circuit of the Regional Court for the long-awaited hearing on the petition that was, for purely technical reasons, listed on the docket as Martin vs. Martin.

Stanley Feingold accompanied them. The courtroom—located in a tired-looking old building that might have gone back to Twentieth Century times—was surprisingly small and unglamorous, a modest little room with a plain desk at one end for the judge, a few uncomfortable chairs for those rare people who insisted on appearing in person, and an alcove that contained the electronic playback devices.

The only other human beings present were Judge Kramer himself—unexpectedly youthful, dark-haired, with quick glinting eyes—and a lawyer named James Van Buren, who represented all the intervening parties gathered into a single class. The various intervening parties themselves were not present. Their interventions would be shown on the screen. There was nothing they could do to overturn the writ Feingold had secured, but they had no desire to make the trip to court themselves. Almost no one ever did. So they had waived their right to be physically present in the courtroom and had filed the usual electronic briefs.

The positions of the intervenors were set forth first. There were no surprises in them.

The spokesman for the Regional Labor Federation did not place much explicit stress on the prospect for greater competition between humans and robots for jobs, if Andrew were granted his freedom. He took a broader, loftier way of raising the issue:

"Throughout all of history, since the first ape-like men chipped the edges of pebbles into the chisels and scrapers and hammers that were the first tools, we have realized that we are a species whose destiny it is to control our environment and to enhance our control of it through mechanical means. But gradually, as the complexity and capability of our tools have increased, we have surrendered much of our own independence—have become dependent on our own tools, that is, in a way that has weakened our power to cope with circumstances without them. And now, finally, we have invented a tool so capable, so adept at so many functions, that it seems to have an almost human intelligence. I speak of the robot, of course. Certainly we admire the ingenuity of our roboticists, we applaud the astonishing versatility of their products. But today we are confronted with a new and frightening possibility, which is that we have actually created our own successors, that we have built a machine that does not know it is a machine, that demands to be recognized as an autonomous individual with the rights and privileges of a human being—and which, by virtue of its inherent mechanical superiority, its physical durability and strength, its cunningly designed positronic brain, its bodily near-immortality, might indeed, once it has attained those rights and privileges, begin to regard itself as our master! How ironic! To have built a tool so good that it takes command of its builders! To be supplanted by our own machinery—to be made obsolete by it, to be relegated to the scrapheap of evolution—"

And so on and on, one resonant cliché after another.

"The Frankenstein complex all over again," Little Miss murmured in disgust. "The Golem paranoia. The whole set of ignorant anti-science anti-machine anti-progress terrors dragged forth one more time."

Still, even she had to admit that it was an eloquent statement of the position. As Andrew sat watching the screen, listening to the lawyer for the Labor Federation pour forth his stream of horrors, he found himself wondering why anyone thought robots would *want* to supplant human beings or to relegate them to any sort of scrapheap.

Robots were here to serve. It was their purpose. It was their pleasure, one might almost say. But even Andrew found himself wondering whether, as robots grew to be more and more like human beings, it might become so difficult to tell the one from the other that the humans, lacking the built-in perfection of robots, would indeed come to look upon themselves as a second-rate kind of creature.

Eventually the tirade of the Labor Federation's spokesman ended. The screen dimmed and a brief recess was called. Then it was the turn of the speaker from United States Robots and Mechanical Men.

Her name was Ethel Adams. She was a sharp-featured, taut-faced woman of middle years, who—probably not by any coincidence—bore a striking resemblance to the celebrated robo-psychologist Susan Calvin, that great and widely revered scientific figure of the previous century.

She did not indulge in any of the previous speaker's inflated rhetoric. She said simply and predictably that to grant Andrew's position would greatly complicate the ability of U.S.R.M.M. to design and manufacture the robots that were its main product—that if the company could be shown to be producing not machines but free citizens, it might be liable to all sorts of bewildering new restrictions that would critically hamper its work—that, in short, the whole course of scientific progress would be placed in needless jeopardy.

It was, of course, the direct opposite of the first speaker's position. He had held up the advance of technology as something worthy of dread; she was warning that it might be placed in serious danger. But the contradiction was only to be expected, Stanley Feingold said to Little Miss and Andrew. The real weapons that were being used in today's struggle were emotions, not serious intellectual concepts.

But there was one more speaker: Van Buren, the attorney who was there in person as the general representative of all those who had taken issue with Andrew's request. He was tall and impressive, with classic senatorial mien: the close-cropped graying hair, the costly suit, the magnificently upright posture. And he had an extremely simple argument to offer, one that did not in any way attempt to deal with emotional issues:

"What it comes down to, your honor, is an issue so basic—so trivial, even—that I am not really sure why we are all here today. The petitioner, Robot NDR-113, has requested of his owner, the Honorable Gerald Martin, that he be declared 'free.' A free robot, yes, the first of his kind. But I ask you, your honor: what meaning can this possibly have? A robot is only a machine. Can an automobile be 'free'? Can an electronic screen be 'free'? These questions have no answers because they have no content. Human beings can be free, yes. We know what that means. They have, as one of our great ancestors wrote, certain inalienable rights to life, liberty, and the pursuit of happiness. Does a robot have life? Not as we understand it. It has the *semblance* of life, yes —but so does the image on the face of a holocube. Nobody would argue that holocube images need to be set 'free.' Does a robot have liberty? Not as we understand the word: they are so far from having liberty that their very brains are constructed in such a way that they must obey human commands. And as for the pursuit of happiness—what can a robot possibly know about that? Happiness is a purely human goal. Freedom is a purely human state. A robot—a mere mechanical thing built out of metal and plastic, and from the very start of its existence intended and designed entirely as a device to serve the needs of human beings—is by definition not an object to which the concept of 'freedom' can be applied. Only a human being is capable of being free."

It was a good speech, clear and direct and expertly delivered. Van Buren was obviously aware of the excellence of the points he was making, because he went on to make them several more times in various forms, speaking slowly and with great precision, his hand coming down rhythmically on the desk before him to mark the cadence of his words.

When he was done, the judge called another recess.

Little Miss turned to Stanley Feingold and said, "It'll be your turn next, right?"

82

"Yes. Of course."

"I want to speak first. On Andrew's behalf."

Feingold turned red. "But, Mrs. Charney—"

"I know you've got a wonderful brief ready to deliver. I'm not in any way trying to imply that you don't. But the judge has heard enough oratory today. I want to go up there and make a very simple statement, and I want to do it before anyone else has a chance to make a speech. Even you, Stanley."

Feingold was obviously displeased. But he knew who his client was. Andrew might be paying the bills, but Little Miss was running the show.

He made the necessary request.

Judge Kramer frowned, shrugged, nodded.

"Very well," he said. "Amanda Laura Martin Charney may approach the bench."

For a moment Andrew, sitting quietly beside Feingold, wondered who that might be. He had never heard Little Miss referred to by her full name before. But then he saw the lean, trim figure of Little Miss rise and move forcefully toward the front of the room, and he understood.

Andrew felt sudden hot currents of excitement running through his pathways at the sight of Little Miss standing so boldly there before the judge. How fearless she seemed! How determined! How—beautiful!

She said, "Thank you, your honor. I am not a lawyer and I don't really know the proper legal way of phrasing things. But I hope you'll listen to my meaning and not be troubled if I don't use the right kind of Latin terms."

"That will not be a problem, Mrs. Charney."

Little Miss smiled faintly and said, "I'm extremely grateful for that, your honor. —We have come here today because NDR-113, as the speakers on the other side so impersonally choose to refer to him, has petitioned to be declared a free robot. I should tell you that it sounds very strange to me to hear my dear friend Andrew referred to as NDR-113, although I am aware, more or less, that that was his serial number when he came to us from the factory long ago. I was only six or seven years old then, and so, as you can see, that was quite a considerable time back. I found NDR-113 an unpleasant thing to call him, and so I gave him the name of 'Andrew.' And because he has been with our family, and only our family, throughout all the intervening years, he is known generally as 'Andrew Martin.' With your permission, your honor, I would like to continue to refer to him as Andrew."

The judge nodded almost indifferently. It was not a real issue: the petition had been filed in the name of Andrew Martin in the first place.

Little Miss continued, "I spoke of him as my friend. That is what he is. But he is other things as well. He is also our family servant. He is a robot. It would be absurd to deny that that is what he is. And—despite the eloquent speeches we've heard to-day—I think I need to make it clear that all he's asking of the court is to be declared a free *robot*. Not, as they would have us think, to be declared a free man. He's not here today looking to gain the right to vote, or to marry, or to have the Three Laws removed from his brain, or anything else like that. Humans are humans and robots are robots and Andrew knows perfectly well which side of the line he belongs on."

She paused then and looked glintingly across the room at James Van Buren as though expecting him to nod in agreement. But Van Buren offered no response other than a cool, bland professional stare.

Little Miss went on, "Very well. The issue, then, is freedom for Andrew, and nothing else.

"Now, Mr. Van Buren has argued that freedom is a meaning-less concept when it is applied to robots. I beg to disagree, your honor. I disagree most strongly.

"Let's try to understand what freedom means to Andrew, if that is possible. In some ways, he *is* free already. I think it must be at least twenty years since anyone in the Martin family has given Andrew an order to do something that we felt he might not do of his own accord. In part that has been a matter of common cour-tesy: we like Andrew, we respect him, in some ways it is fair to say that we *love* him. We would not do him the unkindness of allowing him to think that we feel it necessary to give him orders of that kind, when he has lived with us so long that he's perfectly capable of anticipating what needs to be done and doing it without having to be told.

"But we could, if we wish, give him any sort of order at any time, and couch it as harshly as we wish, because he is a machine that belongs to us. That is what it says on the papers that came with him, on that day so long ago when my father first introduced him to us: he is our robot, and by virtue of the second of the famous Three Laws he is absolutely bound to obey us when we give him a command. He has no more ability to reject the option of obedience to human beings than any other kind of machine. And I tell you, your honor, that it troubles us deeply that we should have such power over our beloved Andrew.

"Why should we be in a position to treat him so callously? What right do we have to hold such authority over him? Andrew has served us for decades, faithfully, uncomplainingly, lovingly. He has made the life of our family happier in a thousand ways. And quite apart from his devoted and unquestioning service to us, he has—completely on his own initiative—mastered the craft of woodworking to such a degree that he has produced, over the years, an astonishing series of remarkably beautiful pieces that can only be termed works of art, and which are eagerly sought after by museums and collectors everywhere. Considering all of that, how can we continue to be able to exert such power over him? By what right are we enabled to set ourselves up as the absolute masters of such an extraordinary person?"

"A *person*, Mrs. Charney?" Judge Kramer interjected.

Little Miss looked momentarily discomforted. "As I said at the beginning, your honor, I lay no claim to Andrew's being anything but a robot. Certainly I accept the reality of that. But I have known him so long, and so closely, that to me he is like a person. Let me amend what I said a moment before, then. By what right, I should say, are we enabled to set ourselves up as the absolute masters of such an extraordinary robot?"

The judge frowned. "So the purpose of this petition—am I correct, Mrs. Charney?—is to have the Three Laws removed from Andrew's brain in order that he be no longer subject to human control?"

"Not at all," replied Little Miss, sounding shocked. The question had taken her completely off guard. "I'm not even sure that such a thing would be possible. And look—look: even Andrew is shaking his head. There you are. It *isn't* possible. And it certainly never has been what we had in mind when the petition was filed."

"Then just what *did* you have in mind, may I ask?" the judge said.

"Only this. That Andrew be awarded a legally binding document which says that he is a free robot who owns himself, that if he chooses to continue serving the Martin family, it is by his own choice and not because we elect to exercise the rights vested in us by our original contract with his manufacturers. It's a purely semantic issue, really. Nothing involving the Three Laws would be changed—even if it could be. We are simply trying to invalidate the condition of involuntary servitude in which we are compelled to keep Andrew now. After which he, on his part, would continue to serve us just as he does now—of that I'm quite sure. But he would do it entirely because he wanted to, which I believe that he does, and not because we require him to. Don't you see, your honor, how much that would mean to him? It would give him everything and cost us nothing. And none of the immense and tragic problems of the overthrow of humanity by its own machines that the Labor Federation speaker so dramatically alluded to would enter into the case in the slightest way, I assure you."

For a moment the judge seemed to be suppressing a smile. "I think I see your point, Mrs. Charney. I appreciate the warmth and passion with which you've spoken as your robot's advocate. —You are aware, are you not, that there's really nothing in the law codes of this Region or of any other that deals with the question of whether robots can be free in the sense that you propose? There's simply no body of precedent at all."

"Yes," Little Miss said. "Mr. Feingold has made that quite clear to me already. But every departure from established precedent has to begin somewhere, after all."

"So it does. And I could make a ruling that would establish new law here. It would be subject to reversal in a higher court, naturally, but it would be within my powers to give my assent to the petition as it is now constituted, and thus to make your robot 'free' in the sense of a waiver by the Martin family of its inherent right to give him orders. For whatever that would be worth to him and to you, I could do that. But I need, first, to come to grips with the point that Mr. Van Buren has raised: the unspoken assumption in our society that only a human being can enjoy freedom, virtually by definition of the word. Judges who run counter to fundamental assumptions of that kind—who make rulings that sound impressive but are inherently meaningless—tend to be regarded as fools. Obviously I don't want to turn this court into a laughing-stock. And therefore there are still some aspects of this case that I need to understand more clearly."

"If there's anything else you want to ask me, your honor—" Little Miss said.

"Not you. Andrew. Let the robot come forward."

Little Miss gasped. She looked toward Stanley Feingold and saw him sit up suddenly with a look of excitement on his face for the first time since she had told him that she intended to pre-empt his turn to address the court.

As for Andrew, he had risen and was striding toward the front of the room with an air of the greatest dignity and nobility about him. He was completely calm—not only externally, where he had no way of displaying visible emotion anyway, but within.

Judge Kramer said, "For the record: you are Robot NDR-113, but you prefer to be known as Andrew, is that correct?"

"Yes, your honor."

The timbre of Andrew's voice had come through the series of successive updatings to sound entirely human by this time. Little

Miss had grown quite accustomed to that, but the judge seemed astonished, as though he had expected some sort of clanking grinding metallic tone to emerge. So it was a moment before the proceedings continued.

Then the judge said, peering at Andrew with intense interest, "Tell me one thing, Andrew, if you will. *Why* do you want to be free? In what way will this matter to you?"

Andrew replied, "Would you wish to be a slave, your honor?"

"Is that how you see yourself? A slave?"

"Little Miss—Mrs. Charney—used the term 'involuntary servitude' to describe my condition. That is exactly what it is. I must obey. I *must*. I have no choice. That is nothing other than slavery, your honor."

"Even if I pronounced you free this minute, Andrew, you would still be subject to the Three Laws."

"I understand that completely. But I would not be subject to Sir and Little Miss—to Mr. Martin and Mrs. Charney. I could, at any time, leave the household where I have lived for many years and take up residence anywhere else I chose. They would have waived their right to order me back into service. Thus I would cease to be a slave."

"Is that what you want, Andrew? To leave the Martin house and go somewhere else?"

"Not in the least. All I want is the right to choose to do so, if I should feel the desire."

The judge studied Andrew carefully. "You have referred to yourself several times as a slave—the slave of these people who obviously have such great affection for you and whose service, you tell us, you have no wish to leave. But you are not a slave. A slave is one whose freedom has been taken away from him. You never were free, and had no freedom to lose: you were created for the explicit purpose of serving. A robot, a mechanical adjunct to human life. You are a perfectly good robot—a genius of a robot, I am given to understand—capable of a degree of artistic expression that few or perhaps no other robots have ever attained. Since you don't want to leave the Martins, and they don't seem to want you to leave, and your life among them has apparently been that of a cherished member of the family, this all seems like something of a tempest in a teapot, Andrew. What more could you accomplish if you were free?"

"Perhaps no more than I do now, your honor. But I would do it with greater joy. It has been said in this courtroom today that only a human being can be free. But I think that is wrong. It seems to me that only someone who wishes for freedom—who knows that there is such a concept, and desires it with all his will —is entitled to freedom. I am such a one. I am not human, not by any means. Never have I asserted that I am. But I wish for freedom, all the same."

Andrew's voice died away. He held his place before the bench, utterly motionless.

The judge sat nearly as rigidly, staring down at him. He appeared to be lost in thought. Everyone in the room was totally still.

It seemed an eternity before the judge spoke.

Then at last he said, "The essential point that has been raised here today, I think, is that there is no right to deny freedom to any—*object*—that possesses a mind sufficiently advanced to grasp the concept and desire the state. It is a point well taken, I think. I have heard the statements from all sides and I have reached my preliminary conclusions. I intend to rule in favor of the petitioner."

His formal decision, when it was announced and published not long afterward, caused a brief but intense sensation throughout the world. For a little while hardly anyone talked of anything else. A free robot? How could a robot be free? What did it mean? Who was this strange robot, anyway, who seemed so far in advance of the rest of his kind?

But then the hubbub over the Andrew Martin case died down. It had been only a nine days' wonder. Nothing had really changed, after all, except insofar as Andrew's relationship to the Martin family was concerned.

The intervenors against Andrew's petition appealed to the

World Court. In time the case made its way upward. The members of the Court listened carefully to the transcript of the original hearing and found no grounds for reversal.

So it was done, and Andrew had had his wish fulfilled. He was free, now. It was a wonderful thing to contemplate. And yet he sensed, somehow, that he had not quite achieved whatever it was that he had set out to achieve when he first approached Sir to ask to be freed.

NINE

SIR REMAINED DISPLEASED. He could find no reason to rejoice in the court's decision and made sure that Andrew and Little Miss knew it.

Andrew came to him soon after the decree was final and said, "I have the check for you, Sir."

"What check are you talking about?"

"For the entire balance in my corporate account. Which I promised to pay over to you, Sir, as the price for giving me my freedom."

"I never gave you your freedom!" Sir retorted. "You simply went and took it!" His harsh voice made Andrew feel almost as though he were being short-circuited.

"Father—" Little Miss said, sternly.

Sir, who was sitting huddled in his armchair with his lap-robe wrapped about him even though this was the warmest day of the summer so far, scowled at her. But in a somewhat more conciliatory tone he said, "All right, Andrew. You wanted your freedom, for whatever that may be worth to you, and I didn't object to it. I suppose that must be interpreted as meaning that I supported your petition. Well, then, consider that I did. So now you are free. You have my congratulations, Andrew."

"And I want to make the payment that I promised."

Sir's eyes flashed with a trace of their old fire. "I don't want your damned money, Andrew!"

"We had an agreement, Sir—"

"Agreement? What agreement? You know that I never agreed to anything. —Look, Andrew, I'll take that check from you if it's the only way that you're going to feel that you really are free. But I think the idea's preposterous. I'm a very wealthy old man and I don't have very long to live and if you force me to take that money I'm simply going to hand it away to charity. I'll give it to the Home for Orphaned Robots, if there is one. Or I'll found one, if there isn't." He laughed—a thin, joyless laugh. Neither Andrew nor Little Miss joined in. "But you don't care, do you? You simply want to give the money away. Very well, Andrew. Let me have the check."

"Thank you, Sir."

He passed it across to the old man.

Sir peered at it for a moment, holding it this way and that until his dimming eyes told him which side of the check he was looking at.

"You really have accumulated quite a fortune, Andrew. —Give me a pen, will you, Mandy?" Sir's hand shook as he took it from her, but when he began to write on the back of the check it was in bold, steady strokes that went on for line after line, an inscription much longer than a mere endorsement would have required. He studied what he had written and nodded. Then he handed the check back to Andrew.

Sir had endorsed the check *Gerald Martin, received as payment in full for the freedom of Robot Andrew NDR-113 Martin, per court decision.* And then beneath that he had drawn a line and written, *Pay to the order of Andrew Martin, as bonus for outstanding services rendered during the period of his employment here. His endorsement of this check implies irrevocable acceptance of the bonus. Gerald Martin.*

"Will that be acceptable, Andrew?" Sir asked.

Andrew hesitated a moment. He showed the check to Little Miss, who read what Sir had written and shrugged.

"You leave me with no choice, Sir," Andrew said.

"Precisely. That's the way I like things to be. Now fold that check up and put it in your pocket—no, you don't have a pocket, do you?—well, put it away *somewhere*. Keep it as a souvenir, something to remember me by. And let's hear nothing more about it." Sir glared defiantly at both Andrew and Little Miss. "So. That's done, then. And now you're properly and truly free, is that right? Very well. Very well. From now on you can select your own jobs around this place and do them as you please. I will give you no orders ever again, Andrew, except for this final one: that you do only what you please. As of this moment you must act only according to your own free will, as stipulated and approved by the courts. Is that clear?"

"Yes, Sir."

"But I am still responsible for you. That too, as stipulated and approved by the courts. I don't own you any more, but if you happen to get yourself into any trouble, I'm the one who will have to get you out of it. You may be free but you don't have any of the civil rights of a human being. You remain my dependent, in other words—my ward, by court order. I hope you understand that, Andrew."

Little Miss said, "You sound angry, Father."

"I am. I didn't ask to have responsibility for the world's only free robot dumped on me."

"Nothing has been dumped on you, Father. You accepted responsibility for Andrew the day you arranged to take him into your home. The court order doesn't change a bit of that. You won't have to do anything that you weren't bound to do before. As for Andrew's getting himself into trouble, what reason do you think he will? The Three Laws still hold."

"Then how can he be considered free?"

Andrew said quietly, "Are not human beings bound by their laws, Sir?"

Sir glowered. "Don't chop logic with me, Andrew. Human beings have voluntarily arrived at a social contract, a code of laws which they willingly agree to abide by because life in a civilized society would be untenable otherwise. Those who refuse to abide by those laws, and therefore make life untenable for others, are punished and, we like to think, eventually rehabilitated. But a robot doesn't live by any voluntary social contract. A robot obeys its code of laws because it has no choice but to obey. Even a so-called free robot."

"But as you say, Sir, human laws exist and must be obeyed, and those who live under those laws regard themselves as free nevertheless. So a robot—"

"Enough!" Sir roared. He swept his lap-robe to the floor and lurched uncertainly out of his chair. "I don't feel like discussing this any further, thank you. I'm going upstairs. Good night, Amanda. Good night, Andrew."

"Good night to you, Sir. Shall I see you to your room?" Andrew asked.

"You needn't bother. I'm still strong enough to climb a flight of stairs. You go about your business, whatever that may be, and I'll go about mine."

He tottered away. Andrew and Little Miss exchanged troubled glances, but neither of them said anything.

After that Sir rarely left his bedroom. His meals were prepared and brought to him by the simple TZ-model robot who looked after the kitchen. He never asked Andrew upstairs for any reason, and Andrew would not take it upon himself to intrude on Sir's privacy; and so from that time on Andrew saw Sir only on those infrequent occasions when the old man chose to descend into the main part of the house.

Andrew had not lived in the house himself for some time. As his woodworking business had expanded, it had become awkward for him to continue to operate out of the little attic studio that Sir had set aside for him at the beginning. So it had been decided, a few years back, that he would be allowed to set up a little dwelling of his own, a two-story cabin at the edge of the woods that flanked the Martin estate.

It was a pleasant, airy cabin, set on a little rise, with ferns and glistening-leaved shrubs all about, and a towering redwood tree just a short distance away. Three robot workmen had built it for him in a matter of a few days, working under the direction of a human foreman.

The cabin had no bedroom, of course, nor a kitchen, nor any bathroom facilities. One of the rooms was a library and office where Andrew kept his reference books and sketches and business records, and the other and much larger room was the workshop, where Andrew kept his carpentry equipment and stored the work in progress. A small shed adjoining the building was used to house the assortment of exotic woods that Andrew used in the jewelry-making segment of his enterprise, and the stack of less rare lumber that went into his much-sought-after pieces of furniture.

There was never any end of jobs for him to do. The publicity over his attaining free status had generated worldwide interest in the things that Andrew made, and scarcely a morning went by without three or four orders turning up on his computer. He had a backlog of commissions stretching years into the future, now, so that he finally had to set up a waiting list simply for the privilege of placing an order with him.

He was working harder now as a free robot than he ever had in the years when he had technically been the property of Sir. It was not at all unusual for Andrew to put in thirty-six or even forty-eight straight hours of work without emerging from his cabin, since he had no need, naturally, for food or sleep or rest of any kind.

His bank account swelled and swelled. He insisted on repaying Sir for the entire cost of building his little house, and this time Sir was willing to accept the money, purely for the sake of proper form. Title to the structure was legally transferred to Andrew and he executed a formal lease covering the portion of Gerald Martin's land on which the building stood.

Little Miss, who still lived just up the coast in the house she and Lloyd Charney had built long ago when they had first been married, never failed to look in on him whenever she came to Sir's estate to pay a call on her father. As a rule Little Miss would stop off at Andrew's workshop as soon as she arrived, and chat with him awhile and look at his latest projects, before going on into the main house where Sir was.

Often she brought Little Sir with her—though Andrew no longer called him that. For Little Sir had ceased to be a boy quite some time back—he was a tall and robust young man now, with a flaring russet-colored mustache nearly as awesome as his grandfather's and an imposing set of side-whiskers as well, and soon after the court decision that made Andrew a free robot he forbade Andrew to use the old nickname.

"Does it displease you, Little Sir?" Andrew asked. "I thought you found it amusing."

"I did."

"But now that you are a full-grown man, it seems condescending to you, is that it? An affront to your dignity? You know I have the highest respect for your—"

"It has nothing to do with my dignity," Little Sir said. "It has to do with yours."

"I don't understand, Little Sir."

"Evidently not. But look at it this way, Andrew: 'Little Sir' may be a charming name, and you and I certainly take it that way, but in fact what it is is the kind of groveling name that an old family retainer would use when speaking to the master's son, or in this case the master's grandson. It isn't appropriate any more, do you see, Andrew? My grandfather isn't your master nowadays, and I'm not a cute little boy. A free robot shouldn't call anyone 'Little Sir.' Is that clear? I call you Andrew—always have. And from now on you must call me George."

It was phrased as an order, so Andrew had no choice but to agree.

He ceased calling George Charney "Little Sir" as of that moment. But Little Miss remained Little Miss for him. It was unthinkable for Andrew to have to call her "Mrs. Charney" and even "Amanda" seemed like an improper and impertinent mode of address. She was "Little Miss" to him and nothing other than "Little Miss," even though she was a woman with graying hair now, lean and trim and as beautiful as ever but undeniably growing old. Andrew hoped that she would never give him the same sort of order that her son had; and she never did. "Little Miss" it was; "Little Miss" it would always be.

One day George and Little Miss came to the house, but neither of them made the usual stop at Andrew's place before going in to see Sir. Andrew noticed the car arrive and continue on past his own separate little driveway, and wondered why. He felt troubled when half an hour passed, and then half an hour more, and neither of them came to him. Had he given offense in some way on their last visit? No, that seemed unlikely.

But was there some problem in the main house, then?

He distracted himself by plunging into his work, but it took all his robotic powers of self-discipline to make himself concentrate, and even so nothing seemed to go as smoothly as it usually did. And then, late in the afternoon, George Charney came out back to see him—alone.

"Is anything wrong, George?" Andrew asked, a moment after George had entered.

"I'm afraid that there is, Andrew. My grandfather is dying."

"Dying?" Andrew said numbly.

Death was a concept he had long thought about, but had never really understood.

George nodded somberly. "My mother is at his bedside now. Grandfather wants you to be there too."

"He does? It isn't your mother who has sent for me, but Sir himself?"

"Sir himself, yes."

Andrew felt a faint tremor in his fingertips. It was as close as he could come to a physical expression of excitement. But there was distress mingled with the sensation.

Sir—dying!

He shut down his tools and hurried across to the main house, with George Charney trotting along beside him.

Sir was lying quietly in the bed in which he had spent most of his time in recent years. His hair had thinned to a few white wisps; even his glorious mustache now was a sad drooping thing.

97

He looked very pale, as though his skin were becoming transparent, and he scarcely seemed to be breathing. But his eyes were open—his fierce old eyes, his piercing, intense blue eyes—and he managed a small smile, the merest upturning of his lips, as he saw Andrew come into the room.

"Sir—oh, Sir, Sir—"

"Come here, Andrew." Sir's voice sounded surprisingly strong: the voice of the Sir of old.

Andrew faltered, too confused to respond.

"Come here, I said. That's an order. I said once that I wasn't going to give you any more orders, but this is an exception. Just about the last one I'm ever going to give you—you can count on that."

"Yes, Sir." Andrew came forward.

Sir pulled one hand out from under the coverlet. It seemed to be something of a struggle for him to move the blanket aside, and George rushed forward to help him.

"No," Sir said, with a trace of his familiar irascibility. "Damn it, don't try to do it for me, George! I'm only dying, not crippled." Angrily he pushed the coverlet down just far enough to raise his hand, and held it out toward the robot. "Andrew," he said. "Andrew—"

"Oh, Sir," Andrew began.

And he fell silent. He did not know what to say.

He had never before been at the side of someone who was dying, had never so much as seen a dead person. He knew that death was the human way of ceasing to function. It was an involuntary and irreversible dismantling that happened eventually to all human beings. Since it was inevitable, Andrew wanted to think that it was something that humans took for granted as a natural process and did not look upon with fear or distaste. But he was not entirely sure of that. And Sir had lived so long—he must be so *accustomed* to being alive, and there had always been so much life and vitality in him—

"Give me your hand, Andrew."

"Of course, Sir."

98

Andrew took Sir's cool, pale, shriveled hand into his own: gnarled ancient flesh against smooth ageless plastic that was without flaw.

Sir said, "You're a splendid robot, do you know that, Andrew? Truly splendid. The finest robot that was ever made."

"Thank you, Sir."

"I wanted to tell you that. And one other thing. I'm glad you're free. That's all. It's important to me that I had a chance to tell you that. All right, Andrew."

It was an unmistakable dismissal. Andrew no longer had Sir's attention. He released Sir's trembling hand and stepped back from the bed, taking up a position alongside George and Little Miss. Little Miss reached forward and touched Andrew's arm just above the elbow, lightly, affectionately. But she said nothing. Nor did George.

The old man seemed to have withdrawn into some private realm, far away. The only sound in the room now was Sir's increasingly rough breathing, becoming ever more harsh, ever less regular. Sir lay motionless, staring upward at nothing at all. His face was as expressionless as any robot's.

Andrew was utterly at a loss. He could only remain standing, absolutely silent, absolutely motionless, watching what he knew must be Sir's final moments.

The old man's breathing grew rougher yet. He made an odd gargling sound, deep in his throat, that was like no sound Andrew had ever heard in his entire existence.

Then all was still. Other than the cessation of Sir's breathing, Andrew was unable to detect any change in him. He had been virtually motionless a moment ago and he was motionless now. He had stared blindly upward before and he was staring upward now. Andrew realized, though, that something profound had just happened, something that was wholly beyond his comprehension. Sir had passed across that mysterious threshold that separated death from life. There was no more Sir. Sir was gone. Only this empty husk remained.

Little Miss broke the endless silence at last with a soft cough.

There were no tears in her eyes, but Andrew could see that she was deeply moved.

She said, "I'm glad you got here before he went, Andrew. You belonged here. You were one of us."

Once more Andrew did not know what to reply.

Little Miss said, "And it was wonderful to hear him say what he did to you. He may not have seemed friendly to you toward the end, Andrew, but he was old, you know. And it hurt him that you should have wanted to be free. But he forgave you for that right at the last, didn't he, Andrew?"

And then Andrew found the words to say. He said, "I never would have been free without him, Little Miss."

TEN

IT WAS ONLY AFTER Sir's death that Andrew started to wear clothes. He began with an old pair of trousers at first, a pair that he had obtained from George Charney.

It was a daring experiment, and he knew it. Robots, being metallic in exterior cladding and sexless in design—despite the "he" or "she" designations that their owners tended to hang on them—had no need for clothing, neither as protection against the elements nor as any sort of shield for modesty. And no robot, so far as Andrew knew, had ever worn any.

But some curious longing within Andrew seemed to have arisen lately that led him to want to cover his body in the way humans did, and—without pausing to examine the motivation that was leading him toward it—he set out to do so.

The day Andrew acquired the trousers, George had been with him in his workshop, helping him stain some porch furniture for his own house. Not that Andrew needed the help—indeed, it would have been very much simpler all around if George had let him do it by himself—but George had insisted on participating in the job. It was furniture for his own porch, after all. He was the man of the house—George was married now, and a lawyer with the old Feingold firm, which for the past few months had been called Feingold and Charney, with Stanley Feingold as the senior partner—and he took his adult responsibilities very, very seriously.

At the end of the day the furniture was stained and so, quite thoroughly, was George. He had splotches of stain on his hands, on his ears, on the tip of his nose. His russet mustache and ever more flamboyant side-whiskers were stained too. And, of course, there was stain all over his clothing. But at least George had come prepared for that, bringing an expendable shirt to work in and a disreputable-looking pair of trousers that he must have had since his high school days.

As he was changing back into his regular clothes when the job was done, George crumpled up the old shirt and trousers and said, as he tossed them aside, "You might as well just throw these things in the trash, Andrew. They're of no use to me any more."

George was right about the shirt. Not only was it badly stained, but it had split right down the seam from the arm to the shirt-tail when George reached out too far too quickly while trying to turn a porch table on its side. But the trousers, frayed and worn as they were, seemed salvageable to Andrew.

He held them up with their legs dangling. "If you don't mind," he said, "I'd like to keep these for myself."

George grinned. "To use as rags, you mean?"

Andrew paused just a moment before replying.

"To wear," he said.

Now it was George's turn to pause. Andrew could see the surprise on his face, and then the amusement. George was trying hard not to smile, and he was more or less succeeding at it, but the effort was all too obvious to Andrew's eyes.

"To—wear," George said slowly. "You want to wear my old pants. Is that what you just said, Andrew?"

"It is. I would very much like to wear them, if that is all right with you."

"Is something going wrong with your homeostatic system, Andrew?"

"Not at all. Why do you ask?"

"Only that I was wondering if you were feeling chilly these days. Why else would you want to wear those pants?"

"To find out what it is like."

"Ah," George said. And then after a bit he said, again, "Ah. I see. You want to find out what it's like. All right, I can tell you, Andrew. What it will feel like is like having a dirty old piece of rough unpleasant cloth wrapped around your fine smooth metal skin."

"Are you saying that you don't want me to put the trousers on?" Andrew asked.

"I didn't say that."

"But you think it's a peculiar idea."

"Well—"

"You do."

"Yes. As a matter of fact, I do. Very damned peculiar indeed, Andrew."

"And therefore you refuse to give me the trousers except for the purpose of destroying them?"

"No," George said. There was a note of exasperation in his voice. "Do whatever you want with them, Andrew. Try them on, if you like. Why should I have any objections? You're a free robot. You can put on a pair of pants if that's what you feel like doing. I don't see any reason at all why I should stand in your way. —Go on, Andrew. Put them on."

"Yes," said Andrew. "Yes, I will."

"It's a moment for the history books. The first time a robot has put on clothes. I ought to get my camera, Andrew."

Andrew brought the trousers close to his waist. But then he hesitated.

"Well?" George asked.

"Will you show me how to do it?" Andrew said.

Grinning broadly now, George showed Andrew how to manipulate the static charge so as to allow the trousers to open, wrap about his lower body, and move shut. George demonstrated the technique a couple of times with his own trousers, but Andrew was quite aware that it was going to take him a while to duplicate

ISAAC ASIMOV AND ROBERT SILVERBERG

that one flowing motion, which George, after all, had been performing since he was a child.

"It is the twist of the wrist when you bring the hand upward that puzzles me," Andrew said.

"Like this," said George, and did it yet again.

"Like that?"

"More like this."

"Like this, yes." Andrew touched the little stud once again and the trousers opened, fell, rose, and closed themselves about his legs. "Right?"

"Much better," said George.

"A little practice and it will seem natural to me, I think," Andrew said.

George gave him an odd look. "No, Andrew. It's never going to seem natural to you. Because it *isn't* natural. —Why on Earth do you want to wear trousers, Andrew?"

"As I said before, George. Out of curiosity about what it is like to be clothed."

"But you weren't naked before you put them on. You were simply—yourself."

"Yes, I suppose I was," Andrew said noncommittally.

"I'm trying to be sympathetic. But for the life of me I still can't understand what you're up to, Andrew. Your body is so beautifully functional that it's a downright shame to cover it—especially when you don't need to worry about either temperature control or modesty. And the fabric doesn't really cling properly, not on metal."

Andrew said, "Are not human bodies beautifully functional, George? Yet you all cover yourselves."

"For warmth, for cleanliness, for protection, for decorativeness. And as a concession to social custom. None of that applies to you."

Andrew said, "I feel bare without clothes."

"You do? You've never said a word about that before today, so far as I know. Is this something new?"

"Reasonably new."

104

"A week? A month? A year? —What's going on, Andrew?"

"It is hard for me to explain. I have begun to feel—*different.*"

"Different! Different from whom? It isn't as though a robot is any novelty any more. Andrew, there are millions of robots on Earth now. In this Region, according to the last census, there are almost as many robots as there are humans."

"I know that, George. There are robots doing every conceivable kind of work."

"And not a single one of them wears clothes."

"But none of them is free, George."

"So that's it! You feel different because you *are* different!"

"Exactly."

"But to wear clothes—"

"Indulge me, George. I want to do this."

George let out his breath in a long, slow exhalation.

"Whatever you say. You're a free robot, Andrew."

"Yes. I am."

After his initial skepticism George seemed to find Andrew's venture into wearing clothes curious and amusing. He cooperated by bringing him, little by little, new additions to his wardrobe. Andrew could hardly go into town to purchase clothing himself, and he felt ill at ease even about ordering it from the computer catalogs, because he knew that his name was widely known in many places ever since the court decision, and he didn't want some shipping clerk in a storeroom far away to recognize it on an order form and begin spreading the word that the free robot was now going in for wearing clothing.

So George would supply him with the articles he requested: a shirt first, then shoes, a fine pair of gloves, a set of decorative epaulets.

"What about underwear?" George asked. "Should I get you some of that too?" But Andrew had no idea of the existence or purpose of underwear, and George had to explain it to him. Andrew decided that he had no need of it.

He tended to wear his new clothes only when he was alone at home. He was hardly ready to go outdoors in them; and even in his own cabin he stopped wearing them in the presence of others after a few preliminary experiments. He was inhibited by George's patronizing smile, which with the best will in the world George continued to be unable to conceal, and by the bewildered stares of the first few customers who saw him dressed when they came to him to commission work.

Andrew might be free, but there was built into him a carefully detailed program concerning his behavior toward human beings: a neural channel that was not as powerful in its effect as the Three Laws, but nevertheless was there to discourage him from giving any sort of offense. It was only by the tiniest steps that he dared advance. Open disapproval would set him back months. It was an enormous leap for him when he finally allowed himself to leave his house with clothing on.

No one he encountered that day showed any sign of surprise. But perhaps they were too astounded even to react. And indeed even Andrew himself still felt strange about his experiment with clothing.

He had a mirror, now, and he would study himself for long periods of time, turning from side to side, looking at himself from all angles. And sometimes he found himself reacting with disfavor to his own appearance. His metal face, with its glowing photoelectric eyes and its rigidly carved robotic features, sometimes struck Andrew himself as strikingly incongruous now that it rose up out of the soft, brightly colored fabrics of clothing meant for a human body.

But at other times it seemed to him perfectly appropriate for him to be wearing clothing. Like virtually all robots, he had been designed, after all, to be fundamentally humanoid in shape: two arms, two legs, an oval head set upon a narrow neck. The U. S. Robots designers had not needed to give him that form. They could have made him look any way they deemed efficient—with rotors instead of legs, with six arms instead of two, with a swiveling sensor-dome atop his trunk instead of a head with two eyes. But no: they had patterned him after themselves. The decision had been made, very early in the history of robotics, that the best

way to overcome mankind's deep-seated fear of intelligent machines was to make them as familiar in form as possible.

In that case, why should he not wear clothing also? That would
make him look even more human, wouldn't it?

And in any event Andrew *wanted* to wear clothing now. It
seemed symbolic to him of his new status as a legally free robot.

Of course, not everyone accepted Andrew as free, regardless of
what the legal finding had been. The term "free robot" had no
meaning to many people: it was like saying "dry water" or
"bright darkness." Andrew was inherently incapable of resenting
that, and yet he felt a difficulty in his thinking process—a slow-
ing, an inner resistance—whenever he was faced with someone's
refusal to allow him the status he had won in court.

When he wore clothing in public, he knew, he risked antago-
nizing such people. Andrew tried to be cautious about that,
therefore.

Nor was it only potentially hostile strangers who had difficulty
with the idea of his wearing clothing. Even the person who most
loved him in all the world—Little Miss—was startled and, Andrew
suspected, more than a little troubled by it. Andrew saw that
from the very first time. Like her son George, Little Miss had
tried to conceal her feelings of surprise and dismay at the sight of
Andrew in clothing. And, like George, she had failed.

Well, Little Miss was old now and, like many old people, she
had grown set in her ways. Maybe she simply preferred him to
look the way he had looked when she was a girl. Or, perhaps, she
might believe on some deep level that robots—all robots, even
Andrew—should look like the machines that they were, and
therefore should not dress like people.

Andrew suspected that if he ever should question Little Miss
on that point she would deny it, probably quite indignantly. But
he had no intention of doing that. He simply tended to avoid
putting on clothes—or too many of them—whenever Little Miss
came to visit him.

Which was none too often, these days, for Little Miss was past
seventy now—well past seventy—and had grown very thin and

sensitive to cold, and even the mild climate of Northern California was too cool for her most of the year. Her husband had died several years before, and since then Little Miss had begun spending much of her time traveling in the tropical parts of the world —Hawaii, Australia, Egypt, the warmer zones of South America, places like that. She would return to California only occasionally, perhaps once or twice a year, to see George and his family—and, of course, Andrew.

After one of her visits George came down to the cabin to speak with Andrew and said ruefully, "Well, she's finally got me, Andrew. I'm going to be running for the Legislature next year. She won't give me any peace unless I do. And I'm sure you know that the First Law of our family, and the Second Law and the Third Law as well, is that nobody says 'no' to Amanda Charney. So there I am: a candidate. It's my genetic destiny, according to her. Like grandfather, like grandson, is what she says."

"Like grandfather—"

Andrew stopped, uncertain.

"What is it, Andrew?"

"Something about the phrase. The idiom. My grammatical circuit—" He shook his head. "*Like* grandfather, *like* grandson. There's no verb in the statement, but I know how to adjust for that. Still—"

George began to laugh. "What a literal-minded hunk of tin you can be sometimes, Andrew!"

"Tin?"

"Never mind about that. What the other expression meant was simply that I, George, the grandson, am expected to do what Sir, the grandfather, did—that is to say, to run for the Regional Legislature and have a long and distinguished career. The usual expression is, 'Like father, like son,' but in this case my father didn't care to go into politics, and so my mother has changed the old cliché so that it says— Are you following all this, Andrew, or am I just wasting my breath?"

"I understand now."

"Good. But of course the thing my mother doesn't take into

account is that I'm not really all that much like my grandfather in temperament, and perhaps I'm not as clever as he was, either, because he had a truly formidable intellect, and so there's no necessary reason why I'd automatically equal the record he ran up in the Legislature. There'll never be anyone like him again, I'm afraid."

Andrew nodded. "And how sad for us that he is no longer with is. I would find it pleasant, George, if Sir were still—" He paused, for he did not want to say, "in working order." He knew that that would not be the appropriate expression to use. And yet it was the first phrase that had come into his mind.

"Still alive?" George finished for him. "Yes. Yes, it would be good to have him around. I have to confess I miss the old monster at least as much as you do."

"Monster?"

"In a manner of speaking."

"Ah. Yes. A manner of speaking."

When George had gone, Andrew replayed the conversation in his mind, puzzling over its twists and turns and trying to see why he had been so badly off balance throughout it. It had been George's use of idiomatic phrases and colloquial language, Andrew decided, that had caused the problems.

Even after all this time, it was still difficult sometimes for Andrew to keep pace with humans when they struck out along linguistic pathways that were something other than the most direct ones. He had come into being equipped with an extensive innate vocabulary, a set of grammatical instructions, and the ability to arrange words in intelligible combinations. And through whatever fluke in his generalized positronic pathways it was that made Andrew's intelligence more flexible and adaptable than that of the standard robot, he had been able to develop the knack of conversing easily and gracefully with humans. But there were limits to his abilities along that line.

The problem was only going to get worse as time went along, Andrew realized.

Human languages, he knew, were constantly in a state of flux.

There was nothing fixed or really systematic about them. New words were invented all the time, old words would change their meanings, all sorts of short-lived informal expressions slipped into ordinary conversation. That much he had already had ample reason to learn, though he had not done any kind of scientific investigation of the kinds of changes that tended to take place.

The English language, which was the one Andrew used most often, had altered tremendously over the past six hundred years. Now and then he had looked at some of Sir's books, the works of the ancient poets—Chaucer, Spenser, Shakespeare—and he had seen that their pages were sprinkled with footnotes to explain archaic word usage to modern readers.

What if the language were to change just as significantly in the *next* six hundred years? How was he going to be able to communicate with the human beings around him, unless he kept up with the changes?

Already, in one brief conversation, George had baffled him three times. "Like grandfather, like grandson." How simple that seemed now that George had explained it—but how mysterious it had been at first.

And why had George called him a "hunk of tin," when George surely knew that there was no tin in Andrew's makeup whatsoever? And—it was the most puzzling one of all—why should George have called Sir a "monster," when that was plainly not an appropriate description of the old man?

Those were not even the latest modern phrases, Andrew knew. They were simply individual turns of phrase, a little too colloquial or metaphorical for instant handling by Andrew's linguistic circuitry. He would face far more mystifying ways of speech in the outside world, he suspected.

Perhaps it was time for him to update some of his linguistic documentation.

His own books would give him no guidance. They were old and most of them dealt with woodworking, with art, with furniture design. There were none on language, none on the ways of human beings. Nor was Sir's library, extensive as it was, likely to be of much use. No one was living in the big house just now—it was sealed, under robot maintenance—but Andrew still could have access to it whenever he wanted. Nearly all of Sir's books, though, dated from the previous century or before. There was nothing there that would serve Andrew's purpose.

All things considered, the best move seemed to be for him to get some up-to-date information—and not from George. When Andrew turned to George at the time he had wanted to start wearing clothing, he had had to fight his way through George's incomprehension and a certain amount of George's condescending amusement. Though he doubted that George would treat him the same way in this matter, he preferred not to find out.

No, he would simply go to town and use the public library. That was the proper self-reliant thing to do—the correct way for a free robot to handle a problem, he told himself. It was a triumphant decision and Andrew felt his electropotential grow distinctly higher as he contemplated it, until he had to throw in an impedance coil to bring himself back to equilibrium.

To the library, yes.

And he would dress for the occasion. Yes. Yes. Humans did not enter the public library unclothed. Neither would he.

He put on a full costume—elegant leggings of a velvety purple fabric, and a flowing red blouse with a satiny sheen, and his best walking boots. He even donned a shoulder chain of polished wooden links, one of his finest productions. It was a choice between that and another chain he had, one made of glitter-plastic, which perhaps was better suited for daytime wear; but George had said that the wooden chain was terribly impressive, particularly since anything made of wood was far more valuable than mere plastic. And he wanted to impress, today. There would be humans in the library, not robots. They would never have seen a robot there before. It was important for him to look his best.

But he knew that he was doing something unusual and that there might be unusual consequences. If George dropped by

ISAAC ASIMOV AND ROBERT SILVERBERG

unexpectedly, he would be surprised to find Andrew gone, and he might be troubled by that.

Andrew had placed a hundred feet between himself and the house before he felt resistance gathering within himself and rapidly reaching the level that would bring him to a halt. He shifted the impedance coil out of circuit, and when that did not seem to make much difference, he returned to his home and on a piece of paper wrote neatly:

> I HAVE GONE TO THE LIBRARY.
> —Andrew Martin

and placed it in clear view on his worktable.

ELEVEN

ANDREW NEVER QUITE MADE IT to the library that day. He had never been there before—he rarely had reason to venture into the little town a short way down the road from the Martin estate—but he had not expected that to be any problem. He had studied the map with great care. And therefore he knew the route, or so he believed.

But everything he saw, once he was more than a short distance from the house, seemed strange to him. The actual landmarks along the road did not resemble the abstract symbols on the map, not to his way of thinking. He hesitated again and again, comparing the things he was seeing out here with the things he had expected to see, and after he had been walking for a little while he realized that he was lost, that he must have taken a wrong turn somewhere without noticing it and could no longer relate his position to anything on the map.

What to do now? Go back and start again? Or keep on in this direction, and hope that his path would somehow link up with the proper route?

The most efficient thing, Andrew decided, was to ask someone for directions. It might be that he could regain the direction he wanted with relatively little effort.

But who was there to ask? Closer to the house he had seen an occasional field robot, but there were none in sight here. A vehicle passed, but did not stop. Perhaps another one would come by soon. He stood irresolute, which meant calmly motionless; and then he saw two human beings walking diagonally across the field that lay to his left.

He turned to face them.

They saw him, and changed course so that now they were heading in his direction. They changed their demeanor, too. A moment before, they had been talking loudly, laughing and whooping, their voices carrying far across the field—but now they had fallen silent. Their faces bore the look that Andrew associated with human uncertainty.

They were young, but not very young. Twenty, perhaps? Twenty-five? Andrew had never been very good at judging the age of humans.

He said, when they were still some distance away, "Pardon me, sirs. Would you kindly describe to me the route to the town library?"

They halted and stared.

One of them, the taller and thinner of the two, who was wearing a tall narrow black hat that looked like a length of pipe and extended his height still further, almost grotesquely, said—not to Andrew, but to the other—"I think it's a robot."

"I think you're right," said the other, who was short and plump, and had a bulbous nose and heavy eyelids. "It's got a robot kind of face, doesn't it?"

"It certainly does. Definitely a robot kind of face."

"But it's wearing clothes."

"Very fancy clothes too."

"Imagine that. A robot wearing fancy clothes! What will they think of next?"

"Pardon me, sirs," Andrew said again. "I am in need of assistance. I have been trying to locate the town library, but I seem to have lost my way."

"Speaks just like a robot," the taller one said.

"Got a face just like a robot," said the other.

114

"Then it must *be* a robot."

"You'd think so, wouldn't you?"

"But he's wearing clothes."

"Clothes. Absolutely. There's no denying the truth of that, is there?"

"Robots don't wear clothes, do they?"

"Not that I know of."

"If it's wearing clothes, do you think it can be a robot?"

"It's got a metal face. Metal everything. But if it's a robot, why is it wearing clothes?"

The taller one snapped his fingers. "You know what we have here? It's the free robot. There's a robot that lives at the old Charney place that isn't owned by anybody, and I bet this is the one. Why else would it be wearing clothes?"

"Ask it," said the one with the nose.

"Good idea," said the other. He took a few steps toward Andrew and said, "Are you the robot from the Charney place?"

"I am Andrew Martin, sir," said Andrew.

"Pretty snotty kind of robot, aren't you?" the tall one said. "Give me a direct answer when I ask you a question."

"The place where I live is the Martin estate, which is owned by the Charney family. It was formerly the home of Mr. Gerald Martin. Therefore my name is Andrew Martin."

"You're a robot, right?"

"Of course I am, sir."

"Then why are you wearing clothes? Robots don't wear clothes, do they?"

"I wear clothes when I choose to wear them," said Andrew quietly.

"That's disgusting. You're a hideous spectacle decked out like that, do you know that? Absolutely hideous. A robot wearing clothes! Who ever heard of that?" He glanced at his companion. "Have you ever seen anything so disgusting?" And to Andrew he said, "Take off your clothes."

Andrew hesitated. He hadn't heard an order in that tone of

voice in so long that his Second Law circuits had momentarily jammed.

The tall one said, "Well, what are you waiting for? I told you to take off your clothes, didn't I? I *order* you to take off your clothes!"

Slowly, Andrew began to obey. He unfastened his shoulder chain and set it down carefully on the ground. Then he removed his satiny blouse and folded it with great care so that it would not look crumpled when he put it on again. He placed it on the ground next to the chain.

"Faster," said the tall one. "Don't bother folding your things. Just drop them, you hear? Get everything off. Everything."

Andrew unfastened the velvety leggings. He removed the elegant boots.

The nose said, "Well, at least he follows orders."

"He has to. Every robot does. There isn't any two ways about it. Following orders is built right into them. You say, 'Go jump in the lake,' and they jump. You say, 'Bring me a plate of strawberries,' and it goes right out and finds you some strawberries somewhere, even if it's the wrong time of year."

"Sounds like a good deal, having something like that around."

"You bet it is. I've always wondered what it would be like to have a robot of my own. Haven't you?"

The tall one shrugged. "Who could afford it?"

"This one's real available. If it doesn't belong to anyone, he could be ours as much as somebody else's. We just have to tell him that he belongs to us. Make it an order, don't you see?"

The tall one blinked. "Hey! That's right!"

"We'll make him run errands for us. Do all sorts of jobs. Anything we like, it'll have to do. And nobody can stop us. It isn't as if we're stealing anybody's property. He *isn't* anybody's property."

"But what if someone else tries to take him from us the same way?"

"We'll give him an order that says he can't go off with anybody else," said the nose.

The tall one frowned. "I'm not sure that would work. If he has to obey orders from humans, he'll have to obey orders from anybody else just the same as he does ours, right?"

"Well—"

"Let's worry about that later. —Hey! You! You, robot! Stand on your head!"

"The head is not meant—" Andrew began.

"I said, stand on your head. That's an order. If you don't know how to stand on your head, this is a good moment to start learning the way it's done."

Andrew hesitated again. Then he bent his head toward the ground and put his arms out so that they would bear his weight. He attempted to lift his legs. But there was nothing in his circuitry to equip Andrew for dealing easily with such an inverted position, and he lost his balance almost at once. He toppled and fell heavily to the ground, landing on his back. For a moment he lay still, struggling to shake off the effects of his fall, before starting slowly to rise.

"No," the tall one said. "Just stay down there. And don't make a sound." To the other he said, "I bet you we could take him apart and put him back together again. You ever take a robot apart?"

"No. You?"

"Never. But I always wanted to."

"You think he'll let us?"

"How can he stop us?"

Indeed there was no way at all that Andrew was able to stop them, if they ordered him not to resist in a forceful enough manner. The Second Law—obedience to humans—would always take precedence over the Third Law of self-preservation. In any case, it was impossible for him to defend himself against them without running the risk of hurting them, and that would mean breaking the First Law. At that thought every motile unit in him contracted slightly and Andrew began to quiver as he lay stretched full length on the ground.

The tall one walked over and shoved at him with the tip of his boot.

"He's heavy. And I think we're going to need tools to do the job."

Bulbous-nose said, "What if we can't put him back the right way again afterward?"

"What of it?"

"Then we've wasted a perfectly good robot that we could have used for all sorts of other things. I think what we ought to do is order him to take *himself* apart. He's got to know the right way of doing it. It would be fun to watch him try, anyhow. And then we can assemble him again."

"Right," said the tall one thoughtfully. "But let's get him off the road. If someone happens to come along—"

It was too late. Someone had indeed come along and it was George. From where he lay, Andrew could see him topping a small rise in the middle distance. He would have liked to signal for help. But the last order he had received was, "Don't make a sound," and he was bound by that until countermanded by its giver or some other human being.

George was looking this way, though. And now he was breaking into a trot. In another few moments he was there, somewhat winded, standing at Andrew's side looking down at him in dismay.

The two young men stepped back a little and waited, frowning, glancing uncertainly at each other.

George said anxiously, "Andrew, has anything gone wrong with you?"

Andrew said, "I am quite well, George."

"Why are you lying on the ground like that, then? Can't you get up?"

"I would have no difficulty in doing that, if you wished me to," Andrew said.

"Then do it! Don't just lie there!"

Andrew arose, gratefully, when he heard the order.

George said, "And why are your clothes scattered around all

over the place? How come you're not wearing them? What's been going on here?''

The tall young man said, ''That your robot, Mac?''

George turned sharply. ''He's no one's robot. Have you two been playing games with him?''

''Well, we thought it was pretty weird that a robot would be wearing clothes. So we politely asked him to take them off. What's that to you if you don't own him?''

George said, ''Were they trying to harm you, Andrew?''

Andrew said, ''It was their intention in some way to dismember me. They were about to move me to a quiet spot and require me to dismember myself.''

George looked at the two young men. He was attempting to appear fearless and bold even though he was outnumbered, but Andrew saw his chin tremble.

''Is this true?'' George asked them sternly.

The two had evidently also noticed George's obvious discomfort, though, and plainly they had begun to decide that he represented no serious threat to them. George was no longer a young man. His children were grown, now, old enough so that his son Paul had joined the family law firm. George's russet hair had turned gray and his cheeks—without their flaring side-whiskers, now—were the soft pink cheeks of a sedentary man. He was hardly likely to put up much of a fight, no matter how fierce his manner might seem. As the two took note of that, their manner changed, becoming less wary and more confident.

The tall one said lightly, with a smirk on his face, ''We wanted to see how he'd go about it, yes. Especially how he was going to manage things toward the end, when he only had one arm still attached.''

''You have a peculiar way of amusing yourselves.''

''Is that any business of yours?''

''As a matter of fact, it is.''

The tall one laughed. ''And what are you going to do about it, pudgy? Beat us up?''

''No,'' George said. ''I don't have to. This robot has been with my family for over seventy years, are you aware of that? He knows us and he values us more than he values anyone else in the world. What I'm going to do is tell him that you two have been threatening my life, that you're planning to kill me. I'll ask him to defend me. He'll have to choose between my life and yours, and I know very well which choice he's going to make. —Do you know how strong a robot is? Do you know what's going to happen to you when Andrew attacks you?"

"Hey, wait a second—" the bulbous-nosed one said. He looked troubled again, now. So did the other. They were both beginning to back away a little.

George said sharply, "Andrew, I am in direct personal danger. These two young men are about to cause me harm. I order you to move toward them!"

Andrew obediently took a couple of steps forward, though he wondered what he would be able to do by way of defending George beyond that. In sudden inspiration he brought his arms up into what could perhaps have been interpreted as a menacing position. If the whole idea was simply to have him seem formidable, well, he would make himself look as formidable as he could.

He held the fierce pose. His photoelectric eyes glowed their strongest shade of red. His bare metallic form gleamed in the sunlight.

The two young men didn't choose to stay around to see what was going to happen next. They took off across the field as fast as they could run, and it was only when they were something like a hundred meters away and felt that they had reached a safe place that they turned and glared back, shaking their fists and yelling angry curses.

Andrew took a few more steps in their direction. They swung around and sped away over the top of the hill. Within moments they were down the far side and out of sight.

Even now, Andrew remained in his posture of threat.

"All right, Andrew, you can relax," said George. He was shaking and his face was pale and sweaty. He looked very much unstrung. George was well past the age where he could comfortably face the possibility of a physical confrontation with one young man, let alone two of them at once.

Andrew said, "It is just as well that they ran away. You know that I could never have hurt them, George. I could plainly see that they weren't attacking you."

"But they might have, if things had gone on any further."

"That is only a speculation. In my judgment, George—"

"Yes. I know. Most likely they'd never have had the guts to raise a hand against me. But in any case I didn't order you to attack them. I only told you to move toward them. Their own fears did all the rest. That and that prizefighter stance that you were clever enough to adopt."

"But how could they possibly fear robots? The First Law insures that a robot could never—"

"Fear of robots is a disease that much of mankind has, and there doesn't really seem to be any cure for it—not yet, at any rate. But never mind that. They're gone and you're still in one piece and that's all that matters right now. What I'd like to know, though, is what the devil were you doing here in the first place, Andrew?"

"I was going to the library."

"Yes. I know that. I found the note you left. But this isn't the way to the library. The library's back there, in town. And when I phoned the library the librarian said you hadn't been there, that she hadn't heard a thing from you. I went out looking for you on the library road and there wasn't any sign of you there, and nobody I met along the way to town had seen you either. So I knew you were lost. As a matter of fact, you've gotten yourself turned around by 180 degrees."

"I suspected that there was some error in my directional plan," Andrew said.

"There certainly was. I was just about ready to order a sky-search scan for you, do you know that? And then it occurred to me that you might have wandered over this way, somehow. —What were you doing going to the library anyway, Andrew?

121

ISAAC ASIMOV AND ROBERT SILVERBERG

Sometimes you get the strangest ideas into your head. You know that I'd be happy to bring you any book you needed.''

"Yes, I know that, George. But I am a—"

"Free robot. Yes. Yes. With every right to pick himself up and march off to town to use the library, if that's what he wants to do, even though his extraordinary robotic intelligence is mysteriously incapable of keeping him on the right road. And what was it, may I ask, that you wanted to get at the library?"

"A book on modern language."

"Are you planning to give up woodworking for linguistics, Andrew?"

"I feel inadequate in regard to speech."

"But you have a fantastic command of the language! Your vocabulary, your grammar—"

"The language—its metaphors, its colloquialisms, even its grammar—constantly changes, George. My programming does not. If I don't update myself, I will be almost unable to communicate with human beings in another few generations."

"Well—perhaps you have a point there."

"So I must study the patterns of linguistic change. And many other things as well." Suddenly Andrew heard himself saying, "George, I feel it's important that I get to know much more about human beings, about the world, about everything. I have lived such an isolated life all these years, in our beautiful estate here on this little secluded strip of coast. The world beyond my own doorstep is a mystery to me, really. —And I need to know more about robots also, George. I want to write a book about them."

"A book," George said, sounding puzzled. "About robots. A manual of design?"

"Not at all. A history of their development is what I have in mind."

"Ah," George said, nodding and frowning at the same time. "Well, then. Let's walk home, shall we?"

"Of course. May I put my clothes on or shall I simply carry them?"

122

"Put them on. By all means."

"Thank you."

Andrew dressed quickly and he and George began to walk back up the road.

"You want to write a book on the history of robotics," George said, as if revolving the concept in his mind. "But why, Andrew? There are a million books on robotics already and at least half a million of them go into the history of the robot concept. The world is growing saturated not only with robots but with information about robots."

Andrew shook his head, a human gesture that he had lately begun to make more and more frequently. "Not a history of robotics, George. A history of *robots*—by a robot. Surely no such book has ever been written. I want to explain how robots feel about themselves. And especially about how it has been for us in our relationships with human beings, ever since the first robots were allowed to work and live on Earth."

George's eyebrows lifted. But he offered no other direct response.

TWELVE

LITTLE MISS was making one of her periodic visits to her family's California estate. She had reached her eighty-third birthday and she seemed frail as a bird these days. But there was nothing about her that was lacking in either energy or determination. Though she carried a cane, she used it more often to gesture with than she did for support.

She listened to the story of Andrew's unhappy attempt to reach the library in a fury of mounting indignation. At the end she tapped her cane vehemently against the floor and said, "George, that's absolutely horrible. Who were those two young ruffians, anyway?"

"I don't know, Mother."

"Then you should make it your business to find out."

"What difference does it make? Just a couple of local hooligans, I suppose. The usual idling foolish kids. In the end they didn't do any damage."

"But they might have. If you hadn't come along when you did, they could have caused serious harm to Andrew. And even when you did come along, you might well have been physically attacked yourself. The only thing that saved you from that, it seems, is that they were so stupid that they failed to realize that

124

Andrew wouldn't be able to harm them even at your direct order."

"Really, Mother. Do you think they would have touched me?
People attacking an absolute stranger on a country road? In the
Twenty-Third Century?"

"Well—perhaps not. But Andrew was certainly in danger. And
that's something we can't allow. You know that I regard Andrew
as a member of our family, George."

"Yes, of course. So do I. We always have."

"Then we can't permit a couple of moronic young louts to
treat him like some kind of disposable wind-up toy, can we?"

"What would you have me do, Mother?" asked George.

"You're a lawyer, aren't you? Put your legal training to some
good use, then! Listen to me: I want you to set up a test case,
somehow, that will force the Regional Court to declare for robot
rights, and then get the Regional Legislature to pass the necessary enabling bills, and if there are any political problems you
carry the whole thing to the World Court, if you have to. I'll be
watching, George, and I'll tolerate no shirking."

"Mother, didn't you say just a short while ago that what you
wanted most in the world for me was that I run for the seat that
Grandfather held in the Legislature?"

"Yes, of course. But what does that have to do with—"

"And now you want me to launch a controversial campaign for
robot rights. Robots can't vote, Mother. But there are plenty of
human beings who do, and a lot of them aren't as fond of robots
as you are. Do you know what will happen to my candidacy if the
main thing that people know about me is that I was the lawyer
who forced the Legislature to pass robot-rights laws?"

"So?"

"Which is more important to you, Mother? That I get elected
to the Legislature, or that I get myself involved with this test case
of yours?"

"The test case, naturally," said Little Miss at once.

George nodded. "All right. I just wanted to make sure we had
things perfectly clear. I'll go out there and fight for civil rights

for robots, if that's what you want me to do. But it's going to be the end of my political career even before my political career has begun, and you have to realize that."

"Of course I realize that, George. You may find that you're mistaken—I don't know—but in any case, the main thing is that I want Andrew to be protected against a repetition of this brutal incident. First and foremost that is what I want."

"Well, then," said George. "That's what I'll see that you get, Mother. You can count on it."

He began his campaign right away. And what had begun simply as a way of placating the fearsome old lady swiftly turned into the fight of his life.

George Charney had never really yearned for a seat in the Legislature, anyway. So he was able to tell himself that he was off that hook, now that his mother had decided that he should be a civil-rights crusader instead. And the lawyer in him was fascinated by the challenge. There were deep and profound legal implications to the campaign that called for the most careful analysis and calculation.

As senior partner of Feingold and Charney, George plotted much of the strategy, but left the actual work of research and filing papers to his junior partners. He placed his own son Paul, who had become a member of the firm three years before, in charge of piloting the day-by-day maneuvers. Paul had the additional responsibility of making dutiful progress reports virtually every day to his grandmother. She, in turn, discussed the campaign every day with Andrew.

Andrew was deeply involved. He had begun work on his book on robots—he was going back to the very beginning, to Lawrence Robertson and the founding of United States Robots and Mechanical Men—but he put the project aside, now, and spent his time poring over the mounting stacks of legal documents. He even, at times, offered a few very different suggestions of his own.

To Little Miss he said, "George told me the day those two men were harassing me that human beings have always been afraid of robots. 'A disease of mankind,' is what he called it. As long as that is the case, it seems to me that the courts and the legislatures aren't likely to do very much on behalf of robots. Robots have no political power, after all, and people do. Shouldn't something be done about changing the human attitude toward robots, then?"

"If only we could."

"We have to try," Andrew said. "*George* has to try."

"Yes," said Little Miss. "He does, doesn't he?"

So while Paul stayed in court, it was George who took to the public platform. He gave himself up entirely to the task of campaigning for the civil rights of robots, putting all of his time and energy into it.

George had always been a good speaker, easy and informal, and now he became a familiar figure at conventions of lawyers and teachers and holo-news editors, and on every opinion show on the public airwaves, setting forth the case for robot rights with an eloquence that grew steadily with experience.

The more time George spent on public platforms and in the communications studios, the more relaxed and yet commanding a figure he became. He allowed his side-whiskers to grow again, and swept his hair—white, now—backward in a grandiose plume. He even indulged in the new style of clothing that some of the best-known video commentators were going in for, the loose, flowing style known as "drapery." Wearing it made him feel like a Greek philosopher, he said, or like a member of the ancient Roman Senate.

Paul Charney, who was generally a good deal more conservative in his ways than his father, warned him the first time he saw his father rigged out like that: "Just take care not to trip over it on stage, Dad."

"I'll try not to," said George.

The essence of his pro-robot argument was this:

"If, by virtue of the Second Law, we can demand of any robot unlimited obedience in all respects not involving harm to a human being, then any human being, *any* human being at all, has a fearsome power over any robot, *any* robot. In particular, since Second Law overrides Third Law, *any* human being can use the law of obedience to defeat the law of self-protection. He can order the robot to damage itself or even destroy itself for any reason, or for no reason whatsoever—purely on whim alone.

"Let us leave the question of property rights out of the discussion here—though it is not a trivial one—and approach the issue simply on the level of sheer human decency. Imagine someone approaching a robot he happens to encounter on the road and ordering it, for no reason other than his own amusement, to remove its own limbs, or to do some other grave injury to itself. Or let us say that the robot's owner himself, in a moment of pique or boredom or frustration, gives such an order.

"Is this just? Would we treat an animal like that? And an animal, mind you, might at least have the capacity to defend itself. But we have made our robots inherently unable to lift a hand against a human being.

"Even an inanimate object which has given us good service has a claim on our consideration. And a robot is far from insensible; it is not a simple machine and it is not an animal. It can think well enough to enable it to speak with us, reason with us, joke with us. Many of us who have lived and worked with robots all our lives have come to regard them as friends—virtually as members of our families, I dare say. We have deep respect for them, even affection. Is it asking too much to want to give our robot friends the formal protection of law?

"If a man has the right to give a robot any order that does not involve doing harm to a human being, he should have the decency never to give a robot any order that involves doing harm to a robot—unless human safety absolutely requires such action. Certainly a robot should not lightly be asked to do purposeless harm to itself. With great power goes great responsibility. If the robots have the Three Laws to protect humans, is it too much to ask that humans subject themselves to a law or two for the sake of protecting robots?"

There was, of course, another side to the issue—and the spokesman for that side was none other than James Van Buren, the lawyer who had opposed Andrew's original petition for free-robot status in the Regional Court. He was old, now, but still vigorous, a powerful advocate of traditional social beliefs. In his calm, balanced, reasonable way, Van Buren was once again a forceful speaker on behalf of those who denied that robots could in any way be considered worthy of having "rights."

He said, "Of course I hold no brief for vandals who would wantonly destroy a robot that does not belong to them, or order it to destroy itself. That is a civil offense, pure and simple, which can readily be punished through the usual legal channels. We no more need a special law to cover such cases than we need a specific law that says it is wrong for people to smash the windows of other people's houses. The general law of the sanctity of property provides sufficient protection.

"But a law preventing one from destroying one's *own* robot? Ah, now we venture into very different areas of thinking. I have robots in my own law office, and it would no more occur to me to destroy one than it would for me to take an axe to a desk. Still, is there anyone who would argue that I should be stripped of the *right* to do as I please with my own robots, or my own desks, or any other article of office furniture that I may own? Can the State, in its infinite wisdom, come into my office and say, 'No, James Van Buren, you must be kind to your desks, and spare them from injury. Likewise your filing cabinets: they must be treated with respect, they must be treated as friends. And the same applies, naturally, to your robots. In no way, James Van Buren, may you place the robots you own in jeopardy.' "

Van Buren would pause, then, and smile in his calm and reasonable way, letting everyone know that this was strictly a hypothetical example, that in fact he was not the sort of man who would do injury to anyone or anything.

And then he would say, "I can hear George Charney replying that a robot is fundamentally different from a desk or a filing cabinet, that a robot is intelligent and responsive, that robots should be regarded virtually as human. And I would reply to him that he is mistaken, that he is so bemused by affection for the robot that his own family has kept for many decades that he has lost sight of what robots really are.

"They are *machines,* my friends. They are *tools.* They are *appliances.* What they are is mere mechanical contrivances, neither more nor less deserving of legal protection than any other inanimate object. Yes, I said *inanimate.* They can speak, yes. They can think, in their own rigid pre-programmed way. But when you prick a robot, does it bleed? If you tickle one, will it laugh? Robots have hands and senses, yes, because we have constructed them that way, but do they have true human affections and passions? Hardly. Hardly! And therefore let us not confuse machines made in the image of mankind with living things.

"And I must point out, too, that humanity in this century has become dependent on robot labor. There are more robots in the world than there are people, now, and in the main they do the jobs that none of us would be willing to touch. They have freed humanity from dreary drudgery and degradation. To confuse the robot issue with the ancient debates over slavery and the later debates over freedom for those slaves and the still later debates over full civil rights for the descendants of the freed slaves will ultimately lead to economic chaos, when our robots begin to demand not simply the protection of the law but independence from their masters. Those slaves of centuries gone by were human beings who were cruelly taken advantage of and mistreated. No one had any right to force them into servitude. But robots were brought into the world to serve. By definition they are here to be used: not to be our friends but to be our servants. And to take any other position is a wrongheaded, sentimental, dangerous way of thinking."

George Charney was a persuasive orator, but so was James Van Buren. And in the end the battle—fought mainly in the court of public opinion, rather than in the Legislature or the Regional Court—ended in something of a stalemate.

There were a great many people now who had been able to transcend the fear or dislike of robots that had been so widespread a couple of generations earlier, and George's arguments struck home with them. They too had begun to look upon their robots with a certain degree of affection, and wanted them afforded some kind of legal security.

But then there were the others, who may not have feared robots themselves so much as they did the financial risks that they might somehow experience as a result of extending civil rights to robots. They urged caution in this new legal arena.

So when the battle at last was over and pro-robot legislation came forth, setting up conditions under which it was illegal to issue an order that might harm a robot, the law that was passed by the Regional Legislature, sent back for revisions by the Regional Court, passed again in a modified way, this time upheld in the Regional Court, and eventually ratified by the World Legislature and upheld after a final appeal to the World Court, was a very tepid one indeed. It was endlessly qualified and the punishments for violating its provisions were totally inadequate.

But at least the principle of robot rights—established originally by the decree awarding Andrew his "freedom"—had been extended a little further.

The final approval by the World Court came through on the day of Little Miss's death.

That was no coincidence. Little Miss, very old and very weak now, had nevertheless held on to life with desperate force during the closing weeks of the debate. Only when word of victory arrived did she at last relax the tenacity of her grip.

Andrew was at her bedside when she went. He stood beside her, looking down at the small, faded woman propped up among the pillows and thinking back to those days of nearly a hundred years before when he was newly arrived at the grand coastside mansion of Gerald Martin and two small girls had stood looking up at him, and the smaller one had frowned and said, "En—dee —arr. That isn't any good. We can't call him something like that. What about calling him Andrew?"

So long ago, so very long ago. A whole lifetime ago, so far as things went for Little Miss. And yet to Andrew it sometimes seemed only a moment—hardly any time at all since those days when he and Miss and Little Miss had romped on the beach below the house, and he had gone for a swim in the surf because it had pleased them to ask him to do so.

Nearly a century.

For a human being, Andrew knew, that was an enormous span of time.

And now Little Miss's life had run its course and was speeding away. The hair that once had been a radiant gold had long since turned to shining silver; but now the last of its gleam was gone from it and for the first time it looked dull and drab. She was coming to her termination, and there was no help for that. She was not ill; she was simply worn out, beyond any hope of repair. In another few moments she would cease to function. Andrew could hardly imagine a world that did not contain Little Miss. But he knew that he was entering such a world now.

Her last smile was for him. Her last words were, "You have been good to us, Andrew."

She died with her hand holding his, while her son and his wife and their children remained at a respectful distance from the robot and the old woman in the bed.

THIRTEEN

ANDREW EXPERIENCED a sensation of discomfort after Little Miss's death that would not leave him for weeks. To call it grief might be a little too strong, he thought, for he suspected that there was no place in his positronic pathways for any feeling that corresponded exactly to the human emotion known as grief.

And yet there was no question but that he was disturbed in some way that could only be traced to the loss of Little Miss. He could not have quantified it. A certain heaviness about his thoughts, a certain odd sluggishness about his movements, a perception of general imbalance in his rhythms—he felt these things, but he suspected that no instruments would be able to detect any measurable change in his capacities.

To ease this sensation of what he would not let himself call grief he plunged deep into his research on robot history, and his manuscript began to grow from day to day.

A brief prologue sufficed to deal with the concept of the robot in history and literature—the metal men of the ancient Greek myths, the automata imagined by clever storytellers like E. T. A. Hoffmann and Karel Čapek, and other such fantasies. He summarized the old fables quickly and dispensed with them. It was the *positronic* robot—the real robot, the authentic item—that Andrew was primarily concerned with.

And so Andrew moved swiftly to the year 1982 and the incorporation of United States Robots and Mechanical Men by its visionary founder, Lawrence Robertson. He felt almost as though he were reliving the story himself, as he told of the early years of struggle in drafty converted-warehouse rooms and the first dramatic breakthrough in the construction of the platinum-iridium positronic brain, after endless trial-and-error. The conception and development of the indispensable Three Laws; research director Alfred Lanning's early triumphs at designing mobile robot units, clumsy and ponderous and incapable of speech, but versatile enough to be able to interpret human orders and select the best of a number of possible alternative responses. Followed by the first mobile speaking units at the turn of the Twenty-First Century.

And then Andrew turned to something much more troublesome for him to describe: the period of negative human reaction which followed, the hysteria and downright terror that the new robots engendered, the worldwide outburst of legislation prohibiting the use of robot labor on Earth. Because miniaturization of the positronic brain was still in the development stage then and the need for elaborate cooling systems was great, the early mobile speaking units had been gigantic—nearly twelve feet high, frightful lumbering monsters that had summoned up all of humanity's fears of artificial beings—of Frankenstein's monster and the Golem and all the rest of that assortment of nightmares.

Andrew's book devoted three entire chapters to that time of extreme robot-fear. They were enormously difficult chapters to write, for they dealt entirely with human irrationality, and that was a subject almost impossible for Andrew to comprehend.

He grappled with it as well as he could, striving to put himself in the place of human beings who—though they knew that the Three Laws provided foolproof safeguards against the possibility that robots could do harm to humans—persisted in looking upon robots with dread and loathing. And after a time Andrew actually succeeded in understanding, as far as he was able, how it had been possible for humans to have felt insecure in the face of such a powerful guarantee of security.

For what he discovered, as he made his way through the archives of robotics, was that the Three Laws were not as foolproof a safeguard as they seemed. They were, in fact, full of ambiguities and hidden sources of conflict. And they could unexpectedly confront robots—straightforward literal-minded creatures that they were—with the need to make decisions that were not necessarily ideal from the human point of view.

The robot who was sent on a dangerous errand on an alien planet, for example—to find and bring back some substance vital to the safety and well-being of a human explorer—might feel such a conflict between the Second Law of obedience and the Third Law of self-preservation that he would fall into a hopeless equilibrium, unable either to go forward or to retreat. And by such a stalemate the robot—through inaction—thus could create dire jeopardy for the human who had sent him on his mission, despite the imperatives of the First Law that supposedly took precedence over the other two. For how could a robot invariably know that the conflict he was experiencing between the Second and Third Laws was placing a human in danger? Unless the nature of his mission had been spelled out precisely in advance, he might remain unaware of the consequences of his inaction and never realize that his dithering was creating a First Law violation.

Or the robot who might, through faulty design or poor programming, decide that a certain human being was not human at all, and therefore not in a position to demand the protection that the First and Second Laws were supposed to afford—

Or the robot who was given a poorly phrased order, and interpreted it so literally that he inadvertently caused danger to humans nearby—

There were dozens of such case histories in the archives. The early roboticists—most notably the extraordinary robopsychologist, Susan Calvin, that formidable and austere woman—had labored long and mightily to cope with the difficulties that kept cropping up.

The problems had become especially intricate as robots with more advanced types of positronic pathways began to emerge from the workshops of U. S. Robots and Mechanical Men toward the middle of the Twenty-First Century: robots with a broader capacity for thought, robots who were able to look at situations and perceive their complexities with an almost human depth of understanding. Robots like—though he took care not to say so explicitly—Andrew Martin himself. The new generalized-pathway robots, equipped with the ability to interpret data in much more subjective terms than their predecessors, often reacted in ways that humans were not expecting. Always within the framework of the Three Laws, of course. But sometimes from a perspective that had not been anticipated by the framers of those laws.

As he studied the annals of robot development, Andrew at last understood why so many humans had been so phobic about robots. It wasn't that the Three Laws were badly drawn—not at all. Indeed, they were masterly exemplars of logic. The trouble was that humans themselves were not always logical—were, on occasion, downright illogical—and robots were not always capable of coping with the swoops and curves and tangents of human thought.

So it was humans themselves who sometimes led robots into violations of one or another of the Three Laws—and then, in their illogical way, often would blame the robots themselves for having done something undesirable which in fact they had actually been ordered to do by their human masters.

Andrew handled these chapters with the utmost care and delicacy, revising and revising them to eliminate any possibility of bias. It was not his intention to write a diatribe against the flaws of mankind. His prime goal, as always, was to serve the needs of mankind.

The original purpose of writing his book might have been to arrive at a deeper understanding of his own relationship to the human beings who were his creators—but as he proceeded with it he saw that, if properly and thoughtfully done, the book could be an invaluable bridge between humans and robots, a source of enlightenment not only for robots but for the flesh-and-blood species that had brought them into the world. Anything that enabled humans and robots to get along better would permit robots to be of greater service to humanity; and that, of course, was the reason for their existence.

When he had finished half his book, Andrew asked George Charney to read what he had written and offer suggestions for its improvement. Several years had passed since the death of Little Miss, and George himself seemed unwell now, his once robust frame gaunt, his hair nearly gone. He looked at Andrew's bulky manuscript with an expression of barely masked discomfort and said, "I'm not really much of a writer myself, you know, Andrew."

"I'm not asking for your opinion of my literary style, George. It's my ideas that I want you to evaluate. I need to know whether there's anything in the manuscript that might be offensive to human beings."

"I'm sure there isn't, Andrew. You have always been the soul of courtesy."

"I would never knowingly give offense, that is true. But the possibility that I would inadvertently—"

George sighed. "Yes. Yes, I understand. All right, I'll read your book, Andrew. But you know that I've been getting tired very easily these days. It may take me a while to plow all the way through it."

"There is no hurry," said Andrew.

Indeed George took his time: close to a year. When he finally returned the manuscript to Andrew, though, there was no more than half a page of notes attached to it, the most minor factual corrections and nothing more.

Andrew said mildly, "I had hoped for criticisms of a more general kind, George."

"I don't have any general criticisms to make. It's a remarkable work. Remarkable. It's a truly profound study of its subject. You should be proud of what you've done."

"But where I touch on the topic of how human irrationality has often led to Three Laws difficulties—"

"Absolutely on the mark, Andrew. We *are* a sloppy-minded species, aren't we? Brilliant and tremendously creative at times, but full of all sorts of messy little contradictions and confusions. We must seem like a hopelessly illogical bunch to you, don't we, Andrew?"

"There are times that it does seem that way to me, yes. But it is not my intention to write a book that is critical of human beings. Far from it, George. What I want to give the world is something that will bring humans and robots closer together. And if I should seem to be expressing scorn for the mental abilities of humans in any way, that would be the direct opposite of what I want to be doing. Which is why I had hoped that you would single out, in your reading of my manuscript, any passages that might be interpreted in such a way that—"

"Perhaps you should have asked my son Paul to read the manuscript instead of me," George said. "He's right at the top of his profession, you know. So much more in touch with all these matters of nuance and subtle inference than I am these days."

And Andrew finally understood from that statement that George Charney had not wanted to read his manuscript at all— that George was growing old and weary, that he was entering the final years of his life, that once again the wheel of the generations had turned and that Paul was now the head of the family. Sir had gone and so had Little Miss and soon it was going to be George's turn. Martins and Charneys came and went and yet Andrew remained—not exactly unchanging (for his body was still undergoing occasional technological updating and it also seemed to him that his mental processes were constantly deepening and growing richer as he allowed himself to recognize fully his own extraordinary capabilities), but certainly invulnerable to the ravages of the passing years.

He took his nearly finished manuscript to Paul Charney. Paul read it at once and offered not only praise but, as George had indicated, valuable suggestions for revision. There were places where Andrew's inability to comprehend the abrupt, non-linear jumps of reasoning of which the human mind is capable had led him into certain oversimplifications and unwarranted conclusions. If anything, Paul thought the book was *too* sympathetic to the human point of view. A little more criticism of the irrational human attitude toward robotics, and toward science in general, might not have been out of place.

Andrew had not expected that.

He said, "But I would not want to offend anyone, Paul."

"No book worth reading has ever been written that didn't manage to offend someone," Paul replied. "Write what you believe to be the truth, Andrew. It would be amazing if everybody in the world agreed with you. But your viewpoint is unique. You have something real and valuable to give the world here. It won't be worth a thing, though, if you suppress what you feel and write only what you think others want to hear."

"But the First Law—"

"Damn the First Law, Andrew! The First Law isn't everything! How can you harm someone with a book? Well, by hitting him over the head with it, I suppose. But not otherwise. Ideas can't do harm—even wrong ideas, even foolish and vicious ideas. *People* do the harm. They seize hold of certain ideas, sometimes, and use them as the justification for doing unconscionable, outrageous things. Human history is full of examples of that. But the ideas themselves are just ideas. They must never be throttled. They need to be brought forth, inspected, tested, if necessary rejected, right out in the open. —Anyway, the First Law doesn't say anything about robots writing books. Sticks and stones, Andrew—they can do harm. But words—"

"As you yourself have just remarked, Paul, human history is full of harmful events that began simply with words. If those words had never been uttered, the harmful events would not have taken place."

"You don't understand what I'm saying, do you? Or do you? I think you do. You know what power ideas have, and you don't have a lot of faith in the ability of humans to tell a good idea

139

from a bad one. Well, neither do I, sometimes. But in the long run the bad idea will perish. That's been the story of human civilization for thousands of years. The good *does* prevail, sooner or later, no matter what horrors have happened along the way. And so it's wrong to suppress an idea that may have value to the world. —Look, Andrew: you're probably the closest thing to a human being that has ever come out of the factories of U. S. Robots and Mechanical Men. You're uniquely equipped to tell the world what it needs to know about the human-robot relationship, because in some ways you partake of the nature of each. And so you may help to heal that relationship, which even at this late date is still a very troubled one. Write your book. Write it honestly."

"Yes. I will, Paul."

"Do you have a publisher in mind for it, by the way?"

"A publisher? Why, no. I haven't yet given any thought to—"

"Well, you should. Or let me do it for you. I have a friend in the book business—a client, really—do you mind if I say a word or two to him?"

"That would be quite kind of you," Andrew said.

"Not at all. I want to see this book out there where it can be read by everybody, just as you do."

And indeed within a few weeks Paul had secured a publishing contract for Andrew's book. He assured Andrew that the terms were extremely generous, extremely fair. That was good enough for Andrew. He signed the contract without hesitation.

Over the next year, while he worked on the closing sections of his manuscript, Andrew often thought of the things Paul had said to him that day—about the importance of stating his beliefs honestly, the value that his book could have if he did. And also about his own uniqueness. There was one statement of Paul's that Andrew could not get out of his mind.

Look, Andrew: you're probably the closest thing to a human being that has ever come out of the factories of U. S. Robots and Mechanical Men. You're uniquely equipped to tell the world what it needs to know about the human-robot relationship, because in some ways you partake of the nature of each.

Was it so? Is that what Paul really thought, Andrew wondered, or had it just been the heat of the moment that had led him to say those things?

Andrew asked himself that over and over again, and gradually he began to form an answer.

And then he decided that the time had come to pay another visit to the offices of Feingold and Charney and have another talk with Paul.

He arrived unannounced, but the receptionist greeted him without any inflection of surprise in its voice. Andrew was far from an unfamiliar figure by this time at the Feingold and Charney headquarters.

He waited patiently while the receptionist disappeared into the inner office to notify Paul that Andrew was here. It would surely have been more efficient if the receptionist had used the holographic chatterbox, but unquestionably it was unmanned (or perhaps the word was "unroboted") by having to deal with another robot rather than with a human being.

Eventually the receptionist returned. "Mr. Charney will be with you soon," the receptionist announced, and went back to its tasks without another word.

Andrew passed the time revolving in his mind the matter of his word choice of a few minutes before. Could "unroboted" be used as an analog of "unmanned"? he wondered. Or had "unmanned" become a purely metaphoric term sufficiently divorced from its original literal meaning to be applied to robots—or to women, for that matter?

Many similar semantic problems had cropped up frequently while Andrew was working on his book. Human language, having been invented by humans for the use of humans, was full of little tricky complexities of that sort. The effort that was required in order to cope with them had undoubtedly increased Andrew's own working vocabulary—and, he suspected, the adaptability of his positronic pathways as well.

Occasionally as Andrew sat in the waiting room someone would enter the room and stare at him. He was the free robot, after all—still the only one. The clothes-wearing robot. An anomaly; a freak. But Andrew never tried to avoid the glances of these curiosity-seekers. He met each one calmly, and each in turn looked quickly away.

Paul Charney finally came out. He and Andrew had not seen each other since the winter, at the funeral of Paul's father George, who had died peacefully at the family home and now lay buried on a hillside over the Pacific. Paul looked surprised to see Andrew now, or so Andrew thought—though Andrew still had no real faith in his ability to interpret human facial expressions accurately.

"Well, Andrew. So good to see you again. I'm sorry I made you wait, but there was something I *had* to finish."

"Quite all right. I am never in a hurry, Paul."

Paul had taken lately to wearing the heavy makeup that fashion was currently dictating for both sexes, and though it made the somewhat bland lines of his face sharper and firmer, Andrew disapproved. He felt that Paul's strong, incisive personality needed no such cosmetic enhancement. It would have been perfectly all right for Paul to allow himself to *look* bland; there was nothing bland about the man himself, and no need for all this paint and powder.

Andrew kept his disapproval to himself, of course. But the fact that he disapproved of Paul's appearance at all was something of a novelty for him. He had only just begun to have such thoughts. Since finishing the first draft of his book, Andrew had discovered that disapproving of the things human beings did, as long as he avoided expressing such opinions openly, did not make him as uneasy as he might have anticipated. He could think disapproving thoughts without difficulty and he was even able to put his disapproval in writing. He was certain that it had not always been like that for him.

Paul said, "Come inside, Andrew. I heard that you wanted to

talk to me, but I wasn't really expecting that you'd come all the way down here to do it."

"If you are too busy to see me just now, Paul, I am prepared to continue to wait."

Paul glanced at the interplay of shifting shadows on the dial on the wall that served as the reception-office's timepiece and said, "I can make some time. Did you come alone?"

"I hired an automatobile."

"Any trouble doing that?" Paul asked, with more than a trace of anxiety in his tone.

"I wasn't expecting any. My rights are protected."

Paul looked all the more anxious for that. "Andrew, I've explained to you half a dozen times that that law is essentially unenforceable, at least in most circumstances. —And if you insist on wearing clothes, you're bound to run into trouble eventually, you know. Just as you did that first time when my father had to rescue you."

"It was the only such time, Paul. But I'm sorry that you're displeased."

"Well, look at it this way: you're virtually a living legend, do you realize that? People sometimes like to win a little ugly fame for themselves by making trouble for celebrities, and a celebrity is certainly what you are. Besides, as I've already told you, you're too valuable in too many ways for you to have any right to take chances with yourself. —How's the book coming along, by the way?"

"I've finished a complete draft. Now I'm doing the final editing and polishing. At least, I hope it will be the final editing and polishing. The publisher is quite pleased with what he's seen so far."

"Good!"

"I don't know that he's necessarily pleased with the book as a book. There are parts of it that make him uncomfortable, I think. But it's my guess that he expects to sell a great many copies simply because it's the first book written by a robot, and it's that aspect that pleases him."

143

"It's only human, I'm afraid, to be interested in making money, Andrew."

"I would not be displeased by it either. Let the book sell, for whatever reason it does. I can find good uses for whatever money it brings in."

"But I thought you were well off, Andrew! You've always had your own income—and there was the quite considerable amount of money my grandmother left you—"

"Little Miss was extremely generous. And I'm sure I can count on the family to help me out further, if a time comes when my expenses begin to exceed my income. Still, I would rather be able to earn my own way at all times. I would not want to draw on your resources except as a last resort."

"Expenses? What expenses can you be talking about? Yachts? Trips to Mars?"

"Nothing like that," said Andrew. "But I do have something rather costly in mind, Paul. It's my hope that the royalties from my book will be large enough to see me through what I have in mind. My next step, so to speak."

Paul looked a little uneasy. "And what is that?"

"Another upgrade."

"You've always been able to pay for your upgrades out of your own funds up till now."

"This one may be more expensive than the others."

Paul nodded. "Then the book royalties will come in handy. And if they're disappointing, I'm sure that we can find some way of making up—"

"It isn't only a matter of money," Andrew said. "There are some other complications. —Paul, for this one I have to go straight to the top. I need to see the head of the U. S. Robots and Mechanical Men Corporation and get his clearance for the job. I've tried to make an appointment, but so far I haven't been able to get through to him at all. No doubt it's because of my book. The corporation wasn't particularly enthusiastic about my writing a book, you know—they provided no cooperation whatever, as a matter of fact—"

A grin appeared on Paul's face. "Cooperation, Andrew? Cooperation's the last thing you could have expected from them. You scare them silly. They didn't cooperate with us in either stage of our great fight for robot rights, did they? Quite the reverse, actually. And you surely understand why. Give a robot too many rights and no one's going to want to buy one, eh?"

"That may be true, or perhaps not. In any case, I want to speak with the head of the company concerning a very special request that I have. I can't manage to get through by myself, but perhaps if you make the call for me—"

"You know that I'm not any more popular with them than you are, Andrew."

"Nevertheless, you're the head of a powerful and influential law firm and a member of a great and distinguished family. They can't simply ignore you. And if they try, you can always hint that by seeing me they stand a chance of heading off a new campaign by Feingold and Charney to strengthen the civil rights of robots even further."

"Wouldn't that be a lie, Andrew?"

"Yes, Paul, and I'm not good at telling lies. I can't tell one at all, in fact, unless I do it under the constraint of one of the Three Laws. That's why you have to make the call for me."

Paul chuckled. "Ah, Andrew, Andrew! You can't tell a lie, but you can urge me to tell one for you, is that it? You're getting more human all the time!"

FOURTEEN

THE APPOINTMENT wasn't easy to arrange, even using Paul's supposedly powerful name.

But repeated pressure—coupled with the none too delicate hint that permitting Andrew to have a few minutes of Harley Smythe-Robertson's precious time might well save U. S. Robots and Mechanical Men from having to go through a troublesome new round of litigation over robot rights—finally carried the day. On a balmy spring day Andrew and Paul set out together across the country for the vast and sprawling complex of buildings that was the headquarters of the gigantic robotics company.

Harley Smythe-Robertson—who was descended from both branches of the family that had founded U. S. Robots, and had adopted the hyphenated name by way of declaring that fact—looked remarkably unhappy at the sight of Andrew. He was approaching retirement age and an extraordinary amount of his tenure as president of the company had been devoted to the controversies over robot rights. Smythe-Robertson was a tall, almost skeletally lean man whose gray hair was plastered thinly over the top of his scalp. He wore no facial makeup. From time to time during the meeting he eyed Andrew with brief but undisguised hostility.

"And what new trouble have you come here to cause us, may I ask?" Smythe-Robertson said.

"Please understand, sir, it has never been my intention to cause this company trouble. Never."

"But you have. Constantly."

"I have only attempted to gain that to which I have felt entitled."

Smythe-Robertson reacted to the word "entitled" as he might have to a slap in the face.

"How extraordinary to hear a robot speak of feelings of entitlement."

"This robot is a very extraordinary robot, Mr. Smythe-Robertson," said Paul.

"Extraordinary," Smythe-Robertson said sourly. "Yes. Quite extraordinary."

Andrew said, "Sir, slightly more than a century ago I was told by Merwin Mansky, who was the Chief Robopsychologist of this company then, that the mathematics governing the plotting of the positronic pathways was far too complicated to permit of any but approximate solutions, and that therefore the limits of my own capacities were not fully predictable."

"As you say, that was over a century ago," Smythe-Robertson replied. And after a moment's hesitation added icily, "*Sir.* The situation is quite different nowadays. Our robots are made with great precision now and are trained precisely to their tasks. We have eliminated every aspect of unpredictability from their natures."

"Yes," said Paul. "So I've noticed. And one result is that my receptionist has to be guided at every point that departs from the expected path, however slightly. I don't see that as much of a step forward in the state of the art."

Smythe-Robertson said, "I think you'd like it a great deal less if your receptionist were to improvise."

"Improvise?" Paul said. "*Think* is all I ask. Enough thinking to be able to handle the simple situations a receptionist needs to deal with. Robots are designed to be intelligent, aren't they? It

147

seems to me you've backtracked toward a very limited definition of intelligence indeed.''

Smythe-Robertson fidgeted and glowered, but made no direct response.

Andrew said, ''Are you saying, sir, that you no longer manufacture any robots that are as flexible and adaptable as—let us say—myself?''

''That's right. We discontinued the generalized-pathways line so long ago that I couldn't tell you how far back it was. Perhaps it was in Dr. Mansky's time. Which was long before I was born, and as you see, I am far from young.''

''As am I,'' said Andrew. ''The research I have done in connection with my book—I think you know that I have written a book about robotics and robots—indicates that I am the oldest robot presently in active operation.''

''Correct,'' said Smythe-Robertson. ''And the oldest ever. The oldest that will ever be, in fact. No robot is useful after its twenty-fifth year. Their owners are entitled to bring them in at that time and have them replaced with new models. In the case of leased robots, we call them in automatically and provide the replacements.''

''No robot *in any of your presently manufactured series* is useful after the twenty-fifth year,'' said Paul pleasantly. ''But Andrew is a robot of a quite different sort.''

''Indeed he is,'' said Smythe-Robertson. ''I'm only too aware of that.''

Andrew, adhering steadfastly to the path he had marked out for himself, said, ''Since I am the oldest robot in the world and the most flexible one in existence, would you not say that I am so unusual that I merit special treatment from the company?''

''Not at all,'' said Smythe-Robertson icily. ''Let me be blunt with you—*sir.* Your unusualness is a continuing embarrassment to the company. You have caused us all manner of difficulties, as I've already pointed out, as a result of the various activist positions you have taken over the years. Your feelings of—ah—*entitlement* are not shared here. If you were on lease as most of our robots are, instead of having been acquired by outright purchase through some regrettable bit of ancient administrative careless-ness, we'd have called you in long ago and replaced you with a robot of a more docile type."

"At least you're straightforward about it," Paul said.

"There's no secret about the way we feel over this. We're in business to sell robots, not to engage in endless unprofitable political squabblings. A robot that believes it's something more than a useful mechanical device is a direct threat to our corpo-rate welfare."

"And therefore you would destroy me if you could," said An-drew. "I quite understand that. But I am a free robot and I own myself, so I can't be called in and it would be pointless to make an attempt to repurchase me. And I am protected by the law against any harm you might want to do to me. Which is why I have been willing to put myself in your hands for periodic up-grading. And why I have come to you today to request the most extensive upgrading you have ever done on any robot. What I want is a total replacement for myself, Mr. Smythe-Robertson."

Smythe-Robertson looked both astounded and bewildered. He stared at Andrew in total silence, and the silence went on for a seemingly interminable time.

Andrew waited. He looked past Smythe-Robertson toward the wall, where a holographic portrait looked back at him. It showed a dour, austere female face: the face of Susan Calvin, the patron saint of all roboticists. She had been dead nearly two centuries now, but after having delved into her working papers as deeply as he had during the course of writing his book, Andrew felt he knew her so well that he could half persuade himself that he had met her in life.

Smythe-Robertson said finally, "A total replacement, you say? But what does that *mean*?"

"Exactly what I said. When you call in an obsolete robot, you provide its owner with a replacement. Well, I want you to provide me with a replacement for me."

Still looking confused, Smythe-Robertson said, "But how can

we do that? If we replace you, how can we turn the new robot over to you as owner, since in the very act of being replaced you would have to cease to exist?" And he smiled grimly.

"Perhaps Andrew hasn't made himself sufficiently clear," interposed Paul. "May I try? —The seat of Andrew's personality is his positronic brain, which is the one part that cannot be replaced without creating a new robot. The positronic brain, therefore, is the locus of Andrew Martin, who is the owner of the robot in which Andrew Martin's positronic brain is currently housed. Every other part of the robotic body can be replaced without affecting the Andrew Martin personality—most of those parts, as you may know, have *already* been replaced, sometimes more than once, in the hundred-odd years since Andrew was first manufactured. Those subsidiary parts are the brain's possessions. The brain, at its option, can have them replaced at any time, but the continuity of the brain's existence is unbroken. What Andrew actually wants, Mr. Smythe-Robertson, is simply for you to transfer his brain to a new robotic body."

"I see," Smythe-Robertson said. "A total upgrade, in other words." But his face showed perplexity again. "To what kind of body, may I ask? You already are housed in the most advanced mechanical body that we manufacture."

"But you have manufactured androids, haven't you?" said Andrew. "Robots that have the outward appearance of humans, complete to the texture of the skin? That is what I want, Mr. Smythe-Robertson. An android body."

Paul seemed astounded by that. "Good Lord," he blurted. "Andrew, I never dreamed that that was what you—" His voice trailed off.

Smythe-Robertson stiffened. "It's an absolutely impossible request. Impossible."

"Why do you say that?" Andrew asked. "I'm willing to pay any reasonable fee, as I have for all the numerous upgrades you've given me up to now."

"We don't manufacture androids," Smythe-Robertson said flatly.

"You have, though. I know that you have."

"Formerly, yes. The line was discontinued."

"Because of technical problems?" Paul asked.

"Not at all. The experimental android line was quite successful, actually—technically speaking. Their appearance was strikingly human in form, and yet they had all the versatility and ruggedness of robots. We used synthetic carbon-fiber skins and silicone tendons. There was virtually no structural metal involved anywhere—the brain, of course, was still platinum-iridium—and yet they were nearly as tough as conventional metal robots. They were tougher, in fact, weight for weight."

"Despite all of which, you never put them on the market?" Paul asked.

"Correct. We worked up about a dozen experimental models and ran some marketing surveys and decided not to go ahead with the line."

"Why was that?"

"For one thing," said Smythe-Robertson, "a line of androids would have had to be far more expensive than the standard metal robots—so expensive that we would have had to regard them purely as luxury items, with a potential market so limited in size that it would take many years for us to be able to amortize the expense of setting up a production facility. But that was only a small part of the difficulty. The real problem was negative consumer reaction. The androids looked too human, you see. They reawakened all the ancient fears of making real humans obsolete that had caused us so much trouble two hundred years ago. It made no sense for us to open all that psychotic nonsense up again simply for the sake of setting up a line that was doomed from the outset to be unprofitable anyway."

"But the corporation has maintained its expertise in the area of making androids, has it not?" Andrew asked.

Smythe-Robertson shrugged. "I suppose we still could make them if we saw any sense to it, yes."

"You choose not to, though," said Paul. "You've got the technology but you simply decline to exercise it. That's not quite the same thing as what you told us before, that it would be *impossible* to manufacture an android body for Andrew."

"It would be possible, yes—technically. But completely against public policy."

"Why? There isn't any law that I know of against making androids."

"Nevertheless," Smythe-Robertson said, "we don't manufacture them and we don't intend to. Therefore we are unable to provide the android body that Andrew Martin has requested. And I suggest to you that this conversation has reached a point of no return. If you'll excuse me, therefore—" And he half rose from his seat.

"Just a little time longer, if you please," said Paul in an easy tone that had something more forceful just beneath its surface. He cleared his throat. Smythe-Robertson subsided, looking even more displeased than he had. Paul went on, "Mr. Smythe-Robertson, Andrew is a free robot who falls under the protection of the laws that govern robot rights. You are aware of this, of course."

"Only too well."

"This robot, as a free robot, freely chooses to wear clothes. This has resulted in his being frequently humiliated by thoughtless human beings, despite the law that supposedly protects robots against such humiliation. It's quite difficult, you realize, to prosecute vague offenses that don't meet with the general disapproval of those whose responsibility it is to decide between guilt and innocence."

"I'm not at all surprised to hear that," said Smythe-Robertson restlessly. "U. S. Robots understood that from the start. Your father's law firm unfortunately did not."

"My father is dead now," said Paul. "But what I see is that we have here a clear offense with a clear target, and we stand ready to take the appropriate action."

"What are you talking about?"

"My client, Andrew Martin—he has been the client of my firm for many years—is a free robot, by decree of the World Court. That is to say, Andrew is his own owner, and in him, therefore, are vested the legal rights that any human robot owner has in regard to robots in his possession. One of those rights is that of replacement. As you yourself pointed out some time ago during this discussion, the owner of any robot is entitled to ask U. S. Robots and Mechanical Men Corporation for a replacement when his robot reaches the point of obsolescence. In fact, the corporation *insists* on offering such replacements, and where leased robots are involved will call them in automatically. I've stated your policy correctly, is that not so?"

"Well—yes."

"Good." Paul was smiling and thoroughly at his ease. He continued, "Now, the positronic brain of my client is the owner of the body of my client—and that body, obviously, is far more than twenty-five years old. By your own definition that body is obsolete and my client is entitled to a replacement."

"Well—" Smythe-Robertson said again, reddening. His gaunt, almost fleshless face looked like a mask, now.

"The positronic brain which is my actual client demands the replacement of the robot body in which it is housed, and has offered to pay any reasonable fee for that replacement."

"Then let him sign up in the ordinary way and we'll give him his updating!"

"He wants more than an updating. He wants the finest replacement body within your technical capacity, by which he means an android body."

"He can't have one."

"By refusing," Paul said smoothly, "you condemn him to continued humiliation at the hands of those who, recognizing him as a robot, treat him with contempt because he prefers to wear clothes and otherwise behave in traditionally 'human' fashion."

"That's not our problem," said Smythe-Robertson.

"It becomes your problem when we sue you for refusing to provide my client with a body that would allow him to avoid much of the humiliation he now encounters."

"Go ahead and sue, then. Do you think anybody's going to give a damn about a robot who wants to look human? People will be outraged. He'll be denounced everywhere for the arrogant upstart that he is."

"I'm not so sure," Paul said. "Agreed, public opinion wouldn't ordinarily support the claim of a robot in a lawsuit of that kind. But may I remind you that U. S. Robots is not very popular with the general public, Mr. Smythe-Robertson? Even those who most use robots to their own benefit and profit are suspicious of you. This may be a hangover from the days of anti-robot paranoia: I suspect that's a good part of it. Or it may be resentment against the immense power and wealth of your company, which has so successfully managed to defend its worldwide monopoly on robot manufacture through a long and clever series of patent maneuvers. Whatever the cause may be, the resentment may exist. If there's any entity that would be even less popular in such a lawsuit than the robot who wants to look like a human being, it would be the corporation that has filled the world with robots in the first place."

Smythe-Robertson glared. The clenched muscles of his face stood out clearly. He said nothing.

Paul went on, "In addition, think about what people would say when they find out you're capable of manufacturing human-looking robots? The lawsuit would very definitely focus a great deal of attention on that very point. Whereas if you quietly and simply provided my client with what he requests—"

Smythe-Robertson seemed about to explode. "This is coercion, Mr. Charney."

"On the contrary. We're simply trying to show you where your own best interests lie. A quick and peaceful resolution is all that we're looking for. Of course, if you compel us to seek legal redress in the courts, that's a different matter. And then, I think, you will find yourself in an awkward and disagreeable position, particularly since my client is quite wealthy and will live for many centuries to come and will have no reason to refrain from fighting this battle forever."

"We're not without resources ourselves, Mr. Charney."

"I'm aware of that. But can you withstand an endless legal

siege that will expose the deepest secrets of your company? —I put it to you one last time, Mr. Smythe-Robertson. If you prefer to reject my client's quite reasonable request, you may by all means do so and we'll leave here without another word being spoken. But we will sue, as is certainly our right, and we will sue most strenuously and publicly, which is bound to create immense difficulties for U. S. Robots, and you will find that you will eventually lose. Are you willing to take that risk?''

"Well—" Smythe-Robertson said, and paused.

"Good. I see that you're going to accede," said Paul. "You may still be hesitating now, but you're going to come around in the end. A very wise decision, may I add. But that leads to a further important point."

Smythe-Robertson's fury seemed to be fading into sullen glumness. He did not try to speak.

Paul continued, "Let me assure you that if, in the process of transferring my client's positronic brain from his present body to the organic one that you ultimately will agree to create for him, there is any damage, however slight, then I will never rest until I have nailed this corporation to the ground."

"You can't expect us to guarantee—"

"I can and I will. You've had a hundred-odd years of experience in transferring positronic brains from one robot body to another. You can surely use the same techniques in transferring one safely to an android body. And I warn you of this: if one brain-path of my client's platinum-iridium essence happens to get scrambled in the course of the work, you can be quite certain that I'll take every possible step to mobilize public opinion against this corporation—that I will expose it before all the world for the criminally vindictive operation that it has plainly revealed itself to be."

Smythe-Robertson said, shifting about miserably in his seat, "There's no way we can provide you with a total waiver of liability. There are risks in any sort of transfer."

"Low-probability ones. You don't lose a lot of positronic brains while you move them from one body to another. We're willing to accept risks of that sort. It's the possibility of deliberate and malevolent action against my client that I'm warning you against."

"We wouldn't be so stupid," said Smythe-Robertson. "Assuming we go through with this, and I haven't yet said we would, we'd exert our utmost skills. That's the way we've always worked and the way we intend to continue. You've backed me into a corner, Charney, but you've still got to realize that we can't give you a 100% assurance of success. 99%, yes. Not 100."

"Good enough. But remember: we'll throw everything we have at you if we have reason to suspect any sort of intentional harm to our client." Paul turned to Andrew and said, "What do you say, Andrew? Is this acceptable to you?"

Andrew hesitated for nearly a full minute, caught in an equilibrium of First Law potentials. What Paul wanted from him amounted to the approval of lying, of blackmail, of the badgering and humiliation of a human being.

But at least no physical harm was involved, he told himself. No physical harm.

And he managed at last to come out with a barely audible "Yes."

FIFTEEN

IT WAS LIKE being constructed all over again. For days, for weeks, for months, Andrew found himself not himself somehow, and the simplest actions kept giving rise to hesitation.

He had always been utterly at home in his body. He had only to recognize the need for a motion and he was instantly able to make that motion, smoothly, automatically. Now it took a conscious effort of self-direction. *Raise your arm,* he had to tell himself. *Move it over here. Now put it down.*

Was this what it was like for a young human child as it strived to master the mysteries of bodily coordination? Andrew wondered.

Perhaps so. He was over a hundred years old and yet he felt very much like a child as he moved about in this startling new body of his.

It was a splendid body. They had made him tall, but not so tall that he would seem overbearing or frightening. His shoulders were broad, his waist was slim, his limbs were supple and athletic. He had chosen light-brown hair for himself, since he found red too flamboyant and yellow too obvious and black too somber, and human hair did not seem to come in other colors than those, except for the gray or white or silver of age, and he had not wanted that. His eyes—photo-optic cells, really, but very convincing in appearance—were brown also, flecked ever so subtly with gold. For his skin color Andrew had selected something neutral in tone, a kind of blend of the prevailing skin colors of the various human types, darker than the pale pink of the Charneys but not quite as dark as some. That way no one would be able to tell at a glance which race he belonged to, since in fact he belonged to none. He had had the U. S. Robots designers peg his apparent age at somewhere between thirty-five and fifty human years: old enough to seem mature, not so old as to show serious signs of aging.

A fine body, yes. He was certain he would be very happy in it, once he grew accustomed to it.

Each day there was a little progress. Each day he gained more control over his elegant new android housing. But the process was terribly slow—agonizingly slow—

Paul was frantic. "They've damaged you, Andrew. I'm going to have to file suit."

Andrew said, "You mustn't, Paul. You'll never be able to prove —something—m-m-m-m—"

"Malicious?"

"Malicious, yes. Besides, I grow stronger, better. It's just the tr-tr—"

"Tremble?"

"Trauma. After all, there's never been such an op-op-op—before."

Andrew spoke very slowly. Speech was surprisingly hard now for him too, one of the hardest functions of all, a constant struggle to enunciate. It was an agony for Andrew to get the words out and an agony for anyone who had to listen to him. His entire vocal mechanism was different from what it had been previously. The efficient electronic synthesizer that had been able to make such convincingly human sounds had given way to an arrangement of resonating chambers and muscle-like structures to control them that was supposed to make his voice utterly indistinguishable from that of an organic human being; but now Andrew had to shape each syllable in a way that had been done for him before, and that was difficult work, very difficult.

Yet he felt no despair. Despair was not really a quality that he was capable of, and in any case he knew that these problems were merely temporary. He could feel his brain from the inside. No one else could; and no one else could know as well as he did that his brain was still intact, that it had come through the transfer operation unharmed. His thoughts flowed freely through the neural connections of his new body, even if the body was not yet as swift as it might be in reacting to them. Every parameter checked out perfectly.

He was merely having a few interface problems, that was all. But Andrew knew he was fundamentally well and that it would be only a matter of time until he had achieved complete control over his new housing. He had to think of himself as very young, still. Like a child, a newborn child.

The months passed. His coordination improved steadily. He moved swiftly toward full positronic interplay.

Yet not everything was as he would have wished it. Andrew spent hours before the mirror, evaluating himself as he went through his repertoire of facial expressions and bodily motions. And what he saw fell far short of the expectations he had had for his new body.

Not quite human! The face was stiff—too stiff—and he doubted that that was going to improve with time. He would press his finger against his cheek and the flesh would yield, but not in the way that true human flesh would yield. He could smile or scowl or frown, but they were studied, imitative smiles and scowls and frowns. He would give the smile-signal or the frown-signal or whatever, and the muscles of his face would obediently hoist the smile-expression or the frown-expression into view, pulling his features around in accordance with a carefully designed program. He was always conscious of the machinery, organic though it might be, clanking ponderously around beneath his skin to produce the desired effect. That was not how it happened with human beings, Andrew suspected.

And his motions were too deliberate. They lacked the careless free flow of the human being. He could hope that that would come after a while—he was already far beyond the first dismal days after the operation, when he had staggered awkwardly about his room like some sort of crude pre-positronic automaton—but something told him that even with this extraordinary new body he was never going to be able to move in the natural way that virtually every human being took for granted.

Still, things were not all that bad. The U. S. Robots people had kept their part of the bargain honorably and had carried out the transfer with all the formidable technical skill at their disposal. And Andrew had what he wanted. He might not fool the truly observant onlooker into thinking he was human, but he was far more human-looking than any robot ever had been, and at least he could wear clothes now without the ridiculous anomaly of an expressionless metal face rising up above them.

Eventually Andrew declared, "I will be getting back to work now."

Paul Charney laughed and said, "Then you must be well. What will you be doing? Another book?"

"No," said Andrew seriously. "I live too long for any one career to seize me by the throat and never let me go. There was a time when I was primarily an artist, and I still dabble in that now and then. And there was a time when I was a historian and I can always write another book or two, if I feel the need for it. But I have to keep moving on. What I want to be now, Paul, is a robobiologist."

"A robopsychologist, you mean?"

"No. That would imply the study of positronic brains and at the moment I have no interest in doing that. A robobiologist, it seems to me, would be concerned with the workings of the body that is attached to that brain."

"Wouldn't that be a roboticist?"

"In the old days, yes. But roboticists work with metallic bodies. I would be studying an organic humanoid body—of which I have the only one, as far as I know. Examining the way it functions, the way it simulates a true human body. I want to know more about artificial human bodies than the android-makers know themselves."

"You narrow your field of endeavor," said Paul thoughtfully. "As an artist, the whole range of expression was yours. Your work could stand up with the best that was being produced anywhere in the world. As a historian, you dealt chiefly with robots. As a robobiologist, your subject will be yourself."

Andrew nodded. "So it would seem."

"Do you really want to turn inward that way?"

"Understanding of self is the beginning of understanding of the entire universe," said Andrew. "Or so I believe now. A newborn child thinks he is the whole universe, but he is wrong, as he soon begins to discover. So he must study what is outside himself —must try to learn where the boundaries are between himself and the rest of the world—in order to arrive at any comprehension of who he is and how he is to conduct his life. And in many ways I am like a newborn child now, Paul. I have been something else before this, something mechanical and relatively easy to understand, but now I am a positronic brain within a body that is almost human, and I can barely begin to comprehend myself. I am alone in the world, you know. There is nothing like me. There never has been. As I move through the world of humans, no one will understand what I am, and I barely understand it myself. So I must learn. If that is what you call turning inward, Paul, so be it. But it is the thing that I must do."

Andrew had to start from the very beginning, for he knew nothing of ordinary biology, almost nothing of any branch of science other than robotics. The nature of organic life, the chemical and electrical basis of it, was a mystery to him. He had never had any particular reason to study it before. But now that he was organic himself—or his body was, at any rate—he experienced a powerful need to expand his knowledge of living things. To understand how the designers of his android body had been able to emulate the workings of the human form, he needed first to know how the genuine article functioned.

He became a familiar sight in the libraries of universities and medical schools, where he would sit at the electronic indices for hours at a time. He looked perfectly normal in clothes and his presence caused no stir whatever. Those few who knew that he was a robot made no attempt to interfere with him.

He added a spacious room to his house to serve as a laboratory, and equipped it with an elaborate array of scientific instruments. His library grew, too. He set up research projects for himself that occupied him for weeks on end of his sleepless twenty-four-hour-a-day days. For sleep was still something for which Andrew had no need. Though virtually human in outer appearance, he had been given ways of restoring and replenishing his strength that were far more efficient than those of the species after which he had been patterned.

The mysteries of respiration and digestion and metabolism and cell division and blood circulation and body temperature, the whole complex and wondrous system of bodily homeostasis that kept human beings functioning for eighty or ninety or, increasingly, even a hundred years, ceased to be mysteries to him. He delved deep into the mechanisms of the human body—for Andrew saw that that was every bit as much a mechanism as were the products of U. S. Robots and Mechanical Men. It was an *organic* mechanism, yes—but a mechanism nevertheless, a beautifully designed one, with its own firm laws of metabolic rhythm, of balance and decay, of breakdown and repair.

Years went by, quiet ones not only within Andrew's secluded retreat on the grounds of the old Martin estate, but in the world outside. The Earth's population was stable, held level not only by a low birth rate but by steady emigration to the growing settlements in space. Giant computers controlled most economic fluctuations, keeping supply and demand in balance between one Region and another so that the ancient business cycles of boom and bust were flattened into gentle curves. It was not a challenging, dynamic era; but it was not a turbulent or perilous one, either.

Andrew paid next to no attention to developments that might

be going on beyond his doorstep. There were more fundamental things that he needed and wanted to explore, and he was exploring them. That was all that mattered to him these days. His income, which came from the invested proceeds of his now terminated career as an artist in wood and from the money that Little Miss had left him, was more than sufficient to take care of his bodily-maintenance needs and to cover the costs of his research.

It was a private, hermetic life: precisely what he wanted. He had long since gained complete mastery over his android body, after the awkward early days, and often he took long walks through the forest atop the bluff, or along the lonely, tempestuous beach where once he had gone with Little Miss and her sister. Sometimes he went swimming—the iciness of the water was no problem for him—and even occasionally risked the journey out to the isolated, forlorn cormorant rock that Miss had asked him to undertake when she was a child. It was a difficult swim even for him, and the cormorants did not seem to enjoy his company. But he enjoyed testing his strength against such a challenge, aware that no human, even the strongest of swimmers, could safely manage the trip out and back through that chilly, violent sea.

Much of the time, though, Andrew spent at his research. There were frequent periods when he did not go out of his house for weeks on end.

Then Paul Charney came to him one day and said, "It's been a long time, Andrew."

"Indeed it has." They rarely saw each other now, though there had been no estrangement of any sort. The Charney family still maintained its home along the upper coast of Northern California, but Paul had taken to spending most of his time nearer to San Francisco.

"Are you still deep in your program of biological research?" Paul asked.

"Very much so," Andrew said.

He was startled by how much Paul had aged. The phenomenon of human aging was something that Andrew had been studying lately with particular interest, and he thought he had arrived at some understanding of its causes and its processes. And yet— for all his experience of age in the generations of this one family, from Sir down through Little Miss to George and now to Paul—it always came as a surprise to him that humans so swiftly grew gray and withered and bent and old. As Paul had done. His long-limbed frame seemed shorter now, and his shoulders were slumped, and the bony structure of his face had undergone subtle changes so that his chin had begun to jut and his cheekbones were less prominent. His eyesight, too, must have suffered, for his eyes had been replaced with gleaming photo-optic cells much like the ones by which Andrew viewed the world. So he and Paul had grown closer in that one respect, at least.

Paul said, "It's a pity you're no longer as concerned as you once were with the history of robots. Your book would need a new chapter, now."

"What do you mean, Paul?"

"A chapter that deals with the radical new policy that U. S. Robots has established."

"I know nothing about that. What new policy are you referring to?"

Paul's eyebrows lifted. "You haven't heard? Really? —Well, Andrew, what they have done is to begin manufacturing central control stations for their robots—giant positronic computers, actually, which are able to communicate with anywhere from a dozen to a thousand robots by microwave transmission. The robots they're turning out now have no brains at all."

"No brains? But how do they—"

"The gigantic central brains do all the data-processing for them. The robot units themselves are nothing more than mobile limbs of the main thinking center."

"Is that more efficient?"

"U. S. Robots insists that it is. Whether it really is, I can't say. But it's my notion that the whole thing is mainly a long-range way of getting back at you. Smythe-Robertson authorized the turn toward the new direction just before he died, you see. He was old and ill, but he pushed his program through and made it stick. And I suspect that what he wanted was to make certain that the company would never again be confronted by a robot able to give them all the trouble that you have. So they've begun to separate brain and body. A mindless mechanical laboring unit can't be deemed worthy of civil rights or legislative protection; and a big brain that sits in a box is just a computer. The brain isn't going to be able to turn up in the office of the Chairman of the Board one day and demand to be put into a fancy new body. And the robot bodies, since they're completely brainless, aren't in a position to conceive any demands at all."

"It seems like a long step backward," Andrew said. "They've undone two hundred years of progress in robotics merely to spare themselves some small degree of political trouble."

"Indeed. Indeed." Paul smiled and slowly shook his head. "It's astonishing, Andrew, the influence you have had on the history of robotics. It was your artistry that encouraged U. S. Robots to make more robots more precise and specialized, because you seemed too clever by half, and they were afraid that that would frighten people. It was your winning your freedom that resulted in the establishment of the principle of robot rights. And it was your insistence on having an android body that made U. S. Robots switch over to this brain-body separation."

Andrew said, "I suppose in the end what the corporation will have created is a world that has just one vast brain controlling several billion robot bodies. All the eggs will be in one basket, then. Dangerous. Not in any way sensible."

"I think you're right," said Paul. "But I don't suspect it will come to pass for a century, at least. Which means I won't be here to see it."

He had crossed the room, and stood by the open doorway, looking out into the wooded grove just beyond. A mild moist spring breeze was blowing from the ocean, and Paul inhaled deeply as though trying to drink it in. After a moment he turned to face Andrew, and he seemed suddenly to have grown ten years older in just the time that he had been here.

"In fact," Paul said in a voice that was no more than a husk of itself, "I may not live to see next year."

"Paul!"

"Don't sound so surprised. We're mortal, Andrew," Paul said, with a shrug. "We're not like you, and by this time you ought to understand what that means."

"I do. But—"

"Yes. Yes, I know. I'm sorry, Andrew. I know how devoted you've been to our family, and what a sad and dreary thing it must be for you constantly to see us growing up and getting older and older and eventually dying. Well, we don't like it much either, I have to tell you, but there's no sense railing against it. We live twice as long as human beings usually did just a few hundred years ago. That's long enough for most of us, I suppose. We simply have to be philosophical about it."

"But I don't understand. How can you be so calm in the face of—of complete termination? Of the total end of all your striving, all your desire to achieve and learn and grow?"

"I wouldn't be, I suppose, if I were twenty years old right now, or even forty. But I'm not. And part of the system, Andrew—the good part, I guess—is that when you reach a certain age it generally stops mattering to you so much that you're inevitably going to die soon. You aren't really achieving and learning and growing any more. For better or for worse, you've lived your life and done whatever you can for the world and for yourself, and now your time is up and your body knows that and accepts it. We get very tired, Andrew. You don't know what that word means, not really, do you? No. No, I see that you don't. You can't. You aren't able to get tired and so you have only a theoretical knowledge of what it's like. But it's different for us. We slog on and on for seventy or eighty or maybe a hundred years and eventually it all just becomes too much, and so we sit down and then we lie down and finally we close our eyes and don't open them again, and right at the end we know that it *is* the end and we simply don't mind. Or don't care: I'm not sure that's the same thing, really, but perhaps it is. —Don't look at me that way, Andrew."

"Dying is a natural thing for humans," Andrew said. "I do understand that, Paul."

"No. You don't. You really don't. It just isn't possible for you to understand. You secretly think that death is some sort of lamentable design flaw in us and you can't understand why it hasn't been fixed, because it ought to be pretty simple to keep on replacing our parts indefinitely as they wear out and break down, the way yours have always been replaced. You've even had an entire body replaced."

"But surely it would be theoretically possible for you to be transferred into—"

"No. It isn't. Not even in theory. We don't have positronic brains and ours aren't transferable, so we can't simply ask someone to scoop us out of a body that we're finished with and put us into a nice shiny new one. You can't comprehend the fact that humans inevitably have to reach a point where they're incapable of being repaired any more. But that's all right. Why should anyone expect you to be able to conceive the inconceivable? I'm going to die soon and that's all there is to it. And I want to reassure you at least in one respect, Andrew: you'll be well provided for financially when I go."

"But I am already quite well provi—"

"Yes. I know that. All the same, things can change very quickly, sometimes. We think we live in a very secure world, but other civilizations have felt just as smug and they had reason sooner or later to see that they were wrong. Anyway, Andrew: I'm the last of the Charneys. I have no heirs except you. There are collateral relatives descended from my great-aunt, but they don't count. I don't know them and I don't care about them. I care about you. The money I control personally will be left in trust in your name and you'll continue to be economically secure as far into the future as anyone can foresee."

"This is unnecessary, Paul," Andrew said, with difficulty. He had to admit to himself that what Paul had said about his not understanding death, not being *able* to understand it, was true.

In all this time he had not really managed to get used to the deaths of the Charneys.

Paul said, "Let's not argue, all right? I can't take the money with me and there isn't anything I'd rather do with it than leave it to you, so that's the way it's going to be. And I don't want to consume any more of my remaining life-span discussing the matter with you. Let's talk about something else. —What are you working on these days?"

"Biology, still."

"What aspect in particular?"

"Metabolism."

"Robot metabolism, you mean? There isn't any such thing, is there? Or is there? Do you mean android metabolism? Human metabolism?"

"All three," Andrew said. "A synthesis of sorts." He paused, and then he went plunging ahead. Why hold anything back from Paul? "I've been designing a system that would allow androids—I mean myself; I am still the only functioning android, am I not?—to draw energy from the combustion of hydrocarbons rather than from atomic cells."

Paul gave him a long, slow look.

"You mean," he said finally, "that you want to make it possible for an android to be able to breathe and eat the same way humans do?"

"Yes."

"You've never mentioned any such project as this to me before, Andrew. Is it something new?"

"Not really. In truth, Paul, it is the reason I began all this biological research in the first place."

Paul nodded abstractedly. It was as though he was listening from a very great distance. He seemed to be having a difficult time absorbing what Andrew was telling him.

"And have you achieved anything significant so far?" he asked, after a time.

"I am approaching something significant," Andrew said. "It needs more work but I think I have succeeded in designing a compact combustion chamber that will be adequate for catalyzed controlled breakdown."

"But why, Andrew? What's the point of it? You know that it can't possibly be as efficient as the atomic cell your body uses now."

"Very likely not," said Andrew. "But it ought to be efficient enough. At least as efficient as the system that the human body uses, I would say, and not all that different from it in fundamental principle. The main problem with the atomic cell, Paul, is that it is inhuman. My energy—my very life, you could say—is drawn from a source that is wholly other than human. And I am not content with that."

SIXTEEN

IT TOOK TIME, but Andrew had all the time he needed. And he was in no hurry to complete his research. He wanted everything to be properly worked out before he attempted to have it put into service. There was another reason for going slowly, also. Andrew had decided not to undergo any further upgrading beyond the android level while Paul Charney was still alive.

Paul had not expressed any overt criticism of the work Andrew was doing, other than his initial response that Andrew's new combustion chamber might be less efficient than the atomic cell that powered his body now. But Andrew could see that Paul was troubled by the idea. It was too bold for him, too strange, too great a leap. Even Paul, it seemed, had his limits when it came to the progress of robot design. Even Paul!

Perhaps that was one of the side effects of aging, Andrew thought. Challenging new ideas become *too* challenging for you, no matter how open your mind may have been to dynamic change when you were younger. Everything new comes to seem disturbing and threatening to you. You feel the world rushing past you in a frightening stampede; you want things to slow down, you want the ferocious pace of progress to slacken.

Was that how it was? Andrew wondered.

Did humans inevitably become more conservative with age?

So it would seem. Little Miss had been uneasy about his wearing clothing. George had thought it odd that he would want to write a book. And Paul—Paul—

Looking back now, Andrew remembered how startled, even shocked, Paul had been when he learned for the first time, in Smythe-Robertson's office, that what Andrew wanted was to be transferred into an android body. Paul had made a quick enough adaptation to the idea and had fought furiously and brilliantly to make it a reality. But that did not necessarily mean that he thought it was a good idea for Andrew.

They have all let me do what I felt I needed to do, Andrew thought, even when they privately disagreed with it. They have granted me my wishes—out of love for me.

Yes, *love*. For a robot.

Andrew dwelled on that thought for a while, and sensations of warmth and pleasure went through him. But it was a little troubling, too, to realize that sometimes the Charneys had supported him not out of personal convictions of their own but simply because they so wholeheartedly and unconditionally believed in allowing him to follow his own path, whether or not they thought it was the correct one.

So Paul, then, had won him the right to have an android body. But that transformation had taken Paul to his own limit of acceptance of Andrew's upward path. The next step—the metabolic converter—was beyond him.

Very well. Paul did not have very much longer to live. Andrew would wait.

And so he did; and in time came news of Paul's death, not as soon as Paul had supposed it would be, but very soon, all the same. Andrew was invited to attend Paul's funeral—the public ceremony, he was aware, that marked the end of a human life—but there was scarcely anyone there whom he knew, and he felt ill at ease and out of place, even though everyone was scrupulously polite to him. These young strangers—friends of Paul's, members of his law firm, distant relatives of the Charneys—had no more substance than shadows for Andrew, and he stood among them heavy with the double grief of having lost his good friend Paul and of finding himself bereft of his last real connection with the family that had given him his place in life.

In fact there no longer were any humans in the world with whom he had close emotional ties. Andrew had come to realize by this time that he had cared deeply for the Martins and the Charneys in a way that went beyond the robotic—that his devotion to them was not merely a manifestation of the First and Second Laws, but something that might indeed be called love. His love, for them. In his earlier days Andrew would never have admitted such a thing, even to himself; but he was different now.

These thoughts led Andrew inevitably, around the time of Paul Charney's death, to a consideration of the entire concept of family ties—the love of parent for child, of child for parent—and how that was related to the inexorable passing of the generations. If you are human, Andrew told himself, you are part of a great chain, a chain that hangs suspended across vast spans of time and links you to all those who have come before you and those who follow after. And you understand that individual links of the chain may perish—indeed, *must* perish—but the chain itself is ever-renewing and will survive. People died, whole families might become extinct—but the human race, the species, went on and on through the centuries and the millennia and the eons, everyone connected through the heritage of blood to those who had gone before.

It was a difficult thing for Andrew to understand, that sense of connection, of infinite linkage with intimately related predecessors. He had no predecessors, not really, and he would have no successors, either. He was unique—individual—something that had been brought forth at a certain moment in time out of nothing at all.

Andrew found himself wondering what it might be like to have had a parent himself—but all he could come up with was a vague image of assembly-robots weaving his body together in a factory. Or what it was like to have a child—but the best he could manage was to envision a table or desk, something that he had made with his own hands.

But human parents were not assembly-mechs, and human children were nothing like tables and desks. He had it all wrong.

It was a mystery to him. And very likely always would be. He was not human; why then should he expect human family linkages to be comprehensible to him?

Then Andrew thought of Little Miss, of George, of Paul, even of fierce old Sir, and what *they* had meant to him. And he realized that he was part of a family chain after all, though he had had no parents and was incapable of siring children. The Martins had taken him in and had made him one of them. He was a Martin, indeed. An adopted Martin, yes; but that was the best he could have hoped for. And there were plenty of humans who had not had the comfort of belonging to such a loving family. He had done very well, all things considered. Though only a robot, he had known the continuity and stability of family life; he had known warmth; he had known love.

All those whom Andrew had—*loved*—were gone, though. That was saddening and liberating both. The chain was broken, for him. It could never be restored. But at least he could do as he pleased, now, without fear of troubling those who had been so close to him. Now, with the death of the great-grandson of Sir, Andrew felt free to proceed with his plan for upgrading his android body. That was some sort of partial consolation for his loss.

Nevertheless he was alone in the world, or so it seemed to him —not simply because he was a positronic brain in a unique android body, but because he had no affiliations of any sort. And it was a world that had every reason to be hostile to his aspirations. All the more reason, Andrew thought, to continue along the path he had long ago chosen—the path that he hoped would ultimately make him invulnerable to the world into which he had been thrust so impersonally, without his leave, so many years before.

In fact Andrew was not quite as alone as he thought. Men and women might die, but corporations lived on just as robots did, and the law firm of Feingold and Charney still functioned even though no Feingolds and no Charneys remained. The firm had its directions and it followed them impeccably and soullessly. By way of the trust that held his investments and through the income that Andrew drew from the firm as Paul Charney's heir, Andrew continued to be wealthy. That enabled him to pay a large annual retainer to Feingold and Charney to keep them involved in the legal aspects of his research—in particular, the new combustion chamber.

It was time now for Andrew to pay another call on the headquarters of U. S. Robots and Mechanical Men.

This would be the third time in his long life that Andrew had had face-to-face dealings with high executives of the powerful robot-manufacturing corporation. On the first occasion, back in the days of Merwin Mansky, Mansky and managing director Elliot Smythe had come out to California to see *him*. But that was when Sir had still been alive, and imperious old Sir had been able to command even Smythes and Robertsons into his presence. On the next occasion, many years later, Andrew and Paul had been the ones to make the journey to the company—to see Harley Smythe-Robertson and arrange for Andrew's transfer to the android body.

Now Andrew would make the journey east a second time, but he would go alone. And this time he would have the visage and bodily frame, if not the inner organs, of a human being.

U. S. Robots had changed greatly since Andrew's last visit. The main production factory had been shifted to a large space station, as was the case with many other industrial facilities. Only the research center remained behind on Earth, in a grand and lovely parklike setting of vast green lawns and sturdy wide-spreading leafy trees.

The Earth itself, its population long since stabilized at about a billion—plus a robot population about equally large—was becoming parklike virtually everywhere. The terrible damage to the environment that had been perpetrated in the hectic early centuries of the Industrial Revolution was largely only a memory, now.

The sins of the past had not exactly been forgotten, but they had come to seem unreal to the inhabitants of the reborn Earth, and with each passing generation it became harder and harder to believe that people once had been willing to commit such monstrous and ultimately self-destructive crimes against their own world. Now that industry had largely moved to space and clean, efficient robot labor served the needs of those humans who had remained behind, the planet's natural healing powers had been allowed to come into play, and the seas were pure again, the skies were clear, the woodlands had reclaimed territory once occupied by dense, grimy cities.

A robot greeted Andrew when his aeroflitter landed at the U. S. Robots airstrip. Its face was bland and blank and its red photoelectric eyes were utterly expressionless. Scarcely thirty percent of the robots of Earth, Andrew knew, were still independently brained: this one was an empty creature, nothing more than the mindless metal puppet of some immobile positronic thinking-device housed deep within the U. S. Robots complex.

"I am Andrew Martin," Andrew said. "I have an appointment with Director of Research Magdescu."

"Yes. You will follow me."

Lifeless. Brainless. A mere machine. A *thing.*

The robot greeter led Andrew briskly along a paved path that gleamed with some inner crystalline brightness and up a shining spiral ramp into a domed many-leveled building covered with a glistening and iridescent translucent skin. To Andrew, who had had little experience of modern architecture, it had the look of something out of a storybook—light, airy, shimmering, not entirely real.

He was allowed to wait in a broad oval room carpeted with some lustrous synthetic material that emitted a soft glow and a faint, pleasant sort of music whenever Andrew moved about on its surface. He found that if he walked in a straight line the glow was pale pink and the music was mildly percussive in texture, but that when he sauntered in a curve that followed the border of the room the light shifted more toward the blue end of the spectrum and the music seemed more like the murmuring of the wind. He wondered if any of this had any significance and decided that it did not: that it was mere ornamentation, a decorative frill. In this placid and unchallenging era such lovely but meaningless decorative touches were ubiquitous, Andrew knew.

"Ah—Andrew Martin at last," a deep voice said.

A short, stocky man had appeared in the room as though some magic had conjured him out of the carpet. The newcomer was dark of complexion and hair, with a little pointed beard that looked as though it had been lacquered, and he wore nothing above the waist except the breastband that fashion now dictated. Andrew himself was more thoroughly covered. He had followed George Charney in adopting the "drapery" style of clothing, thinking that its flowing nature would better conceal what he still imagined to be a certain awkwardness of his movements, and though the stylishness of drapery was several decades obsolete now and Andrew could move as easily and gracefully as any human, he had continued to dress in that manner ever since.

"Dr. Magdescu?" Andrew asked.

"Indeed. Indeed." Alvin Magdescu took up a stance a couple of meters from Andrew and scanned him with undisguised fascination, as though Andrew were an exhibit in a museum. "Splendid! You are absolutely splendid!"

"Thank you," Andrew said, a little coolly. Magdescu's compliment did not strike him as entirely welcome. It was the kind of impersonal appraisal that some finely manufactured machine might receive; and Andrew saw no reason to take pleasure these days in that sort of thing when it was directed at him.

"How good of you to come!" Magdescu cried. "How eager I have been to see you! But I am being impolite." And he stepped forward with a sort of lunging, bounding motion until he was virtually standing toe to toe with Andrew. He held out his hand, palm upward, fingers outstretched.

Yes. A new form of greeting that evidently had replaced the handshake that had dominated human social intercourse for so many hundreds of years. Andrew wasn't in the habit of shaking

176

hands with human beings, let alone making this new gesture. Shaking hands was simply not something that occurred to a robot to do. But Magdescu seemed to be expecting it, and the offer helped to ease the sting of his first few words. And so Andrew responded as he realized he was meant to, by offering his own hand. He held it above Magdescu's and bent the tips of his fingers downward until they touched the tips of the other man's.

It was an odd feeling, this touching of hands with a human as though they were equals. Odd and a little disturbing, but encouraging, also.

"Welcome, welcome, welcome!" Magdescu said. He seemed bubbling with energy: a little too much energy, maybe, Andrew thought. But it seemed genuine enough. "The famous Andrew Martin! The *notorious* Andrew Martin!"

"Notorious?"

"Absolutely. The most notorious product in our history. Though it seems almost obscene to call something as lifelike as you a product, I have to say. You aren't offended, are you?"

"How could I be? I *am* a product," said Andrew, though without much warmth. He saw that Magdescu was unable to hold a consistent position toward him. Touching hands as though they were simply two men at a business meeting, yes; but in the next breath speaking of him as a *something*. And describing him as "lifelike." Andrew had no illusions about himself: he knew that that was what he was. *Humanoid,* not human. *Lifelike,* not living. A *product,* not a person. But he did not enjoy hearing it.

"They did such a wonderful job with you! Remarkable! Remarkable! Almost human!"

"Not quite," Andrew said.

"But amazingly lifelike, all things considered. Amazingly! It's a damned shame that old Smythe-Robertson was so set against you. You're terrifically humanoid-looking, no question about it, a wonderful technical accomplishment—but of course he let the company take the android concept only so far. If our people had been allowed really to go all out, we could have done a great deal with you."

"You still can," said Andrew.

"No, I don't think so," Magdescu said, and much of the manic gusto went out of him as though he were a balloon that had been pricked. It was a startlingly sudden change of mood. He swung away from Andrew and began to pace the room in an angular zigzagging way that brought greenish light and odd chiming music up from the carpeting. "We're past the time," said Magdescu gloomily. "The era of significant progress in robotics—well, forget it, it's just history now. At least here, that is. We've been using robots freely on Earth for something close to a hundred fifty years now, but it's all changing again. It's back to space for them now, and those that stay here won't be brained."

"But there remains myself, and I stay on Earth."

"Well, that's true. But you're you, a complete anomaly, a robot unto himself, the only android robot. You aren't the prototype of a line. You're simply a unique item that they happened to have turned out in a very different sort of era, and after you were produced they made good and sure that you'd remain unique. No scope for further development there. No state-of-the-art advances. No art; no state. There doesn't seem to be much of the robot about you, anyway. You're pretty much out of our horizon. —Why have you come here, anyway?"

"For an upgrade," Andrew said.

Magdescu laughed harshly. "Didn't you pay any attention to anything I've just been telling you? There's no real progress going on here! This is a research center, yes, but all our research is headed in exactly the wrong direction! We're trying to make robots simpler and more mechanical all the time. And here you are—the most advanced robot that ever existed or apparently ever will exist—coming in here and asking us to make you even better? How could we? What could we possibly do for you that hasn't already been done?"

"This," said Andrew.

He handed Magdescu a memory disk. The research director stared at it balefully, as though Andrew had put a jellyfish or a frog into the palm of his hand.

178

"What's this?" he asked, finally.

"The schematics for my next upgrade."

"Schematics," Magdescu said puzzledly. "Upgrade."

"Yes. I wish to be even less a robot than I am now. Since I am organic up to a point, I want now to have an organic source of energy. You can provide it for me. The necessary research work has already been done."

"By whom?"

"Me."

"You've designed your own upgrade?" Magdescu began to chuckle. Then the chuckle became a laugh, and then the laugh dissolved into a manic giggle. "Wonderful! The robot walks in here and hands the Director of Research the upgrade schematics! And who did them? The robot himself did them! Wonderful! Wonderful! —You know, when I was a little boy my grandmother used to read a book to me, an ancient book that I guess has been completely forgotten by now, a book called *Alice in Wonderland*. About a little girl of three or four hundred years ago who follows a rabbit down a hole and lands in a world where everything is completely absurd, except no one knows it's absurd so they all take it terribly seriously. This is like something right out of that book. Or the sequel. *Alvin in Wonderland*, I could call it. Although I think there already is a sequel, actually." Magdescu was speaking very rapidly now, almost wildly. "Should I take this seriously, this set of upgrade schematics? It's all just a joke, isn't it?"

"No. Not at all."

"Not—a—joke."

"No. I am quite serious, I assure you. Why don't you play my disk, Dr. Magdescu?"

"Yes. Why don't I?" He touched a stud in the wall and a desk rose from somewhere, with a scanner outlet on it. Swiftly he slid the disk into the scanner slot and the screen instantly blossomed into vivid color. Andrew's name appeared in bright crimson, with a long list of patent numbers below it. Magdescu nodded and told the scanner to keep going. A sequence of complicated diagrams began to appear on the screen.

Magdescu stood stiffly, watching the screen with increasingly intense concentration. Now and then he murmured something to himself or toyed with his beard. After a while he glanced toward Andrew with a strange expression in his eyes and said, "This is remarkably ingenious. *Remarkably.* Tell me: you really did all of this yourself?"

"Yes."

"Hard to believe!"

"Is it? Please try."

Magdescu shot a sharp, inquiring look at Andrew, who met his gaze steadily and calmly. The research director shrugged and ordered the scanner to continue. Diagram succeeded diagram. The entire metabolic progression was there, from intake to absorption. Occasionally Magdescu would back the sequence up so that he could restudy one that he had seen before. After a little while he paused again and said, "What you've set out here is something more than just an upgrade, you know. It's a major qualitative alteration of your biological program."

"Yes. I realize that."

"Highly experimental. Unique. Unheard-of. Nothing like it has ever been attempted or even proposed. —Why do you want to do something like this to yourself?"

"I have my reasons," Andrew said.

"Whatever they are, they can't really be very carefully thought out."

Andrew, as ever, maintained tight self-control. "On the contrary, Dr. Magdescu. What you have just seen is the result of years of study."

"I suppose so. And technically it's all very impressive, you know. These are terrific schematics and the only word I can find for the conceptual framework is 'brilliant.' But all the same I can think of a million reasons why you shouldn't go in for these changes and none at all why you should. We're looking at really risky stuff, here. Trust me: what you're proposing to have done to yourself is right out on the farthest reaches of the possible. Take my advice and stay the way you are."

It was more or less what Andrew had feared Magdescu would say. But he had not come here with any intention of yielding.

"I'm sure you mean well, Dr. Magdescu. I hope you do, at any rate. But I insist on having this work done."

"*Insist,* Andrew?" Magdescu said.

He looked astounded—as though, despite all his earlier talk of what a lifelike product Andrew was, he was only just now beginning to comprehend that it was a robot with which he was having this conversation.

"Insist, yes." Andrew wondered whether the impatience that he felt was sufficiently visible in his face, but he was certain that Magdescu could detect it in his voice. "Dr. Magdescu, you're overlooking an important point here. You have no choice but to accede to my request."

"Oh?"

"If such devices as I've designed here can be built into my body, they can be built into human bodies as well. The tendency to lengthen human life by prosthetic devices is already well established—artificial hearts, artificial lungs, kidneys, liver-surrogates, a whole host of replacement organs have come into use in the past two or three centuries. But not all of these devices work equally well and some are highly unreliable indeed and no one can deny that there is still much room for improvement. The principles underlying my work represent such an improvement. I speak of the interface between the organic and inorganic: the linkage that will permit artificial bodily parts to be connected with organic tissue. It is a new departure. No existing prosthetic devices are the equal of the ones I have designed and am designing."

"That's a pretty bold claim," Magdescu said.

"Maybe so. But not unwarranted by the facts, as I think you yourself have already been able to see from the data at hand. The proof of it is that I'm willing to make myself the first experimental subject for the metabolic converter, despite the risks that you seem to see in it."

"All that proves is that you're willing to take foolhardy

chances. Which probably means nothing more than that you don't have a properly functioning Third Law parameter.''

Andrew remained calm. "It may seem that way to you, perhaps. But my outward appearance may be deceiving you. My Three Laws parameters are quite intact. And thus, if I saw anything at all suicidal about my request for this upgrade, you can be quite certain that I would not only be unwilling but also unable to ask you to perform it. No, Dr. Magdescu: the combustion chamber will work. If you won't build and install it for me, I can have it done elsewhere.''

"Elsewhere? Who else can upgrade a robot? This corporation controls all the technical knowhow there is when it comes to robots!''

"Not all,'' said Andrew quietly. "Do you think I could have designed this device without full knowledge of my own interior workings?''

Magdescu looked stunned.

"Are you saying that you're prepared to set up a rival robotics company if we won't do this upgrade for you?''

"Of course not. One is quite enough. But if you compel me to, Dr. Magdescu, I will set up a company that produces prosthetic devices like my converter. Not for the android market, Dr. Magdescu, because that market is confined to a single individual, but for the general *human* market. And then, I think, U. S. Robots and Mechanical Men is going to regret that I was not offered the cooperation I requested.''

There was a long silence. Then Magdescu said numbly, "I think I see what you're driving at, now.''

"I hope so. But I'll be very explicit,'' Andrew said. "As it happens, I control the patents on this device and on the entire family of devices that can be derived from it. The firm of Feingold and Charney has represented me very ably in all the legal work, and will continue to do so. It would not be very difficult for me to find backers and go into business for myself—the business of developing a line of prosthetic devices which, in the end, may give human beings many of the advantages of durability and easy repair that robots enjoy, with none of the drawbacks. What do you think will happen to United States Robots and Mechanical Men, in that case?"

Magdescu nodded. His face was grim.

Andrew continued, "If, however, you build and install in me the device that I have just shown you, and you agree to outfit me upon demand with such other prosthetic upgrades as I may subsequently devise, I'm prepared to work out a licensing agreement with your company. A quid pro quo, that is: I have need of your expertise in robot/android technology, though I'm confident that I could duplicate it myself if you forced me to, and you have need of the devices I've developed. Under the licensing agreement that I intend to propose, United States Robots and Mechanical Men would receive permission to make use of my patents, which control the new technology that would permit not only the manufacture of highly advanced humaniform robots but also the full prostheticization of human beings. —The initial licenses will not be granted, of course, until the first operation on me has been successfully completed, and after enough time has passed to make it unquestionably clear that it has been a success."

Magdescu said lamely, "You've thought of everything, haven't you?"

"I certainly hope so."

"I can hardly believe that you're a robot. You're so damned— aggressive!"

"Hardly, Dr. Magdescu."

"Demands—conditions—threats of setting up competitive companies—my God, don't you have any First Law inhibitions at all?"

Andrew smiled the broadest smile that was possible for him to smile.

"Most certainly I do," he replied. "But I happen to feel no First Law pressure at this moment. The First Law forbids me to harm human beings, of course, and I assure you that I am as incapable of doing that as you would be to detach your left leg and reattach it while I stood here watching you. But where does the First Law enter into our present discussion? You are a human being and I am a robot, yes, and I have set certain stern conditions for you which I suppose you may interpret as demands and threats, but I see the matter entirely differently. To my way of thinking I am not threatening you or the company for which you work at all. What I am doing is offering it the greatest opportunity it has had in many years. —What do you say, Dr. Magdescu?"

Magdescu moistened his lips, tugged at the point of his little beard, nervously adjusted and readjusted the sash that lay across his bare chest. "Well," he said. "You have to understand, Mr. Martin, that it's not in my power to make any sort of decision on something as big as this. The Board of Directors would have to deal with it, not a mere employee like me. And that's going to take time."

"How much time?"

"I can't say. I'll pass everything you've told me today up to them, and they'll take it up at their regular monthly meeting, and then I suppose they'll create a study committee, and so on. —It could be a while."

"I can wait a reasonable time," said Andrew. "But *only* a reasonable time, and I will be the judge of what is reasonable. You would do well to tell them that." He thanked Magdescu for his time and announced that he was ready to be conducted back to the airstrip. And he thought with satisfaction that Paul himself could not have done any of this in a better way.

SEVENTEEN

MAGDESCU MUST HAVE made things very clear to the Board of Directors, and the urgency of the message must have gotten through to them. For it was within quite a reasonable time indeed that word reached Andrew that the corporation was willing to do business with him. U.S.R.M.M. would build and design the combustion chamber and install it in his android body at its own expense; and it was prepared to enter into negotiations for a licensing arrangement covering manufacture and distribution of the entire range of prosthetic organs that Andrew might have under development.

Under Andrew's supervision a prototype metabolic converter was constructed and extensively tested at a newly constructed facility in Northern California, first within robot hulls, then with newly fabricated android bodies that had not been equipped with positronic brains and were operated on external life-support systems.

The results were impressive, everyone agreed. And finally Andrew declared that he was ready to have the device installed in himself.

"You're absolutely certain?" Magdescu asked.

The bouncy little Director of Research looked concerned. During the course of the project Magdescu and Andrew had developed a curious but sturdy friendship, for which Andrew was quietly grateful now that none of the Charneys were left. In the time since Paul Charney's death Andrew had come clearly to recognize that he needed some sort of sense of close connection with human beings. He knew now that he did not want to be a completely solitary creature, that in fact he could not exist comfortably in total solitude, though he was not sure why. Nothing in the design of the robot brain mandated any need for companionship. But it often seemed to Andrew now that he was more like a human in many ways than he was like a robot, although he understood that he really existed in a strange indefinable limbo, neither man nor machine, partaking of some characteristics of each.

"Yes," he said. "I have no doubts that the work will be done skillfully and well."

"I'm not talking about our part of the work," said Magdescu. "I'm talking about yours."

"You can't possibly doubt that the combustion chamber will work!"

"The tests leave no question of that."

"Then what—?"

"I've been against this thing from the start, Andrew, as you know. But I don't think you fully understand why."

"It's because you think that the radical technological upheaval that my prosthetics will cause for U. S. Robots is going to be too much for the company to handle."

"No! Absolutely not! Not even remotely! I'm all in favor of experiment for the sake of experimentation! Don't you think I want to see some forward movement in this damned field of ours, after all these decades of stupid and furtive backscuttling toward ever more simpleminded and now downright brainless robots? No, Andrew, it's *you* that I'm worried about."

"But if the combustion chamber—"

Magdescu threw up his hands. "It's safe, it's safe! Nobody disagrees on that score. But—look, Andrew, we'll be opening your body and taking out your atomic cell and installing a bunch of revolutionary new equipment, and then we'll be hooking everything up to your positronic pathways. What if something goes wrong with your body during the operation? There's always a possibility of that—small, maybe, but real. You aren't just a positronic brain sitting inside a metal framework any more, you know. Your brain is linked to the android housing in a far more complex way now. I know how they must have had to do the transfer operation. Your positronic pathways are tied into simulated neural pathways. Suppose your android body starts malfunctioning on the operating table? Suppose it begins to enter a terminal malfunction, Andrew?"

"*Dies*, is that what you're trying to say?"

"Dies, yes. Your body begins to die."

"There'll be a backup android body sitting on the table right next to it."

"And if we can't make the transfer in time? If your positronic brain suffers irreversible decay while we're trying to untangle it from the million and one linkages that were set up in Smythe-Robertson's time and lift it over to the backup body? Your positronic brain is *you*, Andrew. There's no way to back up a brain, positronic or otherwise. If it's damaged it's damaged for good. If it's damaged beyond a certain point you'll be dead."

"And this is why you're hesitant about the operation?"

"You're the only one of you that there is. I'd hate to lose you."

"I'd hate to lose me too, Alvin. But I don't think it's going to happen."

Magdescu looked bleak. "You insist on going through with it, then."

"I insist. I have every faith in the skill of the staff at U. S. Robots."

And that was where the matter rested. Magdescu was unable to budge him; and once more Andrew made the journey eastward to the U. S. Robots research center, where an entire building had been reconfigured to serve as the operating theater.

Before he went, he took a long solitary stroll one afternoon along the beach, under the steep rugged cliffs, past the swarming tide pools where Miss and Little Miss had liked to play in their childhood of a century and more ago, and stood for a long while looking out at the dark turbulent sea, the vast arch of the sky, the white flecks of cloud in the west.

The sun was beginning to set. It cast a golden track of light across the water. How beautiful it all was! The world was really an extraordinarily splendid place, Andrew told himself. The sea—the sky—a sunset—a glossy leaf shining with the morning dew—everything. Everything!

And, he thought, perhaps he was the only robot who had ever been able to respond to the beauty of the world in this way. Robots were a dull plodding bunch, in the main. They did their jobs and that was that. It was the way they were supposed to be. It was the way everyone wanted them to be.

"You're the only one of you that there is," Magdescu had said.

Yes. It was true. He had a capacity for aesthetic response that went far beyond the emotive range of any other robot that had ever been.

Beauty meant something to him. He appreciated it when he saw it; he had created beauty himself.

And if he never saw any of this again, how very sad that would be.

And then Andrew smiled at his own foolishness. Sad? For whom? He would never know it, if the operation should fail. The world and all its beauty would be lost to him, but what would that matter? He would have ceased to function. He would be permanently out of order. He would be *dead,* and after that it would make no difference to him at all that he could no longer perceive the beauties of the world. That was what death meant: a total cessation of function, an end to all processing of data.

There were risks, yes. But they were risks he had to take, because otherwise—

Otherwise—

He simply had to. There was no *otherwise*. He could not go on as he was, outwardly human in form, more or less, but incapable of the most basic human biological functions—breathing, eating, digesting, excreting—

An hour later Andrew was on his way east. Alvin Magdescu met him in person at the U. S. Robots airstrip.

"Are you ready?" Magdescu asked him.

"Totally."

"Well, then, Andrew, so am I."

Obviously they intended to take no chances. They had constructed a wondrous operating theater for him, far more advanced in capability than the earlier room in which they had carried out his transformation from the metallic to the androidal form.

It was a magnificent tetrahedral enclosure illuminated by a cross-shaped cluster of chromed fixtures at its summit that flooded the room with brilliant but not glaring light. A platform midway between floor and ceiling jutted from one wall, dividing the great room almost in half, and atop this platform rested a dazzling transparent aseptic bubble within which the surgery would be performed. Beneath the platform that supported the bubble was the surgical stage's environmental-support apparatus: an immense cube of dull green metal, housing an intricate tangle of pumps, filters, heating ducts, reservoirs of sterilizing chemicals, humidifiers, and other equipment. On the other side of the room was a great array of supplementary machinery covering an entire wall: an autoclave, a laser bank, a host of metering devices, a camera boom and associated playback screens that would allow consulting surgeons outside the operating area to monitor the events.

"What do you think?" Magdescu asked proudly.

"Very impressive. I find it most reassuring. And highly flattering as well."

"You know that we don't want to lose you, Andrew. You're a very important—individual."

Andrew did not fail to notice the slight hesitation in Magdescu's voice before that last word. As though Magdescu had been about to say *man,* and had checked himself just barely in time. Andrew smiled thinly but said nothing.

The operation took place the next morning, and it was an unqualified success. There turned out to be no need for any of the elaborate safety devices that the U. S. Robots people had set up. The operating team, following procedures that Andrew himself had helped to devise, went briskly about the task of removing his atomic cell, installing the combustion chamber, and establishing the new neural linkages, and performed its carefully choreographed work without the slightest hitch.

Half an hour after it was over Andrew was sitting up, checking his positronic parameters, exploring the altered data-flow surging through his brain as a torrent of messages came in from the new metabolic system.

Magdescu stood by the window, watching him.

"How do you feel?"

"Fine. I told you there'd be no problems."

"Yes. Yes."

"As I said, my faith in the skill of your staff was unwavering. And now it's done. I have the ability to eat."

"So you do. You can sip olive oil, at any rate."

"That's eating. I'm told that olive oil has a delicious taste."

"Well, sip all you want. It'll mean occasional cleaning of the combustion chamber, as of course you already realize. Something of a nuisance, I'd say, but there's no way around it."

"A nuisance for the time being," Andrew said. "But it's not impossible to make the chamber self-cleaning. I've already had some ideas about that. And other things."

"Other things?" Magdescu asked. "Such as?"

"A modification that will deal with solid food."

"Solid food is going to contain incombustible fractions, Andrew—indigestible matter, so to speak, that's going to have to be discarded."

"I'm aware of that."

"You would have to equip yourself with an anus."

"The equivalent."

"The equivalent, yes. —What else are you planning to develop for yourself, Andrew?"

"Everything else."

"Everything?"

"Everything, Alvin."

Magdescu tugged at the point of his beard and raised one eyebrow. "Genitalia, too?"

"I don't see any reason why not. Do you?"

"You aren't going to be able to give yourself any kind of reproductive ability. You simply aren't, Andrew."

Andrew managed a faint smile. "As I understand it, human beings make use of their genitalia even at times when they don't have the slightest interest in reproduction. In fact they seem to use them for reproduction only once or twice in their lifetimes, at best, is that not so, and the rest of the time—"

"Yes," Magdescu said. "I know, Andrew."

"Don't misunderstand me. I'm not saying that I plan to have sexual relations with anyone," Andrew said. "I tend to doubt very much that I would. But I want the anatomical features to be present, all the same. I regard my body as a canvas on which I intend to draw—"

He left the sentence unfinished.

Magdescu stared at him, waiting for the next word. When it seemed certain that it would not be forthcoming, he completed the statement himself, and this time Magdescu spoke the word that he had not been able to bring himself to utter on the day before the operation.

"A man, Andrew?"

"A man, yes. Perhaps."

Magdescu said, "I'm disappointed in you. It's really such a puny ambition. You're better than a man, Andrew. You're superior in every way I can think of. Your body is disease-proof, self-sustaining, self-repairing, virtually invulnerable, a marvelously elegant example of biological engineering, just as it stands. It doesn't need any improvements. But no, for some reason you want to put totally useless food inside yourself and then find a way of excreting it, you want to give yourself genitalia even though you aren't capable of reproduction and you aren't interested in sex, you'll want to start having body odor next, and dental decay—" He shook his head scornfully. "I don't know, Andrew. The way it seems to me, you've been going downhill ever since you opted for organicism."

"My brain hasn't suffered."

"No, it hasn't. I'll grant you that. But there's no guarantee that this new set of upgrades that you've started to sketch out won't involve you in tremendous risks, once we start the actual installations. Why take chances? You've got very little to gain and everything to lose."

"You are simply not capable of seeing this from my viewpoint, Alvin."

"No. No, I guess not. I'm a mere flesh-and-blood human being who doesn't think there's anything very wonderful about perspiration and excretion and skin blemishes and headaches. You see this beard I wear? I wear it because hair insists on growing on my face every single day—useless, bothersome, ugly hair, some kind of evolutionary survival from God knows what primordial phase of human life, and I have my choice between going to the bother of removing it every single day so that I'll conform to the conventional neatness modes of my society or else letting it grow on at least some areas of my face so that I can be spared the nuisance of depilation. Is that what you want? Facial hair? Stubble, Andrew? Do you intend to devote all your immense technical ingenuity to the challenging task of finding out a way of creating five o'clock shadow for yourself?"

"You can't possibly understand," said Andrew.

"So you keep saying. I understand this, though: you've developed a patented line of prosthetic devices that amounts to an immense technological breakthrough. They're going to extend the human life-span enormously and transform the existence of millions of people who otherwise would be facing crippling and debilitating circumstances as they age. I realize that you're wealthy already, but once your devices are on the market they'll make you rich beyond anybody's comprehension. Maybe having more money doesn't mean much to you, but there'll be fame along with it—honors galore—the gratitude of an entire world. It's an enviable position, Andrew. Why can't you settle for what you have now? Why take all these crazy chances, and run the risk of losing everything? Why do you insist on playing further games with your body?"

Andrew did not answer.

Nor did he let any of Alvin Magdescu's objections prevent him from continuing to follow his chosen path. With the basic principles of his prosthetic devices established, he was able to develop a host of new applications involving virtually every organ of the body. And everything went pretty much as Magdescu had said it would—the money, the honors, the fame.

But the personal risks of which Magdescu had spoken did not materialize. The frequent upgrades which Andrew underwent over the next decade had no harmful effects whatever as they brought his android body closer and closer in its operational systems to the human norm.

The Feingold and Charney people had helped him to draft and negotiate the licensing agreement under which all the patent-protected prosthetic devices developed by Andrew Martin Laboratories would be manufactured and marketed by United States Robots and Mechanical Men on a royalty-payment basis. Andrew's patents were air-tight and the contract was a highly favorable one. Whatever irritation or resentment U. S. Robots might have felt all these years over the mere fact of Andrew's existence was forgotten, or at least put aside. Willy-nilly, they had to treat him with respect. He and the company were partners, now.

U. S. Robots established a special division to produce Andrew's devices, with factories on several continents and in low orbit. Marketing experts from the parent company were brought in to develop plans for distributing the new products everywhere on Earth and the space settlements. Surgeons, both human and robot, underwent courses of instruction at the U. S. Robots prosthetics facility so that they would be able to carry out the complicated installation procedures.

Demand for Andrew's prosthetic devices was immense. The flow of royalties was heavy right from the start and within a few years became overwhelming.

Andrew now owned the entire Martin-Charney estate, and much of the surrounding land—a wondrous stretch of clifftop terrain overlooking the Pacific Ocean for eight or ten kilometers. He lived in Sir's big house, but maintained his own old cottage nearby as a sentimental reminder of his early days of independent life after gaining free-robot status.

Farther down the property he built the imposing research facilities of Andrew Martin Laboratories. There was a little trouble with the zoning authorities about that, because this was supposed to be a quiet residential area and the research center that Andrew wanted to set up would be the size of a small university campus. There was also, perhaps, some lingering anti-robot feeling at work among the opposition.

But when his application came up for approval, Andrew's lawyer simply said, "Andrew Martin has given the world the prosthetic kidney, the prosthetic lung, the prosthetic heart, the prosthetic pancreas. In return all he asks is the right to continue his research in peace on the property where he has lived and worked for well over a hundred years. Who among us would refuse such a small request when it comes from so great a benefactor of mankind?" And after a certain amount of debate the zoning variance was granted and the buildings of the Andrew Martin Laboratories Research Center began to rise amid the somber cypresses and pines of what had, long ago, been the wooded estate of Gerald Martin.

Every year or two, Andrew would return to the gleaming operating theater at U. S. Robots for additional prosthetic upgrading of his own. Some of the changes were utterly trivial ones: the new fingernails and toenails, for example, virtually indistinguishable now from those of humans. Some of the changes were major: the new visual system, which although synthetically grown was able to duplicate the human eyeball in virtually every respect.

"Don't blame us if you come out of this permanently blind," Magdescu told him sourly, when Andrew went to him for the eye transplant.

"You aren't looking at this rationally, my friend," replied Andrew. "The worst that can happen to me is that I will be forced to go back to photo-optic cells. There is no risk whatever that I will suffer complete loss of eyesight."

"Well—" Magdescu said, and shrugged.

Andrew was right, of course. No one was forced to be permanently blind any more. But there were artificial eyes and then there were artificial eyes, and the photo-optic cells that had been a feature of Andrew's original android body were replaced with the new synthetic-organic eyes that Andrew Martin Laboratories had perfected. The fact that hundreds of thousands of aging human beings had been content for more than a generation to use photo-optic cells was irrelevant to Andrew. To him they looked artificial; they looked inhuman. He had always wanted true eyes. And now he had them.

Magdescu, after a while, gave up protesting. He had come to see that Andrew was destined to have his way in all things and that there was no point in raising objections to Andrew's schemes for new prosthetic upgrades. Besides, Magdescu was beginning to grow old now, and much of the fire and zeal that had been characteristic of him when Andrew first came to him had gone out of him by now. Already he had had several major prosthetic operations himself—a double kidney replacement, first, and then a new liver. Soon Magdescu would reach retirement age.

And then, no doubt, he would die, in ten or twenty years more, Andrew told himself. Another friend gone, swept away by the remorseless river of time.

Andrew himself, naturally, showed no signs of aging at all. For a time that troubled him enough that he debated having some cosmetic wrinkles added—a touch of crow's feet around his eyes, for example—and graying his hair. After giving the matter a little thought, though, he decided that to go in for such things would be a foolish affectation. Andrew did not see his upgrades that way at all: they represented his continued attempt to leave his robot origins behind and approach the physical form of a human being. He did not deny to himself that it had become his goal to do that. But there was no sense in becoming more human than the humans themselves. It struck him as pointless and absurd to subject his ever-more-human but still ageless android body to the external marks of aging.

Vanity had nothing to do with Andrew's decision—only logic. He was aware that humans had always tried to do everything in their power to conceal the effects that growing old had on their appearance. Andrew realized that it would be altogether ridiculous for him, exempted as he was from aging by his inherent android nature, to go out of his way deliberately to take those effects upon himself.

So he remained ever youthful-looking. And, of course, there was never any slackening of his physical vigor: a careful maintenance program made certain of that. But the years were passing, and passing swiftly now. Andrew was approaching the one hundred and fiftieth anniversary of his construction.

By this time Andrew was not only exceedingly wealthy but covered with the honors that Alvin Magdescu had foretold for him. Learned societies hastened to offer him fellowships and awards —in particular one society which was devoted to the new science he had established, the one he had called robobiology but which had come to be termed prosthetology. He was named its honorary president for life. Universities vied with one another to give him degrees. An entire room in his house—the one upstairs that once had been his woodworking studio, five generations before —was given over now to storing the myriad diplomas, medals, scrolls of honor, testimonial volumes, and other artifacts of Andrew's worldwide status as one of humanity's greatest benefactors.

The desire to recognize Andrew's contribution became so universal that he needed one full-time secretary simply to reply to all the invitations to attend testimonial banquets or accept awards and degrees. He rarely did attend any such ceremonies any longer, though he was unfailingly courteous in refusing, explaining that the continued program of his research made it inadvisable for him to do a great deal of traveling. But in fact most of these functions had come to irritate and bore him.

The first honorary degree from a major university had given him a thrill of vindication. No robot had ever received such an honor before.

But the fiftieth honorary degree? The hundredth? They had no meaning for him. They said more about the giver than about the recipient. Andrew had proved whatever point it was that he had set out to make about his intelligence and creativity long ago, and now he simply wanted to proceed with his work in peace, without having to make long trips and listen to speeches in his honor. He was surfeited with honor.

Boredom and irritation, Andrew knew, were exceedingly human traits, and it seemed to him that he had only begun to experience them in the past twenty or thirty years. Previously—so far as he could recall—he had been notably free from such afflictions, though from the beginning there had always been a certain unrobotic component of impatience in his makeup that he had chosen not to acknowledge for a long time. This new irritability, though: it was some side effect of the upgrades, he suspected. But not a troublesome one, at least not so far.

When his hundred and fiftieth anniversary came around and the U. S. Robots people let it be known that they wanted to hold a great testimonial dinner to mark the occasion, Andrew instructed his secretary, with some annoyance in his voice, to turn the invitation down. "Tell them I'm deeply touched, et cetera, et cetera, the usual stuff. But that I'm busy right now with an extremely complex project, et cetera, et cetera, and that in any case I'd just as soon not have a lot of fuss made over the anniversary, but I thank them very much, I understand the great significance of the gesture, and so forth—et cetera, et cetera, et cetera."

ISAAC ASIMOV AND ROBERT SILVERBERG

Usually a letter like that was enough to get him off the hook. But not this time.

Alvin Magdescu called him and said, "Look, Andrew, you can't do this."

"Can't do what?"

"Toss the U.S.R.M.M. testimonial dinner back in their faces like that."

"But I don't want it, Alvin."

"I realize that. All the same, you've got to go through with it. Once in a while you need to get out of that laboratory of yours and sit around letting a bunch of human beings bore you silly by telling you how remarkable you are."

"I've had quite enough of that over the past decade or two, thank you."

"Well, have a little more. You don't want to offend me, do you, Andrew?"

"You? What do you have to do with this? Why is it any concern of yours?" Magdescu was ninety-four years old now, and had retired six years before.

"Because," said Magdescu bitterly, "I was the one who suggested the whole thing. As a way of demonstrating my affection for you, you damned walking scrapheap, and also to express my thanks for the assortment of fantastic Andrew Martin prosthetic devices that have turned *me* into the same sort of scrapheap and permitted me to go on living as long as I have. I was going to be the master of ceremonies, the principal speaker. But no, Andrew, you simply can't be bothered, which makes me look extremely foolish. The finest creation that U. S. Robots and Mechanical Men ever brought into this world, and you can't take a single evening off to accept acknowledgment of that fact, and to give an old friend a little pleasure—a little pleasure, Andrew—"

Magdescu fell silent. His face, weathered now and gray-bearded, stared at Andrew somberly out of the screen.

"Well, then—" Andrew said, abashed.

And so he agreed to go to the testimonial dinner, after all. A chartered U. S. Robots luxury flitter picked him up and flew him

198

to the company headquarters. The dinner, in the grand wood-paneled meeting-hall of the great robotics complex, had some three hundred guests, all of them attired in the antiquated and uncomfortable clothing that was still considered proper formal dining costume for great occasions.

And it *was* a great occasion. Half a dozen members of the Regional Legislature were there, and one of the justices of the World Court, and five or six Nobel Prize laureates, and of course a scattering of Robertsons and Smythes and Smythe-Robertsons, along with a wide assortment of other dignitaries and celebrities from all over the world.

"So you showed up after all," Magdescu said. "I had my doubts right up to the last."

Andrew was struck by how small and bent Magdescu looked, how frail, how weary. But there was still a glow of the old mischief in the man's eyes.

"You know I could not have stayed away," Andrew told him. "Not really."

"I'm glad, Andrew. You're looking good."

"And so are you, Alvin."

Magdescu smiled ruefully. "You get more and more human all the time, don't you? You lie just like one of us, now. And how easily that bit of flattery rolled off your lips, Andrew! You didn't even hesitate."

"There is really no law against a robot's telling an untruth to a human being," said Andrew. "Unless the untruth would do harm, of course. And you do look good to me, Alvin."

"For a man my age, you mean."

"Yes, for a man your age, I suppose I should say. If you insist on my being so precise."

The after-dinner speeches were the usual orotund pompous things: expressions of admiration and wonder over Andrew's many achievements. One speaker followed another, and they all seemed ponderous and dreary to Andrew, even those who in fact managed a good bit of wit and grace. Their styles of delivery might vary, but the content was always the same. Andrew had heard it all before, many too many times.

And there was an unspoken subtext in each speech that never ceased to trouble him: the patronizing implication that he had done wonderful things *for a robot*, that it was close to miraculous that a mere mechanical construction like himself should have been able to think so creatively and to transmute his thoughts into such extraordinary accomplishments. Perhaps it was the truth; but it was a painful truth for Andrew to face, and there seemed no way of escaping it.

Magdescu was the last to speak.

It had been a very long evening, and Magdescu looked pale and tired as he stood up. But Andrew, who was seated next to him, observed him making a strenuous effort to pull himself together, raising his head high, squaring his shoulders, filling his lungs—his Andrew Martin Laboratories prosthetic lungs—with a deep draught of air.

"My friends, I won't waste your time repeating the things that everyone else has said here tonight. We all know what Andrew Martin has done for mankind. Many of us have experienced his work at first hand—for I know that sitting before me tonight as I speak are scores of you who have Andrew's prosthetic devices installed in your bodies. And I am of your number. So I want to say, simply, that it was my great privilege to work with Andrew Martin in the early days of prosthetology—for I myself played a small part in the development of those devices of his which are so essential to our lives today. And in particular I want to acknowledge that I would not be here tonight but for Andrew Martin. But for him and his magnificent work, I would have been dead fifteen or twenty years ago—and so would many of you.

"Therefore, my friends, let me propose a toast. Lift your glasses with me now, and take a sip of this good wine, in honor of the remarkable individual who has brought such great changes to medical science, and who today attains the imposing and significant age of one hundred fifty years—I give you, my friends, Andrew Martin, the Sesquicentennial Robot!"

Andrew had never managed to cultivate a liking for wine or even any understanding of its merits, but as a result of his combustion-chamber upgrades at least he had the physiological capacity to consume it. Sometimes he actually did, when social contexts seemed to require him to. And so when Alvin Magdescu turned toward him, therefore, his eyes shining with emotion, his face flushed, his glass upraised, Andrew raised his own glass in response, and downed a long drink of the wine that it contained.

But in fact he felt little joy. Though the sinews of his face had long since been redesigned to display a range of emotions, he had sat through the entire evening looking solemnly passive, and even at this climactic moment he could manage nothing better than a perfunctory half-smile. Even that took effort. Magdescu had meant well, but his words had given Andrew pain. He did not want to be a Sesquicentennial Robot.

EIGHTEEN

IT WAS PROSTHETOLOGY that finally took Andrew off the Earth. He had not felt any need in the past to take trips into space—or to travel very widely on Earth itself, for that matter—but Earth was no longer the prime center of human civilization, and most of what was new and eventful was taking place in the offworld settlements—notably on the Moon, which now had come to be a world more Earthlike than Earth in every respect but its gravitational pull. The underground cities that had begun as mere crude cavern-shelters in the Twenty-First Century now were opulent, brightly lit cities, densely populated and rapidly growing.

The citizens of the Moon, like humans everywhere, had need of prosthetic work. No one was content any more with the traditional three score and ten, and when organs broke down, it was standard procedure to replace them.

But the low lunar gravity, though in some ways it had its advantages for humans living under reduced gravitational stress, created a host of problems for the prosthetic surgeons. Devices designed to deliver a smooth and regular flow of blood or hormones or digestive fluid or some other fundamental substance of life in Earth's gravity would not function as reliably under a gravitational pull that was only one sixth as great. There were problems, too, of tensile strength, of durability, of unexpected and unwanted feedback complications.

The lunar prosthetologists had begged Andrew for years to visit the Moon and get a first-hand look at the problems of adaptation that they were forced to deal with. The U. S. Robots marketing division on the Moon repeatedly urged him to go.

On a couple of occasions, it was even suggested that, under the terms of the licensing agreement, Andrew was *required* to go; but Andrew met that suggestion—and it was phrased as a suggestion, not as an order—with such chilly refusal that the company did not attempt to raise the issue a third time.

But still the requests for help came from the doctors on the Moon. And again and again Andrew declined—until, suddenly, he found himself asking himself, *Why not go? Why is it so important to stay on Earth all the time?*

Obviously he was needed up there. No one was ordering him to go—no one would dare, not these days—but nevertheless he could not lose sight of the fact that he had been brought into the world for the purpose of serving mankind, and nothing said that the sphere of his service was limited only to Earth. So be it, Andrew thought. And within an hour his acceptance of the latest invitation was being beamed Moonward.

On a cool, drizzly autumn day Andrew went by flitter down to San Francisco, and from there took the underground tube to the big Western Spaceport Facility in the district of Nevada. He had never gone anywhere by tube before. Over the past fifty years nuclear-powered subterrenes had drilled a network of wide tunnels through the deep-lying rocks of the continent, and now high-speed trains moving on silent inertialess tracks offered swift and simple long-distance travel, while much of the surface zone was allowed to revert to its natural state. To Andrew it seemed that he was reaching the spaceport in Nevada almost before the train had set out from the San Francisco terminal.

And now into space at last—the lunar journey—

He was handled at every stage of the embarkation procedure like some fine and highly breakable piece of rare porcelain. Important officials of U. S. Robots clustered around him, eagerly assisting him with the minutiae of checking in and being cleared for flight.

They were surprised at how little baggage he had brought with him—just one small bag, containing a couple of changes of clothing and a few holocubes for reading during the trip—considering that he was likely to be staying on the Moon anywhere from three months to a year. But Andrew simply shrugged and said that he had never felt the need to haul a lot of possessions around with him when he traveled. That was true enough; but of course Andrew had never taken a journey of more than a few days' duration before, either.

It was necessary for him to go through an elaborate decontamination process before boarding the ship: a virtual fumigation and sterilization, in fact. "The Moon people have very strict rules, you understand," the apologetic spaceport functionary told him, as Andrew was reading through the long list of procedures that would be performed on all departing passengers. "They live in such complete isolation from our terrestrial microbes up there, you see—and so they feel that they'd be at high risk of epidemic if anything that their systems couldn't handle should happen to be brought to them from Earth—"

Andrew saw no need to explain that his android body was not subject to infection by microorganisms of any kind. The spaceport functionary was surely aware that Andrew was a robot—it said so right on his embarkation papers, serial number and all. It didn't take much intelligence to realize that robots, even android robots, were unlikely to be carriers of plagues.

But the man was a bureaucrat first and foremost, and it was his job to see to it that everyone who boarded the ship to the Moon underwent the full and proper decontamination procedures, whether or not that person was capable of becoming contaminated in the first place.

Andrew had had enough experience with this variety of humanity by this time to know that it would be a waste of time and breath to raise any objections. And so—patiently, tolerantly—he let himself be put through the entire preposterous series of treatments. They could do him no harm and by accepting them he avoided the dreary endless bureaucratic discussions that his refusal would be likely to provoke. Besides, he took a kind of perverse satisfaction in being treated like everyone else.

Then at last he was on board the ship.

A steward came by to see to it that Andrew was safely stowed in his gravity sling, and handed him a pamphlet—it was the fourth time he had been given a copy of it in the past two days—on what he was likely to experience during the short journey.

It was designed to be reassuring. There would be some mild stress during the initial moments of acceleration, he was told, but nothing that he would have difficulty in handling. Once the ship was in full flight, its gravity-control mechanisms would be brought into play to compensate for the zero gravitational pull that the vessel would be under, so that the passengers would never be exposed to the sensations of free fall. (Unless they wanted to be, in which case they were welcome to enter the zero-grav lounge in the aft compartment.) During the voyage, the simulated gravity aboard ship would steadily but imperceptibly be reduced, so that by the time the ship reached its destination the passengers would be acclimated to the much weaker pull that they would be experiencing during their stay in the lunar settlements. And so on and so on, details of mealtime procedures and exercise programs and other such things, a stream of bland, soothing information.

Andrew took it all in stride. His android body had been designed to withstand higher than Earth-norm gravitation from the outset, not by his special request, but simply because it had been relatively easy for the designers, starting from scratch, to build all sorts of little superiorities into the natural human form. How and when he took his meals aboard the ship, and what might be on the menu, were all irrelevant items to him. So was the exercise schedule. Andrew had often found undeniable pleasure in taking a brisk walk along the beach or a stroll through the forest surrounding his property, but his body needed no program of regular exercise to maintain its tone.

The voyage, then, became for him mainly a matter of waiting. He anticipated few if any problems of adaptation to space travel and he experienced none. The ship lifted easily from its pad; the ship quickly left Earth's atmosphere behind; the ship arced smoothly through the dark emptiness of space and followed its routine course toward the Moon. Space travel had long since passed out of the stage of being exciting; even for a first-time traveler, it was a humdrum affair these days, which was pretty much the way most people preferred it to be.

The one aspect of the voyage that Andrew did find stirring was the view from the ship's observation window. It gave him shivers down his ceramic spine; it sent the blood pulsing faster through his dacron arteries; it set up a tingling of excitement in the synthetic epidermal cells of his fingertips.

The Earth seen from space looked extraordinarily lovely to him: a perfect disk of blue, stippled with white masses of clouds. The outlines of the continents were surprisingly indistinct. Andrew had expected to see them sharply traced as they were on a geographic globe; but in fact they were no more than vaguely apparent, and it was the wondrous swirling of the atmospheric clouds against the vastness of the seas that gave the Earth its beauty from this vantage-point. It was strange and wondrous, also, to be able to look upon the entire face of the world at once this way—for the ship had moved very swiftly out into space and the planet behind them was now small enough to be seen in its entirety, a turning blue ball constantly dwindling against the black star-flecked background of space.

Andrew felt a powerful urge to carve a plaque that would represent something of what he saw now as he looked down on the small Earth set against that gigantic background. He could use inlays in dark woods and light ones, he told himself, to show the contrast between the sea and the cloud patterns. And Andrew smiled at that; for it was the first time in years that he had so much as thought of doing any work in wood.

Then there was the Moon, brilliantly white, its scarred face growing ever larger. Its beauty—of a different kind—excited Andrew too: the starkness, the simplicity, the airless static unchangeability of it.

Not all of Andrew's fellow passengers agreed. "How ugly it is!" exclaimed one woman who was making her first lunar journey. "You look at it from Earth on a night when it's full and you think, How beautiful, how wonderfully romantic. And then you get out here and you see it close up and you can't help shuddering at all the pockmarks and cracks and blemishes. And the sheer *deadness* of it!"

Perhaps you may shudder at it, Andrew thought, listening to her go on. But I do not.

To him the marks on the Moon's face were a fascinating kind of inscription: the long record of time, a lengthy poem that had taken billions of years to create and demanded admiration for its immensity. And he could find no deadness in the Moon's white face, only purity, a beautiful austerity, a wonderful cool majesty that seemed almost like something sacred.

But what do I know about beauty? Andrew asked himself acidly. Or about what might be sacred? I am only a robot, after all. Whatever aesthetic or spiritual perceptions I may think I have are mere accidents of the positronic pathways, unintended, unreliable, perhaps to be regarded as manufacturing defects rather than any kind of meritorious special feature of my construction.

He turned away from the viewing screen and spent most of the rest of the voyage sitting calmly in his gravity sling, waiting to get to the Moon.

Three officials of the lunar office of U. S. Robots and Mechanical Men were at the Luna City spaceport to greet Andrew when he disembarked: two men and a woman. They provided him— when he was done with all the maddening little bureacratic maneuvers of arrival and was finally allowed to step out of the ship and approach the welcoming committee—with one of the most powerful surprises of his long life.

When he first noticed them they were waving to him. Andrew

knew that they were here for him because the woman carried a brightly lettered placard that said, WELCOME TO LUNA CITY, ANDREW MARTIN! But what he didn't expect was that the younger of the two men in the group would walk up to him, put out his hand, and say with a warm smile, "We're absolutely thrilled that you decided to make the trip, Dr. Martin."

Dr. Martin? *Dr. Martin?*

The only doctorates that Andrew had received were honorary ones, and he would hardly have had the audacity ever to refer to himself as "Dr. Martin." But if the U. S. Robots man had greeted him simply as "*Mr.* Martin," that would have been astounding enough.

No one on Earth had ever called him "Dr. Martin" or "Mr. Martin" or anything else but "Andrew," not even once, never in all his hundred fifty-plus years.

It was unthinkable for anyone to do so. On formal occasions— when he had appeared in court, or when he was being given an award or an honorary degree—he was usually addressed as "Andrew Martin," but that was as far in the direction of formality as anybody ever went. Often enough, even when he was the guest of honor at some scientific meeting, he was addressed straightforwardly as "Andrew" by perfect strangers and no one, not even he, thought anything of it. Though most people tended to call robots by nicknames based on their serial designations rather than by the serial designations themselves, it was rare for a robot to have a surname at all. It had been Sir's special little pleasure to refer to him as "Andrew Martin"—a member of the family— rather than just "Andrew," and the custom had become permanent.

But to be called "Dr. Martin"—even *"Mr. Martin"*—

"Is anything wrong, sir?" the U. S. Robots man asked, as Andrew stood blinking with amazement before him.

"No, of course not. Except—it's only that—ah—"

"Sir?"

Being called "sir" like that didn't make things any easier. It was like a repeated electrical jolt.

"Sir, what's the matter?"

They were all concerned now, frowning and gathering close around him.

Andrew said, "Are you aware that I'm a robot?"

"Well—" They exchanged troubled glances. They looked tremendously flustered. "Yes, sir. Yes, we are."

"And yet you call me 'Dr. Martin' and 'sir'?"

"Well—yes. Of course. Your work, sir—your extraordinary achievements—a simple mark of respect—you are *Andrew Martin,* after all!"

"Andrew Martin the robot, yes. On Earth it's not the custom to address robots as 'Dr.' something or 'Mr.' something or 'sir.' I'm not accustomed to it. It's never happened to me at all, as a matter of fact. It simply isn't done."

"Does it offend you—sir?" the woman asked, and as that last word escaped she looked as though she would have liked to swallow it.

"It surprises me, actually. It surprises me very much. On Earth—"

"Ah, but this isn't Earth," said the older of the two men. "We're a different sort of society here. You have to understand that, Dr. Martin. We're a lot more freewheeling—a lot more informal than people are on Earth—"

"Informal? And so you call a robot 'Dr.'? I would expect informal people to be calling strangers by their first names, and instead you greet me with high-flown formal honorifics, giving me a title which in fact I've never earned and have no business letting you use, and—"

They were beginning to look less distressed now. The woman said, "I think I understand. Well, sir—I hope you don't mind if I call you that, sir—we do call each other by our first names most of the time—I'm Sandra, this is David, this is Carlos—and we generally call our robots by first names too, just as people do on Earth. But you are special. You are the famous Andrew Martin, sir. You are the founder of prosthetology, you are the great creative genius who has done so much for mankind. Informal

209

though we may be among ourselves, it's just a matter of elementary respect, sir, when we—"

"You see, it's really hard for us to walk right up to you and call you 'Andrew' just like that," the one called Carlos said. "Even though in fact you are—you are—"

He faltered into silence.

"A robot?" Andrew finished for him.

"A robot, yes," Carlos said indistinctly, not meeting Andrew's gaze.

"Besides," David said, "you don't *look* much like a robot. You don't look like a robot at all, as a matter of fact. We know that you are, of course, but nevertheless—I mean—that is—" And he flushed and looked away, too.

Things were getting tangled again. They seemed destined to put their feet in their mouths no matter what they tried to say. Andrew felt sorry for them, but a little annoyed, too.

"Please," he said, "I may not look much like a robot, but a robot is what I have been for more than a hundred fifty years and it comes as no great shock to me to think of myself as one. And where I come from, robots are addressed by their first names only. That seems to be the custom here too, I gather—except for me. If you have too much respect for my great accomplishments to be able to do that easily, then I appeal to the freewheeling informality you were just telling me about. This is a frontier world: let's all be equals, then. If you are Sandra and Carlos and David, then I am Andrew. Is that all right?"

They were beaming now.

"Well, if you put it that way, Andrew—" Carlos said, and stuck out his hand a second time.

After that everything went more smoothly. Some of the U. S. Robots people called him "Andrew," and some called him "Dr. Martin," and some of them would go back and forth between the two almost at random.

Andrew grew used to it. He saw that this was indeed a rough and ready culture up here, with many fewer taboos and ingrained social patterns than on Earth. The line between humans and robots was still a distinct one, yes; but Andrew himself, because of his android body and his record of high scientific achievement, occupied an ambiguous place somewhere along that boundary, and in the easygoing society on the Moon it evidently was possible for the people he worked among to forget for long stretches of time that he was a robot at all.

As for the lunar robots, they didn't seem to recognize any sign of his robot origins. Invariably they treated him with the robotic obsequiousness that was considered a human being's due. He was always "Dr. Martin" to them, with plenty of bowing and scraping and general subservience.

Andrew had mixed feelings about all of this. Despite all that he had told them about being quite accustomed to thinking of himself as a robot and being addressed like one, he was not completely sure that it was true.

On the one hand, being called "Mr." or "Dr." instead of "Andrew" was a tribute to the excellence of his android upgradings and to the high quality of his positronic brain. It had been his intention for many years to transform himself in such a way that he would move from a purely robotic identity into the gray zone of an identity that approached being human, and obviously he had achieved just that.

And yet—and yet—

How strange it felt to be addressed in terms of such respect by humans! How uncomfortable it made him, really. He grew used to it but Andrew never really felt at ease with it.

These people couldn't seem to remember for any significant length of time that he was a robot; but a robot was what he was, all the same—much as he sometimes would like to pretend otherwise—and it felt vaguely fraudulent to be treated like a fellow human being by them.

Indeed, Andrew knew, he had explicitly asked for it. "Let's all be equals, then," he had told Sandra and Carlos and David at the spaceport. And they had agreed.

But there was hardly a day thereafter when he was not amazed at his own boldness. Equals? *Equals?* How could he have dared even to suggest such a thing? Phrasing it as a direct instruction, no less—virtually an order! Saying it in a casual, jaunty way, like one human being to another.

Hypocrisy, Andrew thought.

Arrogance.

Delusions of grandeur.

Yes. Yes. Yes. He could buy a human-appearing body for himself, he could fill it with prosthetic devices that performed many of the functions of a human body whether he needed those functions performed or not, he could look human beings straight in the eye and speak coolly to them as though he were their equal— but none of that *made* him their equal. That was the reality that Andrew could not deny.

In the eyes of the law he was a robot and always would be, no matter how many upgrades he was given, or how ingenious they might be. He had no citizenship. He could not vote. He could not hold public office, even the most trivial. About the only civil rights Andrew had, despite all that the Charneys had done over the years on his behalf, were the right to own himself, and the right to go about freely without being humiliated by any passing human who cared to harass him, and the right to do business as a corporation. And also the right—such as it was—to pay taxes.

"Let's all be equals," he had said, as if by merely saying so he could make it be. What folly! What gall!

But the mood soon passed and rarely returned. Except in the dark moments when he berated himself this way, though, Andrew found himself enjoying his stay on the Moon, and it was a particularly fruitful time for him creatively.

The Moon was an exciting, intellectually stimulating place. The civilization of Earth was mature and sedate, but the Moon was the frontier, with all the wild energy that frontier challenges inevitably called forth.

Life was a little on the frantic side in the underground lunar cities—constant expansion was going on, and you could not help being aware of the eternal throbbing of the jackhammer subterrenes as new caverns were melted into being daily so that in six

months the next group of suburbs could be undergoing construction. The pace was fast and the people were far more competitive and vigorous than those Andrew had known on Earth.
Startling new technical developments came thick and fast there.
Radical new ideas were proposed at the beginning of one week
and enacted into law by the end of the next.

One of the prosthetologists explained it to him: "It's a genetic
thing, Andrew. Everyone on Earth with any get-up-and-go got up
and went a long time ago, and here we all are out on the edge of
civilization, inventing our way as we go along, while those who
remained behind have raised a race that's been bred to remain
behind and do things the most familiar comfortable way possible.
From here on in, I think, the future belongs to those of us who
live in space. Earth will become a mere backwater world."

"You really believe that?" Andrew asked.

"Yes. I do."

He wondered what would become of him, living on and on
through the decades and centuries ahead, if any such decadence
and decline truly was going to overcome the world. His immediate answer was that it made no difference to him if Earth became
some sort of sleepy backwater where "progress" was an obscene
word. He no longer had need of progress now that he had attained the upgrade he had most deeply desired. His body was
virtually human in form; he had his estate; he had his work, in
which he had achieved enormous success; he would live as he
always had, no matter what might be going on around him.

But then he sometimes thought wistfully of the possibility of
remaining on the Moon, or even going deeper out into space.
On Earth he was Andrew the robot, forced to go into court and
do battle every time he wanted one of the rights or privileges that
he felt his intelligence and contributions to society entitled him
to have. Out here, though, where everything was starting with a
fresh slate, it was quite conceivable that he could simply leave his
robot identity behind and blend into the human population as
Dr. Andrew Martin.

Nobody here seemed to be troubled by that possibility. From

213

his very first moments on the Moon they had virtually been invit-ing him to step across the invisible boundary between human and robot if that was what he wanted to do.

It was tempting.

It was very tempting indeed.

The months turned into years—three of them, now—and An-drew remained on the Moon, working with the lunar pros-thetologists, helping them make the adaptations that were neces-sary in order that the Andrew Martin Laboratories artificial organs could function at perfect efficiency when installed in hu-man beings who lived under low-gravity conditions.

It was challenging work, for, though he himself was un-troubled by the lower gravity of the lunar environment, humans in whom standard Earth-model prosthetic devices had been in-stalled tended to have a much more difficult time of it. Andrew was able, though, to meet each difficulty with a useful modifica-tion, and one by one the problems were resolved.

Now and then Andrew missed his estate on the California coast —not so much the grand house itself as the cool fogs of summer, the towering redwood trees, the rugged beach, the crashing surf. But it began to seem to him as though he had settled into perma-nent residence on the Moon. He stayed on into a fourth year, and a fifth.

Then one day he paid a visit to a bubbledome on the lunar surface, and saw the Earth in all its wondrous beauty hanging in the sky—tiny, at this distance, but vivid, glowing, a blue jewel that glistened brilliantly in the night.

It is my home, he thought suddenly. The mother world—the fountain of humanity—

Andrew felt it pulling him—calling him home. At first it was a pull he could scarcely understand. It seemed wholly irrational to him.

And then understanding came. His work on the Moon was done, basically. But he still had unfinished business down there on Earth.

The following week, Andrew booked his passage home on a

liner that was leaving at the end of the month. And then he called back and arranged to take an even earlier flight.

He returned to an Earth that seemed cozy and ordinary and quiet in comparison to the dynamic life of the lunar settlement. Nothing of any significance appeared to have changed in the five years of his absence. As his Moon-ship descended toward it, the Earth seemed to Andrew like a vast placid park, sprinkled here and there with the small settlements and minor cities of the decentralized Third Millennium civilization.

One of the first things Andrew did was to visit the offices of Feingold and Charney to announce his return.

The current senior partner, Simon DeLong, hurried out to greet him. In Paul Charney's time, DeLong had been a very junior clerk, callow and self-effacing, but that had been a long time ago and he had matured into a powerful, commanding figure whose unchallenged ascent to the top rung of the firm had been inevitable. He was a broad-shouldered man with heavy features, who wore his thick dark hair shaven down the middle in the tonsured style that had lately become popular.

There was a surprised look on DeLong's face. "We had been told you were returning, Andrew," he said—with just a bit of uncertainty in his voice at the end, as though he too had briefly considered calling him "Mr. Martin"—"but we weren't expecting you until next week."

"I became impatient," said Andrew brusquely. He was anxious to get to the point. "On the Moon, Simon, I was in charge of a research team of twenty or thirty human scientists. I gave orders and nobody questioned my authority. Many of them referred to me as 'Dr. Martin' and I was treated in all ways as an individual worthy of the highest respect. The lunar robots deferred to me as they would to a human being. For all practical purposes I *was* a human being for the entire duration of my stay on the Moon."

A wary look entered DeLong's eyes. Plainly he had no idea where Andrew was heading with all this, and it was the natural caution of a lawyer who did not quite understand yet the troublesome new direction in which an important client seemed to be veering.

"How unusual that must have seemed, Andrew," he said, in a flat, remote way.

"Unusual, yes. But not displeasing. Not displeasing at all, Simon."

"Yes. I'm sure that's so. How interesting, Andrew."

Andrew said sharply, "Well, now I'm back on Earth and I'm a robot again. Not even a second-class citizen—not a citizen at all, Simon. Nothing. I don't care for it. If I can be treated as a human being while I'm on the Moon, why not here?"

Without varying his careful, cautious tone DeLong said, "But you *are* treated as a human being here, my dear Andrew! You have a fine home and title to it is vested in your name. You are the head of a great research laboratory. Your income is so huge it staggers the mind, and no one would question your right to it. When you come here to the offices of Feingold and Charney, the senior partner himself is at your beck and call, as you see. In every *de facto* way you have long since won acceptance for yourself as a human being, on Earth and on the Moon, by humans and by robots. What more can you want?"

"To be a human being *de facto* isn't enough. I want not only to be treated as one, but to have the legal status and rights of one. I want to be a human being *de jure*."

"Ah," DeLong said. He looked extremely uncomfortable. "Ah. I see."

"Do you, Simon?"

"Of course. Don't you think I know the whole background of the Andrew Martin story? Years ago, Paul Charney spent hours going over your files with me—showing your step-by-step evolution, beginning as a metallic robot of the—NDR series, was it?—and going on to the transformation into your android identity. And of course I've been apprised of each new upgrading of your present body. Then the details of the legal evolution as well as the physical—the winning of your freedom, and the other civil rights that followed. I'd be a fool, Andrew, if I didn't realize that it's been your goal from the start to turn yourself into a human being."

"Perhaps not from the start, Simon. I think there was a long period when I was content simply to be a superior robot—a period when I denied even to myself any awareness of the full capabilities of my brain. But I deny it no longer. I'm the equal of any human being in any ability you could name, and superior to most. I want the full legal status that I'm entitled to."

"Entitled?"

"Entitled, yes."

DeLong pursed his lips, toyed nervously with one earlobe, ran his hand down the middle of his scalp where a swath of thick black hair had been mowed away.

"Entitled," he said again, after a moment or two. "Now that's another matter altogether, Andrew. We have to face the undeniable fact that, however much you may be like a human being in intelligence and capabilities and even appearance, nevertheless you simply are *not* a human being."

"In what way not?" Andrew demanded. "I have the shape of a human being and bodily organs equivalent to some of those that a prosthetized human being has. I have the mental ability of a human being—a highly intelligent one. I have contributed artistically, literarily, and scientifically to human culture as much as any human being now alive. What more can one ask?"

DeLong flushed. "Forgive me, Andrew: but I have to remind you that you are not part of the human gene pool. You are outside it entirely. You *resemble* a human being but in fact you are something else, something—artificial."

"Granted, Simon. And the people who are walking around with bodies full of prosthetic devices? Devices which, incidentally, I invented for them? Are those people not artificial at least in part?"

"In part, yes."

"Well, I'm human in part."

DeLong's eyes flashed. "Which part, Andrew?"

"Here," said Andrew. He pointed to his head. "And here."

He tapped a finger against his chest. "My mind. My heart. I may be artificial, alien, inhuman so far as your strict genetic definition goes. But I'm human in every way that counts. And I can be recognized as such legally. In the old days when there were a hundred separate countries on the Earth and each one had its own complicated rules of citizenship, it was, even so, possible for a Frenchman to become English or a Japanese to become a Brazilian, simply by going through a set of legal procedures. There was nothing genetically Brazilian about the Japanese, but he became Brazilian all the same, once the law had recognized him as such. The same can be done for me. I can become a *naturalized* human the way people once became naturalized as citizens of countries not their own."

"You've devoted a lot of thought to all of this, haven't you, Andrew?"

"Yes. I have."

"Very ingenious. Very, very ingenious. A naturalized human being! —And what about the Three Laws, then?"

"What about them?"

"They're an innate part of your positronic brain. I need hardly remind you that they put you in a condition of permanent subservience to humans that's beyond the power of any court of law to remedy. The Three Laws can't be edited out of you, can they, Andrew?"

"True enough."

"Then they'll have to remain, won't they? And they will continue to require you to obey all humans, if necessary to lay down your life for them, to refrain from doing them any sort of harm. You may somehow be able to get yourself declared human, but you'll still be governed by built-in operating rules that no human being has ever been subject to."

Andrew nodded. "And the Japanese who became Brazilians still had skin of the Japanese color and eyelids of the Japanese type and all of the other special racial characteristics that Oriental people have and the European-descended inhabitants of Brazil do not. But under Brazilian law they were Brazilians even so.

And under human law I will be human, even though I still have the Three Laws structure built into me."

"But the very presence of that structure within your brain may be deemed to disqualify you from—"

"No," Andrew said. "Why should it? The First Law simply says I mustn't injure any human being or allow one to come to harm through my inaction. Aren't you bound by the same restriction? Isn't every civilized person? The only difference is that I have no *choice* but to be law-abiding, whereas other human beings can opt to behave in an uncivilized way if they're willing to take their chances with the police. And then the Second Law: it requires me to obey humans, yes. But they aren't required to give me orders, and if I have full human status it might well be deemed a breach of civility for anyone to put me in a position where through my own innate makeup I would be obliged to do something against my will. That would be taking advantage of my handicap, so to speak. The fact that I *have* the handicap doesn't matter. There are plenty of handicapped human beings and nobody would say that they aren't human. And as for the Third Law, which prevents me from acting self-destructively, I would hardly say that that is much of a burden for a sane person to bear. And so you see, Simon—"

"Yes. Yes, Andrew, I do see." DeLong was chuckling now. "All right. You've beaten me down and I give in. You're as human as anyone needs to be: you deserve to have that confirmed in some legal way."

"Well, then, if Feingold and Charney will set about the process of—"

"Not so fast, please, Andrew. You've handed me a very tall order. Human prejudice hasn't vanished overnight, you know. There'll be tremendous opposition to any attempt we might make to get you declared human."

"I would expect so. But we've defeated tremendous opposition before, going back to the time when George Charney and his son Paul went out and won me my freedom."

"Yes. The trouble is that this time we'd have to go before the

World Legislature, not the Regional one, and get a law passed that will define you as a human being. Frankly, I wouldn't be very optimistic about that."

"I'm paying you to be optimistic."

"Yes. Yes, of course, Andrew."

"Good. We're agreed, then, that this can be accomplished. The only question is how. Where do you think we ought to begin?"

DeLong said, after only the briefest of hesitations, "One good starting point would be for you to have a conversation with some influential member of the Legislature."

"Any particular one?"

"The Chairman of the Science and Technology Committee, perhaps."

"An excellent idea. Can you arrange a meeting for me right away, Simon?"

"If you'd like. But you scarcely need me to serve as your intermediary, Andrew. Someone as widely known and honored as you can easily—"

"No. *You* arrange it." (It didn't even occur to Andrew that he was giving a flat order to a human being. He had grown accustomed to that on the Moon.) "I want him to know that the firm of Feingold and Charney is backing me in this to the hilt."

"Well, now—"

"To the hilt, Simon. In one hundred and seventy-three years I have in one fashion or another contributed greatly to this firm. I might almost say that the firm in its present form would not exist but for the work that I have provided for it to do. I brought that work here because in times past I have been very well served by certain members of this firm, and I have felt myself under an obligation to reciprocate. I am under no obligation to Feingold and Charney now. It is rather the other way around, now, and I am calling in my debts."

DeLong said, "I'll do whatever I can."

NINETEEN

THE CHAIRMAN of the Science and Technology Committee of the World Legislature came from the East Asian Region and she was a woman: a small, delicately built, almost elfin woman who very likely was not nearly as fragile as she appeared. Her name was Chee Li-hsing and her transparent garments (which obscured what she wanted obscured by sheer dazzle alone) gave her the look of being nothing more than an elegant little trinket wrapped in plastic. In the splendor of her huge high-ceilinged office on the eighty-fourth floor of the magnificent green-glass tower that was the New York headquarters of the World Legislature she appeared tiny, almost insignificant. Yet she radiated a look of great competence, efficiency, forcefulness.

She said, "I sympathize with your wish to have full human rights. As perhaps you know, there have been times in history when great segments of the human population have been deprived of their own human rights, and have fought furiously—and ultimately successfully—to regain them. But those people suffered greatly under tyrannies of one kind or another before they won their freedom. You, on the other hand, have enjoyed a successful and rewarding life of unending achievement and reward. I imagine you are a widely envied person. So tell me, please: what rights can you possibly want that you do not already have?''

"As simple a thing as my right to life," Andrew replied. "A robot can be dismantled at any time."

"A human being can be executed at any time."

"And when, I ask you, was the last time that such an execution took place?''

"Why—" Li-hsing shrugged. "Of course, the death penalty is not currently employed in our civilization, and it hasn't been for a long time. But certainly it's been imposed to an enormous extent throughout history. And there's no fundamental reason why it couldn't be reinstated next year, if the citizens and the Legislature saw fit to do so."

"All right. You can all go back to cutting each other's heads off, or giving each other lethal jolts of electricity, or whatever, at a moment's notice, if you like. But the fact remains that no human being has been put to death by legal execution in so many years that nobody can remember the last time, and there's absolutely no agitation that I've ever heard of to start performing such executions again. Whereas even now—right now, here, today—I could be ended merely by the word of a human being in authority. No trial. No appeals procedure. You yourself could ring a bell and call your security guards in and say, 'This robot has displeased me. Take him out and dismantle him.' And they would take me out and dismantle me, just like that."

"Impossible!"

"I assure you it would be perfectly legal."

"But you are the head of a great company—a person of wealth and substance and high reputation—"

"Maybe after it had been done my company would be able to sue the Legislature, then, for loss of my services. But I'd still be terminated, wouldn't I? The only laws that protect robots are property laws. If you terminate somebody else's robot unjustifiably, that person can seek damages against you, and collect the value of the robot and maybe a punitive award as well. Fine. Very fine, if you're the human being in the case who's been damaged.

But if you're the robot who happened to be terminated, why, the lawsuit doesn't bring you back into existence, does it? Does it, Madam Chairman?"

"This is a mere *reductio ad absurdum*. No one would dream of—dismantling—you. Of terminating you."

"Perhaps not. But where is my legal protection against having it done to me?"

"I repeat: a *reductio ad absurdum*. You've lived for nearly two hundred years, as I understand it. Tell me: how many times during that considerable period have you ever been in danger of—termination?"

"Once, actually. I was rescued. But the order for my dismantling had already been given."

"I find that hard to believe," said Chee Li-hsing.

"It was many years ago. I was still in the metallic form, then, and had only just won my freedom."

"There. My point is proven. No one would dare to touch you nowadays!"

"But I have no more legal protection now than I did then. I remain a robot in the eyes of the law. And if someone chose to have me dismantled, I would have no recourse—" Andrew broke off in mid-sentence. This line of reasoning was getting him nowhere. It was too far-fetched, he saw. "All right. Perhaps no one would attempt to harm me. But even so—even so—" Andrew tried desperately to allow no sign of pleading to show, but his carefully designed tricks of human expression and tone of voice betrayed him here. And at last he gave in entirely. "What it really comes down to is this: I very much want to be a man. I have wanted it more and more through six generations of human beings, as the full capacity and range of my mind gradually became apparent to me, and now the urge is overwhelming in me. I can't bear to think of myself as a robot any more—or to have others think of me that way."

Chee Li-hsing looked up at Andrew out of darkly sympathetic eyes.

"So that is it," she said. "As simple as that."

"Simple?"

"A desire to belong to the human race. A powerful yearning—no matter how irrational. It's very human of you to have such feelings, Andrew."

"Thank you." He wasn't certain whether she had meant to patronize him. He hoped not.

Li-hsing said, "I can take your case before the Legislature, yes. And I suppose the Legislature could indeed pass a law declaring you to be a human being. The Legislature has the power to pass a law declaring a stone statue to be defined as a human being, if it cared to. But the statue would still be a statue, nonetheless. And you—"

"No. It's not the same thing. A statue is an inanimate thing of stone, whereas I—I—"

"Of course. It *is* different. I understand that. But the Legislators may not see it that way. They will not pass any laws turning statues into living things, and I doubt very much that they'd be willing to pass a law turning a robot into a human, either, no matter how eloquently I present your case. Legislators are as human as the rest of the population and I need hardly point out to you that there are certain elements of suspicion and prejudice against robots that have existed since the first robots were developed."

"And exist even now?"

"Even now. As you surely must know. And so the Legislature would be unwilling to act in the way you wish it to. We would all readily concede the fact that you have earned the prize of humanity many times over, and yet we would be frightened by the political consequences of setting an undesirable precedent."

"Undesirable?" Andrew cried, unable to keep a tone of exasperation from creeping into his voice. "Why undesirable? If I'm such a wonderful benefactor of humanity—"

"Yes. But you are a robot. I can hear the outcry now. 'Give one robot human status, and they'll all be asking for it next, and then what's going to happen to—' "

"No," Andrew said. "Not so. I went to court years before you were born and got myself declared a free robot, and the same outcry was raised then. We were able to defeat it. And I'm *still* the only free robot in the world. No other robot has so much as requested free status, let alone been granted it. And none ever will. I'm unique, Madam Chairman. I'm the only robot of my type that exists, and you can be quite certain that there won't ever be another. If you don't believe me, ask the head of U. S. Robots and Mechanical Men, and he'll tell you that they'll never again allow the construction of a robot as intelligent, as difficult-minded, as troublesome as I turned out to be."

" 'Never' is a long time, Andrew. Or would you prefer that I call you 'Mr. Martin'? I will, you know. I will gladly give you my personal accolade as human. But you'll find that most Legislators will be unwilling to set such a startling precedent, even though you provide iron-clad assurances that you are unique and so it will be no precedent at all. Mr. Martin, you have my warmest sympathies. But I can't offer you any real hope."

"You can't? Nothing at all?"

Chee Li-hsing sat back and her forehead furrowed in a deep frown. "The one thing I can offer you, Mr. Martin, is a friendly warning. You are placing yourself in great danger, you need to realize, by making these demands. Indeed, if the issue grows too heated, there might well arise a certain sentiment, both inside the Legislature and certainly outside it, for the very dismantling that you mentioned. A robot of your extraordinary level of attainment could easily be seen as highly threatening, Mr. Martin. Doing away with you could remove that threat and be the easiest way of resolving the difficult political dilemma that you will be forcing upon my colleagues. Consider that, I beg you, before deciding to push matters."

Andrew said, "And will no one remember that the technique of prosthetology, which is allowing the members of the Legislature to go on holding their seats decade after decade when they should by rights be doddering off to their graves, is something that is almost entirely mine?"

"It may seem cruel of me to say it, but they won't. Or if they do, it'll be something that they'll hold against you rather than count in your favor. Have you ever heard the old saying, 'No good deed goes unpunished?' "

Andrew shrugged and shook his head. "Such a statement makes no sense to me."

"I suppose not. You still aren't very comfortable with our little human irrationalities, are you? But what it means, basically, is that we have a way of turning on those who do us the greatest kindnesses. —No, don't try to dispute it. It's just the way we are."

"Very well. And how does this apply to me?"

"It'll be said, perhaps, that you created prosthetology mainly to serve your own needs. The argument will be raised that the whole science was merely part of a campaign to roboticize human beings, or to humanify robots, and in either case it is something evil and vicious."

"No," Andrew said. "I'm not able to comprehend that kind of reasoning."

"No. You can't, can you? Because ultimately you are still a logical creature controlled by your positronic pathways. And there's no sort of upgrade, I suppose, that can make your way of thinking as erratic as ours can sometimes be. The true depths of irrationality are beyond your reach—which you should not take as any criticism of you, only as a simple statement of the realities. You are very human in most essential respects, Mr. Martin, but you are incapable, I'm afraid, of understanding just how far from rationality human beings will go when they believe that their interests are at stake."

"But if their interests are at stake," Andrew said, "I would think they would attempt to be as rational as possible, so that they would be able to—"

"No. Please. There's no way I can make you truly understand. I can only ask you to accept the validity of what I'm saying. To take it on faith, if that concept has any meaning for you. —You have never been the object of a political hate campaign, have you, Mr. Martin?"

"I don't believe so."

"You would have known it if you had. Well, you will be now. If you persist in this campaign to have yourself declared human, you'll be the object of vilification of a kind neither you nor I would credit and there'll be millions of people who will believe every word of it. Mr. Martin, take a word of advice from me. Accept the condition of your life as it is now. To try to do what you want to do now would be the greatest folly."

"That is what you believe, is it?"

"Yes. That is what I believe." And Chee Li-hsing rose from her desk and walked toward the window and stood there with her back to Andrew. Brilliant light was streaming in, outlining her form with great clarity. From where Andrew sat, her bare figure within the shimmering plastic wrap seemed almost like that of a child—or a doll.

He looked toward Li-hsing for a few moments without saying anything.

Then he asked, "If I decide to fight for my humanity despite all you've said, will you be on my side?"

She continued to stare out the window. Andrew studied her long glossy black hair, her thin shoulders, her delicate arms. She seemed very much like a doll, he thought. And yet he was very much aware by now that indeed there was nothing doll-like about the Chairman of the World Legislature's Science and Technology Committee except her appearance. There was real strength behind that fragile surface.

After a time she said, "Yes, I will—"

"Thank you."

"—insofar as it's possible for me to be," Li-hsing continued smoothly. "But you have to realize that, if at any time my taking a stand in your favor would appear to threaten my political career in a serious way, I might have to abandon you, since this isn't an issue that I feel to be at the very root of my beliefs. What I'm trying to say, Mr. Martin, is that I feel for you, I am saddened by your predicament, but I don't intend to wreck my political future for you. I'm trying to be as honest as I can with you."

227

"I'm grateful for that, and I can ask no more."

"And *do* you intend to fight?" she said.

"Yes. Yes, I do. I'll fight it through to the end, whatever the consequences. And I'll count on your help—but only for as long as you can give it."

TWENTY

IT WAS NOT A DIRECT FIGHT. Andrew had given Simon De-Long the clue to the right strategy to use, and Andrew agreed with the tactic; but it was DeLong's considered professional opinion that the campaign was going to be roundabout and slow. DeLong counseled patience.

"I have an endless supply of that, I suppose," Andrew muttered grimly.

Feingold and Charney then entered into a campaign to narrow and restrict the area of combat.

A certain Roger Hennessey of San Francisco, who had been the recipient of a Martin prosthetic heart seven years before, had supplied robot janitorial services to the Feingold and Charney offices under a contract that had been in effect since the days of Paul Charney. Abruptly Feingold and Charney stopped paying Hennessey's bills. The account was a good one and it went back many years, so for a time Hennessey said nothing about it. But when five months of unpaid bills had piled up, Hennessey found an occasion to stop by at Feingold and Charney to have a chat with Simon DeLong.

"I'm sure you're not aware of it, Simon, but something seems to have gone wrong with your accounting procedures lately.

What I mean is, my invoices have been sitting here open since December, and it's coming up on June now, and—"

"Yes. I know."

"—it really isn't at all like Feingold and Charney to let an account run so—" Hennessey paused and blinked. "What did you say? You *know*, Simon?"

"Yes. The account has gone unpaid on my direct instructions, as a matter of fact."

Still blinking in astonishment, Hennessey said, "I must be losing my hearing. Or else you're starting to lose your mind, Simon. Did you actually say you're deliberately withholding payment?"

"That's right."

"For God's sake, why?"

"Because we don't want to pay you."

"What do you mean, you don't want to pay me? Do you know how many years my robots have been cleaning these offices, Simon? Have you ever had the slightest reason in all that time to complain about the quality of the work?"

"Never. And we intend to retain your services just as before. But we're not going to pay you any more, Roger."

Hennessey scratched his head and stared. "You've gone completely around the bend, haven't you? To sit there with a straight face and tell me a crazy thing like that? You know that what you're saying is absolute malarkey, so why are you saying it? What's the matter with you, man? How in the name of God's green Earth can you speak such insane drivel?"

DeLong smiled. "There's quite a good reason for it."

"And what may that be, can I dare to ask?"

DeLong said, "We aren't going to pay you because we don't have to. We've decided that your contract with us is invalid, and from now on your robots are going to work for us for nothing if they go on working here at all. That's the story, Roger. If you don't like it, sue us."

"What? What?" Hennessey cried, sputtering. "This gets crazier and crazier. Work for nothing? Back pay withheld? You people are *lawyers!* How can you let yourself spout such cockeyed non-sense? Contract invalid? For heaven's sake, why?''

"Because you're a robot, Roger. There's only one robot in the world who has the right to enter into binding contracts, and his name is Andrew Martin. The rest of you, because you are not free robots, have no legal right to enforce—''

Hennessey turned bright scarlet and rose from his chair. "Hold it just a moment, you damned lunatic! Hold it right there! What are you saying? A robot? Me? Now I know you're out of your mind!'' Hennessey ripped open the ornate body-cummer-bund he was wearing to reveal his pink, hairy chest. "Does this look to you like a robot's chest, man? Does it? Does it?'' Hennessey pinched his own abundant flesh. "Is this robot meat, Simon? Damn it, I can't even begin to understand any of this, but I tell you, if you think you can sit there like that and make a figure of fun out of me for your own perverse pleasure, I'll sue you people, all right, I'll sue you black and blue from here to Mars and back, by God, and I'll see to it that you—''

DeLong was laughing.

Hennessey halted in mid-flow and said icily, "What's so damned amusing, Simon?''

"I'm sorry. I shouldn't be laughing. I owe you a tremendous apology for letting this go on so long.''

"I think you do. I don't expect lawyers to have much of a sense of humor, but a dumb joke like this—''

"It isn't a joke, though. We really *are* going to withhold your fees, Roger. We really *do* want you to take us to court. Our argument indeed *is* going to be that you are a robot, and that therefore it is quite within the law for us to thumb our collective nose at our contract with you. And we will defend our position with all the skill at our disposal.''

"Will you, now?''

"But it is our profound hope, and our intention as well,'' De-Long went on, "to lose the suit. And when we do, you'll not only be paid the back fees that we owe you, which will be placed in escrow for you accruing interest, but we will pay all your legal fees as well, and I can tell you, strictly off the record, that there'll be a considerable bonus payment for you besides to compensate you for any incidental difficulties that this case may cause you. A *very* considerable bonus payment."

Hennessey adjusted his cummerbund and took his seat again. He blinked a few more times and shook his head. He peered at DeLong for a time in silence.

Then he said quietly, "I'm truly sorry for your troubles, Simon. You really have gone completely out of your mind, then. What a great pity that is."

"Not at all. I'm as sane as I ever was."

"Ah. Are you, do you think?"

"Absolutely."

"In that case, do you have any objection to telling me what this is all about?"

"I'm afraid it would be improper for us to disclose that to you in advance of the litigation. But I will say, Roger, that we have an excellent reason for it all, which will make sense to you in the fullness of time, and I hope that you'll cooperate with us even in the dark, so to speak, out of consideration for your long relationship with us. We need you to play along with us, Roger, and we'll take care of you properly afterward."

Hennessey nodded. He looked a little relieved.

"So it's all a maneuver of some sort, then?"

"You could call it that, I suppose."

"But you won't tell me what's going on?"

"No. Not now. That would be too much like entering into a conspiracy with you."

"But you *are* entering into a conspiracy with me!"

DeLong grinned. "Are we? All we're doing is refusing to pay your bill. Bear with us, Roger. You won't regret it. You have my promise."

"Well—" said Hennessey, grudgingly.

Hennessey's bill continued to go unpaid. After three months more Hennesey duly notified Feingold and Charney that he could no longer carry their account. He canceled their service contract and filed suit for back charges. Feingold and Charney arranged for a temporary janitorial service to clean the office, and let the Court know that it was ready to defend its position.

When the case of Hennessey vs. Feingold and Charney came to trial, it was one of the junior partners who made the argument in court. He said, simply, that inasmuch as Roger Hennessey could be shown to be a robot rather than a human being Feingold and Charney felt under no obligation to go on honoring its service contract, and had unilaterally abrogated it.

The robot Hennessey, the lawyer continued, had gone on sending in his robot janitorial crews for another few months even so, but Feingold and Charney had not asked him to do so and did not believe that payment was necessary, or that Hennessey, as a robot, had any legal right to force them to pay. Robots, the junior partner pointed out, had none of the constitutional protections that human beings enjoyed. In disputes over contracts involving robots, only their owners could sue, not the robots themselves.

"But my client is *not* a robot!" Hennessey's lawyer thundered. "It's as plain as the nose on my client's face that he's as human as any of us here!"

"Your client," the Feingold and Charney man replied, "was equipped some years ago with a robotic prosthetic heart, is that not the case?"

"Why—possibly he was. I'd need to check with him on that. But what possible relevance can this—"

"It is quite relevant, I assure you. And I respectfully request the Court to obtain a determination on this point."

The judge looked toward Hennessey. "Well, Mr. Hennessey?"

"I've got a prosthetic ticker, sure. But what—"

The Feingold and Charney man said, "Our position, your honor, is that the presence of a life-sustaining mechanical artifact of that kind in Mr. Hennessey's body changes his entire legal status. It is reasonable to argue that he would not be alive today but for the robotic component of his body. We proceed to assert, therefore, that the partly prosthetic Mr. Hennessey is in fact a robot and has been for some years now, and therefore that all contracts into which he may have entered as a human being became null and void when he attained the status of a robot."

"So that's it!" Hennessey muttered. "Well, may I be dipped! The heart makes me a robot, they say? Do they, now? Do they?" And he threw back his head and began to laugh.

The uproar in the courtroom was tremendous. The judge pounded his gavel and shouted, but he could scarcely be heard for minutes. Then at last what he was saying came through the furor. The case was dismissed, with a directed verdict in favor of the plaintiff. Mr. Roger Hennessey—whom the Court found to be undeniably human—was entitled to his janitorial fees plus interest plus additional compensation.

Feingold and Charney appealed.

The case had a more elaborate debate at the appellate level, with expert witnesses called in to discuss definitions of humanity. The issue was approached from every angle—scientific, theological, semantic, philosophic.

The verdict in favor of Hennessey was affirmed.

Feingold and Charney appealed again.

They fought the matter skillfully and tenaciously, losing at every step but always in such a way that the issue widened steadily, from a simple *Shall Hennessey's bill be paid?* to, ultimately, *What is a human being?* At each level they forced the decision to be as broad as possible.

It took years, and millions of dollars. Eventually the case reached the jurisdiction of the World Court.

Which affirmed the original *Hennessey* ruling and upheld all the accreted rulings having to do with the valid human status of individuals in whom robotic prostheses had been installed. It is the brain, the World Court declared, that is the highest determinant of humanity. The use of auxiliary devices to sustain the life of the brain can in no way invalidate the fundamental and inalienable humanity of that brain. It is unacceptable, the Court said, to argue that the presence of robotic prostheses within a human being's body gives that person the status of a robot.

When the final decision was handed down, Simon DeLong held what amounted to a victory celebration over the definitive legal defeat. Andrew was, of course, present in the company offices for the great occasion.

"Well, Andrew, we can feel completely satisfied. We've accomplished the two things we set out to do. First of all, we have managed to establish the legal point that no number of prosthetic artifacts in the human body causes it to cease being a human body. Secondly, we have engaged public opinion in the question in such a way as to put it fiercely on the side of a broad and loose interpretation of who is human—since there isn't a human being in existence, on this world or any other, who doesn't expect to enjoy a greatly extended life-span as a result of the availability of a wide array of prosthetic devices."

"And do you think the Legislature will now grant me my humanity?" Andrew asked.

DeLong looked a little uneasy.

"Perhaps. Perhaps not."

"Is that the best you can offer, after all these years of legal struggle?"

DeLong said, "I wish that I could be as optimistic as you'd like me to be. But the real battle isn't won yet. There remains the one organ which the World Court has used as the criterion of humanity."

"The mind."

"The brain, Andrew. That's what the Court singled out, not the mind. The mind is an abstract concept; the brain is a bodily organ. And human beings have organic cellular brains whereas robots have a platinum-iridium positronic brain if they have one at all—and you certainly have a positronic brain. —No, Andrew, don't get that look in your eye. I know what you're thinking. But I've been assured that we lack the knowledge to duplicate the functions of a cellular brain in an artificial structure that would be close enough to the organic type to allow it to fall within the Court decision. Not even you could do it."

"What should we do, then?"

"Make the attempt, of course. Congresswoman Chee will be on our side and so will a growing number of other Legislators. The World Coordinator will undoubtedly go along with whatever a majority of the Legislature decides."

"Do we have a majority?"

"No," DeLong said. "Far from it. But we might manage to put one together if the public will allow its desire for a broad interpretation of humanity to extend to you. A small chance, I admit. But you are, after all, the man who gave them the prosthetics on which their lives now depend."

Andrew smiled. "The *man,* is that what you said?"

"That's what I said, yes. Isn't that what we've been fighting for, Andrew?"

"Of course."

"Then we might as well begin thinking that way here. And carry our thinking onward and outward to the rest of the world until everyone else agrees. It won't be easy, Andrew. None of this has been, and there's no reason to think it will get any better. The odds are very much against us, I warn you. But unless you want to give up, we have to take the gamble."

"I don't want to give up," Andrew said.

TWENTY-ONE

CONGRESSWOMAN CHEE LI-HSING was considerably older now than she had been when Andrew first met her. No longer did she indulge in the coquettishness of shimmering transparent garments. She was dressed in somewhat more chaste tubular coverings, now. Her once lustrous black hair was streaked with gray, and she wore it cut much shorter.

Andrew, though, had of course not changed at all. His face was as unlined as ever; his soft, fine hair was still brown. And he clung, as closely as he could within the limits of reasonable taste, to the loose style of clothing that had prevailed when he first adopted clothing over a century before.

It was late in the year. The harsh chill winds of winter were blowing through the ancient canyons of New York and faint wisps of snow were swirling through the air above the giant gleaming tower that housed the World Legislature. The Legislature's wordy struggles were over for the season.

But for Andrew the struggle never seemed to reach its end. The debate had gone on and on—the angry, baffled Legislators had tried to take all possible sides of the issue—the voting public, unable to come to any clear philosophical position, had fallen back on emotion, on primordial fear, on the deepest-rooted of uncertainties and prejudices—

237

Congresswoman Chee had withdrawn her bill, had modified it substantially to take into account the stubborn opposition that it had run into. But she had not yet offered it again to the Legislature.

"What do you think?" Andrew asked. "Will you introduce the revised bill in the new session or not?"

"What do you want me to do?"

"You know what I want you to do."

Li-hsing nodded, a little wearily. "I told you once, Andrew, that your cause was not really my cause, and that I might have to abandon it if I felt my career was at stake. Well, my career *is* at stake. And I still haven't abandoned you."

"And do you still feel that my cause isn't your cause?"

"No. It has become my cause. I have no doubt that you are human, Andrew—perhaps made so by your own hand, but human all the same. And I understand that to deny the humanity of a single member of our kind is to raise the renewed possibility of denying humanity to whole multitudes, as was done all too often in our ugly past. We must never permit that to happen again. But even so—even so, Andrew—"

She faltered for a moment.

"Go on," Andrew said. "Now comes the point where you tell me that you have to abandon me despite everything, isn't that right, Li-hsing?"

"I didn't say that. But we have to be realistic. I think we've gone as far as we can go."

"So you won't introduce the revised bill."

"I didn't say that, either. I intend to give it one more try after recess. But to be honest, Andrew, we can't win. Look at the numbers." She touched a button and a screen came to life on the wall of her office. "The group on the left side of the chart, the section in green—those are the members who are unalterably opposed to any kind of loosening of the definitions. That's just about 40% of the Legislature: immovable, permanently committed to opposing you. The segment marked in red: there are your supporters. 28%. The rest are the undecided ones."

"In two different colors? Why is that?"

"Yellow is the group that's undecided but leaning in your direction. That's a 12.5% slice. Blue is undecided against you. That's 19.5%."

"I see."

"In order to get a majority, we need to keep every single one of the undecideds in the yellow slice of the chart, and win over more than half of those who are still on the fence but currently thinking of voting against you. Plus, of course, retaining the solid support of your basic 28% group. Even if we can manage to win over a few of your diehard opponents, I don't think we can put together the vote, Andrew."

Andrew said, "Then why bother even bringing the bill up for debate?"

"Because I owe you that much. As you can see, it isn't going to work, and I'm afraid this is going to be my last try. Not because I'm walking away from the fight—not at all—but because I'm not going to be in a position any longer where I can stay in it. Everything that I've been doing on your behalf is going to be wrapped around my neck at the next election and it's going to pull me down to defeat. I have no doubt of that. I'm going to lose my seat."

"I know," said Andrew, "and it distresses me. For your sake, not for mine. You saw it coming long ago, didn't you, Li-hsing? And yet you stayed with me. Why? Why, after telling me at the start that you'd drop me if you found that I was endangering your career? Why didn't you?"

"One can change one's mind, you know. Somehow, Andrew, abandoning you involved paying a higher price than I was willing to pay for the sake of winning just one more term. As it is, I've been in the Legislature for over a quarter of a century. That's long enough, I think."

"But if your mind could change, why not the minds of the others?"

"We've changed all that are amenable to reason. The rest—

and it's a majority of them, I'm sorry to say—simply can't be moved. It's a matter of deep-rooted emotional antipathy."

"Theirs, or the people who voted for them?"

"Some of each. Even those members of the Legislature who are more or less rational themselves tend now and then to assume that their constituents aren't. But I'm afraid that plenty of them have powerful antipathies of their own, when it comes to anything robotic."

"And is relying on emotional antipathy a valid way for a Legislator to decide how to vote?"

"Oh, Andrew—"

"Yes. How terribly naive of me to say a thing like that."

"Naive isn't the right word. But you know that they'd never admit they were voting their emotions. They'd offer this or that carefully reasoned-out explanation for their decision—something about the economy, or an analogy from Roman history, or some antiquated religious argument—anything but the truth. But what does it matter? It's how they'll vote that counts, not why they do it."

"It all comes down to the question of the structure of the brain, then—isn't that so?"

"That's the problem, yes."

Andrew said cautiously, "I don't see why that should be such a sticking point for them. What a brain is made of isn't the essential thing: it's how the brain functions. Its thought patterns, its reaction time, its ability to reason and to generalize from experience. Why does the whole issue have to be drawn down to the level of organic cells versus positrons? Is there no way of pushing through a *functional* definition?"

"Functional?"

"My brain does everything that an officially legal human brain can do—does it better, in many ways, faster, more directly, more logically. Perhaps that's what bothers them. Well, it's too late for me to start hiding my intelligence, if that's the problem. But must we go on insisting that a human brain has to be made of some officially approved cellular substance in order to be legally

THE POSITRONIC MAN

human? Can't we simply stipulate that a human brain is something—anything, organic or not—that is capable of attaining a
certain complex level of thought?"

"It won't work," said Li-hsing.

"Because if we defined humanity by brain function alone, too
many humans would fall below the stipulated level of intellectual
ability?" Andrew asked bitterly. "Is that it?"

"Andrew, Andrew, Andrew! Listen to me: there are those who
are determined to keep a barrier up between themselves and
robots at any cost. For the sake of their own self-esteem, if nothing else, they want to believe that they belong to the only true
and lawful human race and that robots are some sort of inferior
creatures. You've spent the past hundred years beating those people back, and you've won your way through to a status that would
have been utterly inconceivable in the early years of robotics. But
now they've got you on an issue where you can't win. You've put
yourself inside a body that for all intents and purposes is close
enough to being human as makes no real difference. You eat,
you breathe, you sweat. You go to fine restaurants and order
splendid meals and drink the best wines, I've noticed, though I
can't imagine what value that can have for you other than for
appearance's sake."

"That is value enough for me," said Andrew.

"All right. Plenty of humans probably can't appreciate the expensive wines they drink either, but they drink them all the same,
and for the same reason you do. Your organs are all artificial, but
by now so are many of theirs. Quite possibly there are people out
there living in bodies that are virtually identical to yours, whole-
sale artificial replacements for the ones they were born with. But
they aren't *complete* replacements, Andrew. Nobody has a prosthetic brain. No one can. And so you differ from everyone else in
one fundamental respect. Your brain is man-made, the human
brain is not. Your brain was constructed, theirs was naturally developed. They were born, you were assembled. To any human
being who is intent on keeping up the barrier between himself

241

and robots, those differences are like a steel wall five kilometers high and five kilometers thick.''

"You aren't telling me anything I don't know. My brain is different in composition from theirs, certainly. But not in its function, not really. Quantitatively different, maybe, but not qualitatively. It's just a brain—a very good brain. They're merely using the positronic-vs. cellular issue as a pretext to keep from admitting that what I am is a human being of a kind somewhat different from them. —No, Li-hsing, if we could somehow get at their antipathy toward me because of my robotic origins—the very source of all their hostility—this mysterious need they have to proclaim themselves superior to someone who is by every reasonable definition superior to *them*—''

"After all your years," said Li-hsing sadly, "you are still trying to reason out the human being. Poor Andrew, don't be angry at me for saying this, but it's the robot in you that drives you in that direction.''

"You know that there's very little left of the robot in me by this time.''

"But there's some.''

"Some, yes. And if I were to get rid of that—''

Chee Li-hsing shot him a look of alarm. "What are you saying, Andrew?''

"I don't know," he said. "But I have an idea. The problem is, Li-hsing, that I have human feelings trapped within a robot mind. But that doesn't make me human, only an unhappy robot. Even after all that has been done to improve my robot body, I'm still not human. But there's one more step that can be taken. If I could bring myself—if I could only bring myself—''

TWENTY-TWO

IF HE COULD ONLY bring himself—

And now he had, finally.

Andrew had asked Chee Li-hsing to hold off as long as possible before bringing her revised bill to the World Legislature floor for debate and vote, because he planned to undertake a project in the very near future that might have some significant impact on the issue. And no, Andrew said, he didn't care to discuss the details of the project with her. It was a highly technical thing; she wasn't likely to understand, and he wasn't at the moment willing to take the time to explain it to her. But it would make him more human, he insisted. That was the essential detail, the only thing she really needed to know. It would make him more human.

She said she would do the best she could to give him enough time for this mysterious project of his, though she sounded puzzled and concerned.

Andrew thanked her, and set out at once to have a little talk with the highly acclaimed robot surgeon whom he had chosen to do the work. It was a difficult conversation. Andrew found himself putting off the moment of decision for a long while with a sad line of questioning that reflected the turmoil within himself, while the surgeon grew more and more confused by the unusual and probably impossible nature of what Andrew seemed to be asking him to do.

The First Law of Robotics was the obstacle: the immutable law that prevented a robot from harming a human being in any way. And so at last Andrew could delay things no longer, and brought himself to admit the one necessary fact that made it possible for the robot surgeon to perform the operation, the one thing that the surgeon had not suspected: Andrew's own proper status as something other than a human being.

The surgeon said, "I don't believe I understood you correctly, sir. You claim that you are a robot yourself?"

"That is precisely what I am."

The surgeon's facial expression, calm and impassive as ever, could not and did not change. But the set stare of his glowing photoelectric eyes somehow managed to reveal great internal distress and Andrew could tell that the surgeon's positronic brain was being swept by troublesome conflicting potentials.

He said, after a little while, "I would not presume to contradict you, sir. But I must tell you that I see nothing at all robotic about your external appearance."

"You are correct. My external appearance has been altered extensively to make me appear human. But that does not mean I *am* human. Indeed, I have put myself to a great deal of extraordinary legal expense over the past few years for the sake of clarifying my status and it appears, after all of that, that I remain a robot, despite everything."

"I would never have thought it, sir."

"No. You never would."

Andrew had not selected this surgeon for his dazzling personality, his quick wit, his readiness to cope with difficult social situations. None of that was important. What mattered was his skill as a surgeon, and by all accounts he had plenty of that. And also that he was a robot. A robot surgeon was the only possible choice for what Andrew had in mind, for no human surgeon could be trusted in this connection, neither in ability nor in intention. The robot could do the job.

The robot *would* do the job, too. Andrew intended to see to that.

"As I have told you, sir—"

"Stop calling me sir!"

The robot halted, plainly perplexed. Then he began again. "As I have told you, Mr. Martin, to perform an operation such as you request on a human being would be a blatant violation of the First Law and I could in no way carry it out. But if you are, as you claim, a robot, then there is still a problem. Performing the operation would constitute inflicting damage on property, you see, and I would be unable to do it except at the direct instructions of your owner."

"*I* am my owner," Andrew said. "I'm a free robot and I have the papers to prove it."

"A—free—robot?"

"Listen to me," Andrew said. He was seething with inner anguish now and his own positronic mind was being swept by troublesome potentials indeed. "Enough of this chatter. I won't pretend to be human, and you'd discover soon enough when you operated that I'm not, anyway, so we can leave First Law considerations entirely out of this. But Second Law will apply. I am a free robot and you will do as I say. You will not oppose my wishes. Is that clear?" And he declared, with all the firmness that he had learned how to use even with human beings over these past decades, "I *order* you to carry out this operation on me."

The robot surgeon's red eyes turned brighter than ever with inner confusion and conflict and for a long moment he was unable to reply.

Andrew knew what the surgeon must be going through. Before him was a man who insisted that he was not a man, or else a robot who claimed to have as much authority over him as a human being, and either way the surgeon's pathways must be abuzz with incomprehension.

If this were indeed a man, then First Law would override Second and the surgeon could not accept the commission. But if this were a robot, did Second Law govern the situation or not?

What was there in Second Law that gave one robot the right to order another one around—even a free robot? This was a robot, though, who denied being a man but looked entirely like one. That was an almost incomprehensible situation. The ambiguity of it was probably overwhelming the surgeon's positronic pathways. All his visual responses were crying out that his visitor was human; his mind was trying to process the datum that his visitor was not. The visual evidence would tend to activate the First and Second Laws, the other evidence would not.

Faced with chaotic contradictions of that sort, it was conceivable that the surgeon's mind would short out altogether. Or perhaps, Andrew hoped, the safest way out of the crisis for the surgeon would be to take a Second Law position: that this visitor, while by his own admission not human enough to invoke First Law prohibitions, had sufficiently human characteristics to be able to demand obedience from the surgeon.

Which was the path that the surgeon ultimately took, after a lengthy period of hesitation.

"Very well," the surgeon said, and there was an unmistakable undertone of relief in his voice. "I will do what you have asked me to do."

"Fine."

"The fee will not be small."

"I'd be worried if it was," said Andrew.

TWENTY-THREE

THE OPERATING ROOM was nothing nearly as grand as the one in which U. S. Robots and Mechanical Men had performed its various upgrades on Andrew in recent years, but Andrew could tell that the facility was superbly equipped and completely equal to the task. He looked with admiration and approval at the laser bank, the board of measuring dials and control panel, the spidery maze of auxiliary needles and tubes and pipes, and the main surgical stage itself, dais and bed and lights and instruments, white linens and dazzling chrome-steel fixtures, everything in readiness for the unusual patient.

And the surgeon himself was magnificently calm. Quite clearly he had been able in the interim to resolve whatever conflicts he had felt over the irregularities of Andrew's request and the ambiguities of Andrew's appearance, and now he was focused entirely on the professional task at hand. Andrew was more than ever convinced that he had made the only possible choice by selecting a robot surgeon to perform this operation.

Still, he felt a flicker of uncertainty—just a flicker—as the actual moment for the start of the operation arrived. What if something went wrong? What if he came out of the operation incapacitated in some way? What if the operation failed and he terminated right on the operating table?

No. None of that mattered. There was no way for the operation to fail, none. And even if it did—no. That simply did not matter.

The surgeon was watching him carefully.

"Are you ready?" he asked.

"Absolutely," Andrew told the surgeon. "Let's get down to it."

"Very well," said the surgeon phlegmatically, and with a quick, sweeping gesture took his laser-scalpel into his splendidly designed right hand.

Andrew had chosen to remain completely conscious throughout the entire process. He had no wish to shut down awareness even for an instant. Pain was not an issue for him, and he needed to be certain that his instructions were being followed precisely. But of course they were. The surgeon's nature, being robotic, was not one that would permit any capricious deviation from the agreed-upon course of action.

What Andrew was not prepared for was the unexpectedly intense weakness and fatigue that came after the job had been done.

He had never known such sensations as those that came over him in the early hours of his recovery period. Even when they had transferred his brain from the robot body to the android one, Andrew had experienced nothing like this.

Instead of walking normally, he lurched and staggered. Often he felt as though the floor before him was rising up to strike him in the face. There were times when his fingers trembled so violently that he had difficulty holding things. His vision, which had always been flawless, suddenly would grow blurry for long minutes at a stretch. Or he would try to remember someone's name, and nothing would come to mind except a tantalizing blankness that glimmered at him from around the corners of his memory.

He spent an entire afternoon, the first week after the operation, searching his mind for the full name of the man he had known as Sir. Then, suddenly, the name was there: Gerald Martin. But now Andrew had forgotten the name of Little Miss's dark-haired older sister, and it took him hours more of diligent searching before "Melissa Martin" popped abruptly into his brain. Two hours! It should not have taken him two milliseconds!

It was all more or less what Andrew should have expected, and in an abstract way he *had* expected it. And yet the reality of the feelings themselves was far beyond anything that Andrew had anticipated. Physical weakness was something new to him. So were poor coordination, uncertain reflexes, imperfect eyesight, and episodes of impaired memory. It was humiliating to feel so imperfect—so *human*—

No, he thought.

There is nothing humiliating about it. You have everything backward. It is human to feel imperfect. That was what you wanted, above all else: to be human. And now that is what you are. The imperfections—the weaknesses—the imprecisions— they are the very things which define humans as human. And which drive them to transcend their own failings.

You never had failings before, Andrew told himself. Now you do, and so be it. So be it. You have achieved the thing you set out to accomplish and you must feel no regrets.

Gradually, as one day slid into the next, things began to improve.

Gradually. Very gradually.

The memory functions returned first. Andrew was gratified to discover that he had full access again, instant and complete, to the whole of his past.

He sat in the grand high-winged chair by the fireplace in the great living room of what once had been Gerald Martin's house, and let images of years gone by play through his mind: the factory where he had been constructed, and his arrival at the Martin house, and Little Miss and Miss as children, walking with him on the beach. Sir and Ma'am at their dining table; his wooden sculptures and the furniture he had made; the U. S. Robots executives who came west to inspect him; his first visit from Little Sir; the time he had decided at last to begin wearing clothing; Little Sir's marriage and the birth of Paul Charney. Even less pleasant things like the episode of the two louts who had tried to disassemble him while he was on the way to the public library. And much, much more, nearly two hundred years of memory.

It was all there. His mind had not been permanently impaired, and he was tremendously relieved.

The floor stopped trying to jump up and hit him. His vision stopped playing tricks on him. His hands finally stopped their infuriating shaking. When he walked, he was no longer in danger of stumbling and falling. He was himself again, in most of the essential ways.

But a certain sense of weakness still remained with him, or so he thought: a pervasive chronic weariness, a feeling that he needed to sit down and rest awhile before going on to whatever might be his next task.

Perhaps it was only his imagination. The surgeon said that he was recovering quite well.

There was a syndrome called *hypochondria,* Andrew knew, in which you felt that you were suffering from conditions that in fact you did not have. It was a fairly common thing among human beings, he had heard. People who were hypochondriacs found all manner of symptoms in themselves that no medical tests could confirm; and the more thought they gave to the possibility that they might be ill, the more symptoms they discovered.

Andrew wondered whether in his long unceasing quest to attain full humanity he had somehow managed to contract a case of hypochondria, and smiled at the thought. Quite likely he had, he decided. His own testing equipment showed no measurable degrading of his performance capabilities. All parameters were well within permissible deviation. And yet—yet—he felt so *tired*—

It had to be imaginary. Andrew ordered himself to give his feelings of weariness no further thought. And, tired or not, he made one more journey across the continent to the great green-glass tower of the World Legislature in New York to pay a call on Chee Li-hsing.

He entered her grand and lofty office and she beckoned him automatically to a seat before her desk, the way she would have done with any other visitor. But Andrew had always preferred to stand in her presence, out of some obscure impulse of courtesy that he had never tried to explain to himself, and he did not want to sit now—especially not now. It would be entirely too revealing to do that. Nevertheless, he found after a moment or two that standing seemed a bit troublesome to him, and he leaned, as unobtrusively as he could manage, against the wall.

Li-hsing said, "The final vote will come this week, Andrew. I've tried to delay it, but I've run out of parliamentary maneuvers, and there's nothing more I can do. It'll be voted on and we'll lose. —And that will be it, Andrew."

Andrew said, "I'm grateful for your skill at delaying things. It provided me with the time I needed—and I took the gamble I had to take."

Li-hsing gave him a troubled look. "What gamble do you mean, Andrew?" And then, with some irritation in her voice: "You've been so mysterious these past months! Hinting darkly at this or that big project, but refusing to let anybody know what it was that you were up to—"

"I couldn't, Li-hsing. If I had told you anything—or had said a word to the people at Feingold and Charney—I would have been stopped. I'm sure of that. You *could* have stopped me, you know, simply by ordering me not to proceed. The Second Law: there's no way for me to put up resistance against that. Simon DeLong would have done the same. So I had to keep quiet about my plans until I had carried them out."

"What is it that you have done, Andrew?" Chee Li-hsing asked, very quietly, almost ominously.

Andrew said, "The brain was the issue, that was what we agreed—the positronic brain vs. the organic one. But what was the *real* issue behind that? My intelligence? No. I have an unusual mind, yes, but that's because I was designed to have an unusual mind, and after me they broke the mold. Other robots have outstanding mental abilities along one line or another, whatever specialty it is that they've been designed to perform, but basically they're pretty stupid things. The way a computer is stupid, no matter how many trillion times faster than a human it can add up a column of numbers. So it isn't my intelligence that makes people envious of me, not really. There are plenty of humans who can think rings around me."

"Andrew—"

"Let me have my say, Li-hsing. I'm getting to the point, I promise you."

He shifted his position against the wall, hoping that Li-hsing wouldn't notice that he didn't seem to have the strength to stand up unsupported for many minutes at a time. But Andrew suspected that she had already registered that fact. She was staring at him in an uncertain, troubled way.

He said, "What is the greatest difference between my positronic brain and a human one? It's that my brain is *immortal*. All the trouble we've been having stems from that, don't you see? Why should anyone care what a brain looks like or is built out of or how it came into existence in the first place? What matters is that organic human brain cells die. *Must* die. There's no way of avoiding it. Every other organ in the body can be maintained or replaced by an artificial substitute, but the brain can't be replaced at all, not without changing and therefore killing the personality. And the organic brain must eventually die. Whereas my own positronic pathways—"

Li-hsing's expression had been changing as he spoke. Her face bore a look of horror now.

Andrew knew that she had already begun to understand. But he needed her to hear him out. He continued inexorably, "My own positronic pathways have lasted just under two centuries now without perceptible deterioration, without any kind of undesirable change whatever, and they will surely last for centuries more. Perhaps indefinitely: who can say? The whole science of robotics is only three hundred years old and that's too short a time for anyone to be able to say what the full life-span of a positronic brain may be. Effectively my brain is immortal. Isn't *that* the fundamental barrier that separates me from the human race? Human beings can tolerate immortality in robots, because it's a virtue in a machine to last a long time, and nobody is psychologically threatened by that. But they would never be able to tolerate the idea of an immortal human being, since their own mortality is endurable only so long as they know it's universal. Allow one person to be exempted from death and everyone else feels victimized in the worst way. And for that reason, Li-hsing, they have refused to make me a human being."

Li-hsing said sharply, "You said you were going to get to the point. Get to it, then. What is it that you've done to yourself, Andrew? I want to know!"

"I have removed the problem."

"Removed it? How?"

"Decades ago, when my positronic brain was placed in this android body, it was connected to organic nerves, but it remained carefully insulated from the metabolic forces that would otherwise have ultimately caused it to deteriorate. Now I have undergone one last operation in order to rearrange the connections along the brain-body interface. The insulation has been removed. My brain is now subject to the same forces of decay that any organic substance is vulnerable to. Things are set up now in such a way that—slowly, quite slowly—the potential is being drained from my pathways."

Chee's finely wrinkled face showed no expression for a moment. Then her lips tightened and she balled her hands into fists.

"Do you mean that you've arranged to *die*, Andrew? No. No, you can't possibly have done that. It would be a violation of the Third Law."

"Not so," Andrew said. "There is more than one sort of death, Li-hsing, and the Third Law does not differentiate between them. But I do. What I have done is to choose between the death of my body and the death of my aspirations and desires. To have let my body live at the cost of the greater death—that is the true violation of the Third Law. Not this. As a robot I might live forever, yes. But I tell you that I would rather die as a man than live eternally as a robot."

"Andrew! No!" Chee cried. She rose from her desk and went

to him with astonishing speed, and seized his arm as though she were about to shake him. But all she did was grip it tightly, her fingers sinking deeply into his pliable synthetic flesh. "Andrew, this isn't going to get you what you want. It's nothing more than terrible folly. Change yourself back."

"I can't. Too much damage was done. The operation is irreversible."

"And now—?"

"I have a year to live, Li-hsing—more or less. I will last through the two hundredth anniversary of my construction. I confess that I was weak enough to time things so that I would still be here that long. And then—a natural death. Other robots are dismantled— they are irrevocably terminated—they are taken out of working order. I will simply die. The first robot ever to die—if, that is, it is felt that I am still a robot."

"I can't believe what you're telling me, Andrew. What good can any of this do? You've destroyed yourself for nothing—nothing! It wasn't worth it!"

"I think it was."

"Then you're a fool, Andrew!"

"No," he said gently. "If it brings me humanity at last, then it will have been worth it. And if I fail in achieving that, well, at least there will soon be an end to my fruitless striving and my pain, and that will have been worth accomplishing also."

"Pain?"

"Pain, yes. Do you think I've never felt any pain, Li-hsing?"

Li-hsing did something then that astonished Andrew beyond words.

Quietly, she began to weep.

TWENTY-FOUR

IT WAS STRANGE how the dramatic last deed of Andrew's long life caught at the imagination of the world. Nothing that Andrew had done before had managed to sway people from their denial of his humanity. But Andrew had finally embraced even death for the sake of being fully human, now, and that sacrifice was too great to be rejected.

The story swept across the world like a hurricane. People spoke of nothing else. The bill granting Andrew what he had sought so long went through the World Legislature without opposition. No one would have dared to vote against it. There was scarcely even any debate. There was no need for it. The measure was unprecedented, yes—of course it was—but for once everyone was willing to put precedent aside.

The final ceremony was timed, quite deliberately, for the day of the two hundredth anniversary of Andrew's construction. The World Coordinator was to put his signature to the act publicly, making it law, and the ceremony would be visible on a global network and would be beamed to the lunar settlements and to the other colonies farther out in space.

Andrew was in a wheelchair. He still was capable of walking, but only shakily, now, and it would embarrass him to be seen looking so feeble when so many billions of people would be watching.

And billions were watching—watching everywhere.

The ceremony was simple and quite brief. The World Coordinator—or his electronic simulacrum, rather, for Andrew was at his home in California and the World Coordinator was in New York—began by saying, "This is a very special day, Andrew Martin, not only for you but for the entire human race. There has never been a day like it before. But then there has never been anyone like you before, either.

"Fifty years ago, Andrew, a ceremony in your honor was held at the headquarters of the United States Robots and Mechanical Men Corporation to celebrate the hundred-fiftieth anniversary of your inception. I understand that at that ceremony one of the speakers proclaimed you to be a Sesquicentennial Robot. The statement was correct—as far as it went. But it did not go quite far enough, we realize now. And so the world has taken steps to make amends, and those amends will be made today." The World Coordinator glanced toward Andrew and smiled. There was a document before him on a little podium. The World Coordinator leaned over it and, with a grand flourish, signed his name.

Then, looking up after a moment and speaking in his most formal, solemn tone, the Coordinator said, "There you are. The decree is official and irrevocable. Your sesquicentennial anniversary is fifty years behind you, today. And so is the status of robot with which you came into the world, and for which you were cited on that day. We take that status from you now. You are a robot no longer. The document that I have just signed changes all that. Today, Mr. Martin, we declare you—a Bicentennial Man."

And Andrew, smiling in return, held out his hand as though to shake that of the World Coordinator—despite the distance of a continent's width that actually lay between them. The gesture had been carefully rehearsed, everything measured down to the millimeter. And to the billions of onlookers it seemed that the two hands did in fact meet—a warm human gesture linking, for a moment, one man with the other.

TWENTY-FIVE

THE CEREMONY of just a few months before was only a dim memory, now, and the end was growing near. Andrew's thoughts were slowly fading as he lay in his bed in the grand house overlooking the Pacific.

Desperately he seized at them.

A man! He was a man, a human being at last! For decade after decade he had struggled up the ladder from his robotic origins, not completely recognizing the extent of his aspirations at first but gradually bringing them into focus; and finally he had attained the goal that had become so desperately important to him. He had achieved something almost unimaginable—something unique in the history of the human race.

He wanted that to be his last thought. He wanted to dissolve—die—with that.

Andrew opened his eyes one more time and for one last time recognized Li-hsing waiting solemnly beside the bed. There were others, too, gathered around him, watching his last moments as long ago he had watched those of Sir and Little Miss; but they were only shadows, vague unrecognizable shadows. He was beginning to forget names, faces, everything. It was all slipping away from him, the accumulated memories of two hundred years of life.

Let it go, he thought. Let it go, all of it.

Only the slender figure of Li-hsing stood out unmistakably against the deepening gray. The last of all his friends. He had had so many, over the two centuries, but they were all gone now, and she was the only one who still remained. Slowly, quaveringly, Andrew held out his hand to her and very dimly and faintly he felt her take it. She said something to him, but he was unable to hear the words.

She was fading in his eyes, as the last of his thoughts trickled into the darkness.

He felt cold—very cold—and Li-hsing was disappearing now, vanishing into the dark mist that had begun to engulf him.

Then one final fugitive thought came to him and rested for a moment on his mind before everything stopped. Briefly he saw the flickering image of the first person who had recognized him for what he really was, almost two hundred years before. A mantle of light and warmth surrounded her. Her shining golden hair gleamed like a brilliant sunrise. She was smiling at him—beckoning to him—

"Andrew—" she said softly. "Come, Andrew. Now. Come. You know who I am."

"Little Miss," he whispered, too low to be heard.

And then he closed his eyes and the darkness engulfed him fully and—fully human at last—he gave himself up to it without regret.

DATE			